Chrysalis

Chrysalis

RIE ANDERS

Other Books by Rie Anders

Island Series

Pavey Boulevard
On Island
Hunters Moon

Island Romance Short Stories

Snug Harbor
Meadow Rising
True Blue

Cabin Christmas Romances

Snow & Mistletoe
Dear Santa, Define Good
Naughty & Nice

Crown Family Series

Chrysalis
Solara – Coming Soon
Phoenix – Coming Soon

CHAPTER 1

"CHARLOTTE! CHARLOTTE, ARE you even paying attention?"

The entourage of people around the large cherrywood conference table stared at me, their eyes wide with confusion. They looked a bit concerned and slightly embarrassed for me.

My mind had definitely wandered. What had I been thinking about?

With its plush carpet, cream-colored walls, and elegantly displayed contemporary art, the forty-story building's eighth-floor executive conference room looked out toward the Bayou—which was muddy and stagnant. The dandelion-sculptured fountain and water sparkling in the unusually perfect Houston spring day had entranced me.

Rapidly tapping the top of my pen against the soft laptop mat in front of me, I dug deep (and dug fast) for remnants of the conversation that had taken place before I zoned out. The quick staccato of the clicking brought me back to the present, and I responded confidently.

"I'm sorry, Richard. Yes, I agree with the target demographic, and I feel confident that the campaign will bring in the sales numbers we're looking for."

His response was a slow and agreeable drawl, but his look was still doubtful. "Okay, then."

He stood, grabbed his laptop and phone, and headed out of the conference room, saying over his shoulder as he left, "Charlotte, can I see you in my office?"

Some of my colleagues turned to watch me leave, shrinking down a little in their chairs. Some of them actually avoided eye contact. I could feel them thinking, *She's in way over her head.*

I stood, gathered my belongings, adjusted my periwinkle blue skirt, and then buttoned its matching suit jacket. My expensive high heels dug into the carpet as I left the conference room and followed behind my boss.

His gait was fast. Slowing my pace, I took the time to prepare myself for this conversation.

"Shut the door behind you, Charlotte," he said as he sat down behind his desk. He leaned back in his chair, rested his clasped hands across his belly, and waited until I sat down in front of him.

"What's going on, Charlotte? Are you okay?" His concern was expectedly genuine, different from the tone he had previously used in the conference room. He had mentored me up through this company— which offered financial services, specifically retirement planning—for the past few years. I was ashamed of my distracted behavior.

My career with the company had started right out of college, and I'd been promoted steadily and predictably over the years. Recently, I became vice president of sales; subsequently, I became disillusioned with my life's path.

Apparently, if this little chat was any indication, Richard had begun to sense my restlessness. The fact that I was daydreaming during our Monday morning executive briefing might have also given it away.

"I'm fine, Richard. I'm a little out of sorts today, but I'm totally on point. I promise."

"You do know you deserved your promotion. You earned this position." His eyes were kind and soft, and his tone was gentle.

My shoulders sagged. I forced myself to sit up straighter.

Don't show weakness, I thought.

Even if I didn't understand what was happening to me, I didn't want Richard to have any doubts.

"I know, Richard. You picked the right person." Fake it 'til you make it, I guess.

After a thoughtful pause, he changed topics and moved on to something more personal. "Are you looking forward to your party Saturday night?"

My fiancé, Mark, was hosting a party Saturday night to celebrate my promotion and our engagement. And, of course, to show off our beautiful new home just off Kirby Avenue. The house had a pool and the perfect sized yard for a party tent.

We'd recently purchased an 8,000-square-foot classic Georgian home, and oddly, the size made me feel suffocated, instead of free. Mark had pressured me into buying it, even though I'd insisted I wanted to wait until we were married. But it was what he wanted for our future, and so I went along with his plan. Mark was a stockbroker, and good impressions meant everything to him. Mercedes, check. Large impressive home, check. Beautiful wife, check. (Not to brag.)

Pasting a practiced smile on my face, I made sure it reached my eyes and responded, "Oh, yes! Mark has found the most amazing caterer and a highly recommended string quartet to play. It should be lovely. You are coming, aren't you?"

"Wouldn't miss it!" He leaned back in his chair again, seemingly satisfied that I was going to get back to normal.

"If there's nothing else..." I started to stand. "I want to make sure I get my forecasts for the next quarter completed before the end of the day. You know how the Accounting department can be."

My attempt at levity was well received.

"I'm here for you if you need me, Charlotte. I hope you know that."

I nodded at him, turned around, and shut his door quietly behind me.

Back in my corner office, I removed my jacket and draped it on the hanger on the back of my door.

After shutting the door, I slipped off my shoes and went to stand at the window. My polished appearance reflected in the glass, and I grimaced at the image staring back. The outer shell was classically pretty, but inside was a hollow emptiness that something was missing. I felt unfulfilled. My dark brown hair fell to my shoulders in an asymmetrical cut, meticulously flat-ironed straight. My eyebrows were dark and groomed, framing my dark blue eyes.

I stared vacantly out the window, past my reflection, and longed to rip off this constricting suit and burn it in the nearest trash can. The chains of corporate America were smothering me, and I wasn't sure how much longer I could do this. I wished I could pinpoint the exact moment I became so disillusioned, but I couldn't. The feelings crept up on me until one day—most likely the day of my promotion—I just stopped being happy.

Out the window and across the street, in a strip mall of shops, was a dance studio I'd been going to—a pole dancing studio.

Earlier this year, while working late on the mundane task of annual budget activities, Richard had sent me across the street to a local Irish bar to pick up dinner. The pole dancing studio was just around the corner, and the neon red letters and heart on the marquis had caught my attention.

A few days after that budget meeting, I'd stopped in on my way home and was instantly fascinated with the studio. The lobby was small; it had thick, white carpet, white leather couches, and a mirrored wall. A rack of short, short shorts, and a variety of tanks and sleeveless T-shirts stood up against a wall. Below the shirts sat a shelf of high-heeled platform shoes for sale. The shoes were hot pink and glittered gold, red vinyl and clear plastic. I had touched them (fascinated) as I waited to be helped.

The dark-haired receptionist had addressed me, jolting me from my daydreams.

"Hi, can I help you?" She'd placed the phone back on the receiver as she stood to greet me. I'd stared as she'd unfolded herself from the chair and continued to rise. (She was so tall.)

"Um, yes, maybe, I don't know." I'd laughed at myself and bit the corner of my bottom lip. This was not a world I was familiar with—but it called to me—and I'd hoped she could ease me into it.

"First time?"

I had smiled at her. "Obvious, is it?"

Her eyes had roved down my pantsuit and then back up. She'd shrugged and giggled, crinkling up her nose. "Kind of."

Her youthful laugh had put me at ease, and I'd relaxed.

"Are you interested in classes?"

"I don't know. Maybe?"

She'd reached for a tri-fold brochure and slid it across the desk. Unfolding it, and pointing to a schedule, she'd walked me through the types of classes and cost. I'd glanced at her figure—and her lack of clothing—as she'd talked, and then I'd sucked in my abs a bit.

"You can sign up for ten classes, or fifty, or you can get a membership and come as often as you want to."

"Maybe I'll just start with ten."

Her face had broken into a huge grin. "Great! Do you want to see the studio?"

"Sure!"

As she'd stepped out from behind the desk, I'd glanced down at her feet, noticing that she wore six-inch platforms, leg warmers, and a pair of shorts like the ones on the rack. I'd tried not to gawk, but her body was incredible. While I wasn't on the heavy side, I had gone a little soft in the past few years—my size twelve suits had gotten a little snug.

"Now, you have to take off your shoes when you go into the studio; only bare feet are allowed." She'd lifted one foot, taken off her shoe, and done the same with the other.

I'd slipped off my heels, placed them on a silver shoe rack, and waited for her to open the door. She'd smiled at me patiently, raised her eyebrows, and asked silkily (as if she was unveiling the most delicious secret in the world), "Ready?"

I had nodded at her and followed behind as she opened the door to what appeared to be a ballet studio—but it wasn't. Gleaming gold poles stood floor-to-ceiling, shiny and flawless. The polished wood floors shined up at me, and the red walls at either end gave the room a sultry vibe.

She'd flipped a light switch, and a soft glow had shone from the canister lights recessed into the ceiling. One wall was floor-to-ceiling mirrors; the other was a room separator that opened to a second studio, if needed.

The room had captivated me. I was charmed by the secrets I imagined it held. The room had been quiet and empty, and I'd felt the pull to touch one of the poles. Reaching out, I'd touched it gently and then gripped it with my hand.

Looking over my shoulder at the woman, I'd said, "What's your name?"

She'd smiled at me like she knew the pole goddesses had bitten me. "I'm Erin."

"Hi, Erin, I'm Charlotte. You can call me Charlie."

"Hi, Charlotte. That's a pretty name. I think I'll call you that. Should I sign you up for classes?" She'd had a cheeky grin on her face.

That had been months ago. I'd gotten stronger and leaner since then. My abs were now tighter, my thighs more muscular, and my size ten skirts had replaced my twelves.

I looked down at the studio sign from my office window, and a flicker of excitement and joy washed over me. What time were classes today?

I looked at the pink gym bag under my desk, sat down, and then pulled up the studio website on my phone.

There were two classes tonight: one at 5:00 p.m., and the other at 6:00 p.m. I usually went on Tuesday and Thursday nights, but tonight, I needed a class.

The clock on the wall of my office indicated it wasn't even lunchtime. Sighing heavily, I glanced back at the site. The schedule indicated there was a noon class. Could I make a noon class? Adrenaline rushed through my body at the thought of dancing off the morning's stressful meeting.

I hurriedly slipped my shoes back on, grabbed my bag from under my desk, and my purse from the desk drawer.

Hitching my purse over my shoulder, I ran out of my office. My assistant was typing away at her desk, and I spoke in a clipped tone on my way out.

"Peggy, I need to run an errand. I should be back by 2:00 p.m."

Peggy looked like a Peggy, and she had been with me for years. She stopped typing, glanced at my bag, and then back at me. "And what should I tell Accounting?"

I stopped, paused long enough to pull myself back into the moment, and then looked directly at her. Her eyes were knowing. I felt myself slipping farther from my position. "Tell them I had to taste cake, and I'll have the numbers uploaded by close of business."

"Should I update them for you?" She smiled at me.

"I can do it, Peggy. It won't take me long."

We continued to look at each other a beat longer—a standoff of wills—until I smiled back at her. "I have to go."

She shook her head, and then she went back to typing. "Be careful."

I left the elegant office's hallway and moved toward the elevator, waggling my fingers at her. The glass office doors shut behind me, and I stepped into the elevator, my smile growing the closer I got to the exit.

CHAPTER 2

"Hey, Erin, I thought I would take a noon class today. Can you sign me in?" Since the studio was so close to my office, I arrived with time to change and have a quick chat with her.

She was standing behind the desk, focused on the computer screen in front of her, and jiggling a pen between her fingers. "Sure, Charlotte. Give me a minute, and I'll get you taken care of."

Her clipped tone was unlike the usually bubbly girl I loved to visit. I briefly considered heading back to my office.

Leaning over the counter, I whispered, "Are you okay? Is this a bad time?"

She looked past my shoulder, toward the studio, and then whispered back, "Our owner is in town, and he's super grumpy today. He's leaving this afternoon, and he wanted me to pull some promotion material together for an upcoming competition. I'm a little stressed out."

"There's a competition?" My voice rose. I stood up straight and then smiled.

Her jaw dropped. "Seriously, Charlotte? That's what you got out of my answer?"

I put my right hand on the counter in consolation and used my left hand to shift my bag up higher on my shoulder. "Oh, my goodness, Erin. I'm sorry. I just didn't know there were competitions in this sport. Is there anything I can help you with? I'm really good at marketing campaigns."

A deep, baritone voice spoke from behind me. "Erin, can you call and confirm the car? My flight leaves at 3:00 p.m., and I can't miss it."

I made a goofy face at her, not turning to look at the man standing a few feet behind me.

"Yes, Mr. Crown. I called a short time ago, and they'll be here right at 1:00 p.m."

"Thank you," he responded. His deep voice filled the room.

I waited until Erin relaxed her shoulders and exhaled loudly before giggling and mocking her. "He sounds scary!"

"He's really not that scary. He's just going through a difficult time and seems to be snapping at everyone."

I wanted to sit and gossip, but I also wanted to forget about work. Gossiping would make me more anxious, and that was never a good thing.

Stepping over to the shoe rack, I slipped off my shoes. As I opened the door to the studio, I said, "I'm going to go change. You'll sign me in?"

She nodded briefly at me and added, "Will you really help me with these campaigns?"

"Of course!"

The door swooshed closed behind me, leaving me alone in the studio. It was quiet, alluring. From that very first class, my fascination with it had not changed. Now that I knew there was a competition—I was even more intrigued.

The changing area was in the back, and I shut the dressing room door behind me to change. My bag was packed with a few outfits, and today, I pulled out a pair of red boy-shorts and a matching red sports bra. I slipped a black, backless sweatshirt over my head and put my thumbs through the finger holes at the sleeves' ends. Sometimes, the girls in the class would wear the platform heels, but today I would go barefoot. To keep me warm until we got into the dancing, I wore silver leg warmers that reached my mid-thigh.

Turning my backside to the mirror, I glanced over my shoulder and ran my hands up the backs of my thighs, admiring how my bottom had lifted over the past few months. I giggled at the tiny bit of butt cheek peeking out of the bottom of my boy-shorts.

(Mark would have a heart attack if he knew I was doing this.)

I left my hair down so I could flip it during some of the moves, and then I shoved my work suit into my bag.

I flipped off the light switch as I left the room and shut the door behind me. Turning back to the studio, I came up hard against a solid, male body coming out of one of the offices.

"Oof," I grunted and reached out to him to keep from tripping.

He was almost a head taller than me, and my gaze went directly to his collarbone and strong neck. My hands were firmly gripped on his biceps, and my fingers tightened. The smell of him was intoxicating, hints of amber and sandalwood. I pressed my chest closer to him— he was so warm. I was overwhelmed with a sense of familiarity; of intense intimacy between us. My gaze lifted to his face, and I inhaled sharply, entranced by the heavily lashed brown eyes that met mine.

"Ahh…" My voice sounded foreign to me, breathy and seductive. My breaths came quick, and my chest heaved.

His lips were full and framed by a three-day beard. Hints of silver laced the neatly trimmed hairs. I leaned up, my lips parting. I was enthralled, and I wanted nothing more than to press my body closer to him. His hand slid down to my bottom, brushing the fleshy cheek exposed from under my shorts. I opened my mouth to speak, but only a squeak came out.

Leaning down close to my ear, his deep voice whispered, "I don't usually fuck the dancers, but I could make an exception for you."

The vulgarity of his words brought me back to the moment, and I was embarrassed by my blatant display of wantonness.

Now that I had my bearings, I stepped back out of his arms and straightened my shoulders. "That was rude. I think there's been a misunderstanding. I'm a customer, not a dancer. I mean, I take classes here, so I guess I'm a dancer, but I'm not a *dancer* dancer." I blushed. "Not that there's anything wrong with stripping. I'm just not..." I huffed and then took a deep breath and calmed myself before I spoke again. "I'm not a stripper."

I stood before him stoically, my shoulders drawn back. His eyes wrinkled at the corners as a slow, sexy smile curved the sides of his mouth. He chuckled, and my eyes were drawn to his lips. I licked mine.

"So, you don't want to fuck?" He glanced at his large military-style watch. "I leave in an hour. There's time."

I bristled at his language. I looked at him more closely—the man who had to be Mr. Crown. His jet-black hair was cut short on the sides, longer on top, and it was wavy. A lock had fallen onto his forehead. I followed his hand as he ran it back over his brow, smoothing his hair back into place. His cheekbones were high, and a smattering of golden freckles dotted his nose, making him appear boyish—a direct contrast to the boldness of what he had just spoken.

His crass words turned me on, and that addled me. "No, I don't want to... you know. And I don't think that's an appropriate way to speak to your customers."

He laughed, and his deep belly laugh made my lady parts ache. "Lady, the way you held on to me and panted, I disagree. But, okay. Have a good class." He looked at his watch again and then back up at me. "It starts in one minute."

With that, he walked off and left me standing, bewildered, in the small area between the changing rooms.

Pulling myself together, I stepped into the dance studio, placed my bag on a bench along the wall, grabbed a bottle of antiseptic cleaner and a rag, and picked out a pole to use. I sprayed the pole with the cleaner and then wiped it down, making sure it was dry enough to grip.

A bottle of pole grip was on the shelf next to the speakers. After shaking it, I squirted a small amount onto my hands before starting my stretch routine.

Three other girls came into the studio from the front reception area, followed by an instructor I'd never met.

"Hi, I'm Dani." She extended her hand to me.

"Charlie."

"Hi, Charlie. Are you new?"

"I usually come in the evenings, but I needed a break today, so here I am."

"Great! Welcome."

Dani was wearing an outfit similar to mine, except it was black. She was short, had a pixie haircut, and reminded me of Tinkerbell. She introduced me to the other three girls.

"They're rehearsing for the competition, so they're going to be moving really fast for this lesson. Just do what you can to keep up."

I tugged on the hem of my shorts. Again, I had that feeling I was intruding. The past fifteen minutes had been so surreal. *What had motivated me to come to a class I don't usually attend? Oh, I remember, budget forecasts.*

Dani moved (almost bounding) over to the stereo system against the wall and scrolled through her iPhone for her playlist. She hit a button on the screen and flipped a light switch before walking back to the center of the room.

I'd taken a pole in the back row; one of the other girls took a pole next to me; the other two girls took the ones in front of us. The poles were placed so that all students could watch themselves in the mirrors.

Sultry music started playing on the speakers overhead, and I forgot all about work. I forgot to be self-conscious, and I *almost* forgot about the sexy, crass man in the back room. Almost.

Dani put her hands above her head, clasping her hands, and swinging her hips side to side. "Okay, ladies, let's get started."

Dani led us through a stretching routine and then a floor routine. The floor routine was awkward for me, and I tried my best to just let go of my inhibitions. It had always felt a little too erotic to me—ass in the air and chest to the floor.

The effortless movement of the other girls fascinated me. Their bodies moved like liquid gold, seducing me through the motions. I watched covertly, mesmerized. They appeared to be making love, yet lost in their own seduction. The girls in my evening classes weren't this good; I was inspired.

"Good job, Charlotte, you look amazing." Dani complimented me as we finished with the floor work and moved on to pole moves.

She talked us through a routine of spins and slides, transitioning from one move to the other with fluid movements. I was lost in the music, the sultry beat and erotic tones lulling me into an almost sexual state. When I moved from a wiggle into pole frisking, I bent at the waist, flipped my hair back, and imagined the man I'd met in the back room caressing me from behind. It was wishful thinking, but I was so lost in my fantasy that I didn't realize Dani had stopped dancing. She was clapping for us and our hard work for the day.

Gradually bringing myself back to real life, I cleaned off the pole, and then took long gulps from my water bottle.

"Thank you for a great class, Dani."

"You're welcome. I hope you come back."

"Definitely." I grabbed my bag off the bench and went out into the reception area to talk with Erin.

She was busy on the phone, so I sat down on one of the white couches backed up against the window and waited for her to finish the call. I sat primly and stared out at the parking lot, watching as a black limousine pulled up in front of the building.

Ending the call, Erin pushed an intercom button and waited until a deep voice answered, "Paxton."

"Mr. Crown, your ride is here."

"Thanks, Erin. I'll be right out."

Erin looked up at me, her eyes wide. She bit her lower lip.

I tilted my head and asked her, "Still need my help?"

Mr. Crown emerged from a side door, rolling a suitcase behind him. A black leather messenger bag's strap crossed his chest. Underneath it, he wore a black, mandarin-collared leather jacket over a black T-shirt. His stance was solid; his attention was resolute.

He started a conversation with Erin, and I took that time to admire his firm backside filling out his worn jeans. I scanned down; his jeans tapered into leather motorcycle boots. As I scanned back up, he turned and glanced at me over his shoulder, catching my eye. I looked away quickly (down at my hands) and then back out the window.

He said to Erin, "I'll see you in three weeks for the event. Send me your ideas this afternoon. I'll look them over tonight after I land."

"Yes, sir, I'll have them for you right away."

He left without another glance toward me. I stared as he walked toward the limo. I stared as the driver opened the door for him and took his bag. I was—still—staring when he turned toward me and gave me a wickedly handsome smile before stepping into the back. I sucked in air and stared back, watching as the door shut and the limo drove away.

I felt branded.

CHAPTER 3

"CHARLOTTE, I ONLY have three hours until Mr. Crown is back on the ground. He'll be checking his email on the plane, so I can't use that as an excuse for not delivering." Erin stood behind the receptionist desk wringing her fingers, her brows drawn together.

I sighed heavily. "Okay, let me call my secretary and tell her I'm not coming back this afternoon. Give me a few minutes, and then I can focus on your plan."

Taking my cell phone out of my bag, I stepped back into the studio so I could have some privacy, and called Peggy. She answered on the second ring. "Should I update the numbers for you?"

I loved this woman!

"Yes, please. The spreadsheet is in my budget folder on the shared drive. All you need to do is check the formulas and upload the numbers by account. I won't be back this afternoon."

I was pacing back and forth across the studio while I talked, forefinger and thumb at my temple. "Move my leadership meeting to tomorrow morning. Also, can you call Mark and tell him I'll be late tonight?" I pulled my lips in between my teeth and looked at the ceiling, briefly closing my eyes. I hated asking Peggy to lie for me, but I was tired today, and he would hear the deceit in my voice.

"And if Richard is looking for you?"

I pinched the bridge of my nose. "Well, cake tasting doesn't usually last all day… Tell him Neiman-Marcus called and my dress for the party needs to be altered."

"Charlotte…" She drawled slowly, caution in her tone.

"I know, Peggy, I know." Silence sat between us. She was worried about me. "I just need a few more days, and I'll be back to being me. I promise."

We said our good-byes and hung up. Then I called my best friend, and realtor, Suzanne Madden.

Suzanne and I had been roommates at Arizona State University, and we had stayed close all of these years. On our senior trip to Cozumel, she introduced me to Mark, a former—casual—boyfriend of hers. We were all from Scottsdale, Arizona, but had never met until college. I went to a private high school; Mark and Suzanne went to a public one. She was sassy, sophisticated, and could sell hay to a wheat farmer. Suzanne and Mark had dated in high school but discovered they were better off as friends.

Her phone went directly to voicemail, so I sent her a text: *Bring me a dress please… let's have dinner*

I followed up with the address of the studio and went back out to help Erin.

Slouching behind the reception desk, Erin was staring blankly at the computer monitor in front of her. I pulled up a stool next to her and hopped up on it.

Rubbing my hands together eagerly and then placing my palms on my thighs, I asked, "Okay, what have you got?"

She turned sad eyes to me and then swiveled the screen so I could read it. Nothing. It was blank.

"Erin! Does he know you haven't even started?"

She shook her head, tears welling in her eyes.

"When is the event?"

"Three weeks."

"Oh, jeez. Okay, not a problem. First, we need to create an event on Facebook and set up an advertisement. Do you have a budget?"

Tears rolled down her face.

I jumped off the stool and pushed her off hers. "Trade me places."

Placing my hands above the keyboard, I closed my eyes and waited for inspiration. A feeling of calm settled over me. Once I started the creative process, the plan just flowed from me.

I pulled up a website to make quick, creative flyers, and Erin told me the information while I typed. I put her to work researching local yoga studios to contact. We'd need somewhere to hang these flyers.

Facebook advertisements were easy; I used my personal credit card to run the ads.

"Don't you think we should run this by Mr. Crown before we do it?" She started biting her nails.

"No. He strikes me as the type that prefers action." I didn't look up as I typed out an ad. "Tell him what you've done and be confident about it. He wants publicity and a high turnout. This is his business, Erin. It's not a charity."

My eyes bugged, and I was struck with a shot of adrenaline. "Oh, a charity! That is a *great* idea. Does he feel strongly about anything? A cause? Animals?"

Her face turned pensive and a little sad. "Well, his wife was recently involved in an accident."

"What? He's married?" My shock wouldn't seem strange, given that she had no idea what had transpired in the back room. My stomach clenched. A hot flash of embarrassment ran through my body, and my eyes burned. I shook my head to clear it, the hypocrisy of my feelings shaming me. I calmed myself and said in a more neutral tone, "Huh, I wouldn't have thought."

Then I looked back at the computer screen so I wouldn't keep talking.

"I think they've been separated for a while. She worked in the Phoenix studio as an instructor. I don't know much about her before that, but she might have been a stripper."

I glanced at her in warning. "You shouldn't assume if you don't know."

"Sorry," she said meekly.

"What about a charity?"

"Right. I was getting to that." She continued with her story. "They were married for a few years. Rumor has it..." She looked pointedly at me so I wouldn't cut her off. "*Rumor* has it that he wanted a family, and she wanted to keep competing. Having a baby would ruin her figure—or so she said. She started an affair with a Harley Davidson salesperson, and Mr. Crown was filing for divorce when a drunk driver pushed her and her boyfriend off the side of the road. Her boyfriend was killed, and she's in the hospital," Erin paused, "in Phoenix."

My fingers had frozen above the keyboard, and I looked at her in shock. "Wow." It was a lame response, but I had nothing else to say.

She reverted to her young, chipper self. "Yeah, so that kind of sucks, and it's probably why he's been so grumpy."

I stared at her incredulously, torn between desperately wanting to ask more about him and chastising her for her lack of empathy. Instead, I focused on Erin's most pressing problem. "The charity?"

"Oh, right. So, maybe we do something like Mothers Against Drunk Driving."

"Huh. Okay. Well, that one you *do* need to run by him. I'll help you draft an email, and you can recommend it. We'll definitely run the Facebook ad. Is there an opportunity to do an exposition here at the studio? Maybe a preview of local competitors?"

"The event is in three weeks, Charlotte. How do I do that?"

"You have a mailing list of all the members of the studio?"

"Yes."

"Current and inactive?"

"Yes."

"Great! Let's call a couple of competitors to perform their routine here at the studio. Maybe the night before, we'll host a little party, and serve champagne and snacks. Send out an invite to members. Build their interest again, and maybe they'll come watch the competition."

"Why do you keep saying, 'we'?"

My head jerked back just a bit, and I shook my head. "I don't know. Uh, I guess I was just getting excited for you."

The grin on her face grew, and she leaned in to hug me. "Ahh, you love us!"

At the risk of getting too attached, I teasingly brushed her off. "Whatever. Let's finish this up and send off the email."

In the email to Mr. Crown, we drafted an outline of the plan: what she had done so far (I made her take the credit), her recommendation on the charity, and her idea about the expo. I told her to start calling the competitors to see if they were interested, and I gave her a list of caterers that would be on the less expensive side. The Facebook ad would start running as soon as it was approved, and I told her to blame me if he was upset with her.

"Charlotte, thank you so much! I couldn't have done this without you. You saved my job."

I almost (sardonically) agreed with her. Instead, I took the less offensive path and told her she did great.

"He'll be impressed, Erin, I'm positive. And if you need any more help, here's my personal cell number." I took a post-it off the counter, wrote my number on it with a fine tip marker, and handed it to her. "You can call me anytime."

She took the post-it and put it in the top drawer, thanking me.

My phone vibrated on the counter, and I looked down to see a text from Suzanne: *I think you gave me the wrong address, this is a strip club*

Laughing out loud, I texted back: *Right address, not a strip club, come inside*

A moment later, Suzanne sashayed in with a fancy leather tote bag resting on her left forearm. As she removed her sunglasses with movie star flair, she said, "Well, this is interesting."

She glanced pointedly at me and then gave the room a cursory look.

When her gaze returned to mine, I introduced my friends to each other. "Erin, this is my friend, Suzanne. Suzanne, Erin." I gestured to both of them and watched as Suzanne crossed the room on gazelle-like legs to shake Erin's hand.

"It's nice to meet you," Erin mumbled back. I could tell she was intimidated.

Suzanne was stunning: perfect model body, tall, porcelain skin. She didn't believe in tanning and was high-maintenance from her pedicured toes to her perfectly arched eyebrows. She was also razor-sharp-smart and wasted no time with pleasantries. "Why are we here?"

"Well, I have been taking pole dancing classes, and today, I took the day off from work. I was helping Erin with some marketing ideas and thought you might want to join me for dinner. I didn't want to put my work clothes back on, so I asked you to bring me a dress. Did you bring me a dress?"

She squinted at me, saying nothing. Then she rested her arm on the counter and started strumming her fingertips across the surface. The rippling clicking of her nails annoyed me. I slapped my hand down on top of hers, trying not to laugh. "Stop it!"

She stopped, but continued to stare at me. "I don't understand, Charlie. What's going on here?"

Erin giggled. When I glanced at her, she lowered her chin to her chest and her eyes to the computer screen in front of her. A slight smile still sat on her face.

"Did you bring me a dress?" I asked again, brusquely.

She removed her arm from the counter and pulled a silk halter dress from her bag. "It's all I could find that would fit you."

I took it from her and gave her a pointed look. "I'll be right back."

"Should I just wait out here?"

I glanced from her to Erin. Erin's eyes went wide. She shook her head, mouthing, "No, no, no."

Suzanne turned to look at her just as she mouthed her last 'no,' and then rolled her eyes and went to sit on the couch.

"I'll just sit over here. Erin, could you please get me a glass of water?"

She responded, "Yes, ma'am," which got her another raised eyebrow.

I quickly went into the back room, took off my workout clothes, and put the dress on over my head. Suzanne was usually only like this in front of other people. I had seen her party and cry and joke with the people she was closest to. When it came to strangers, however, she always pulled the Cruella de Ville act. I usually ignored her.

I grabbed my gym bag and my purse and went back out into the lobby. I put my shoes on the floor and slipped my feet back into them. "Ready?"

Suzanne stood from the couch, once again placing her tote bag on her forearm. "Yes."

She was polite as we left, acknowledging Erin and pleasantly telling her, "Have a good evening."

I stood in front of the counter for just a moment, giving Erin a few final instructions.

"Text me if he responds; call me if you need help. You did a great job today, and you'll be fine."

She stepped around the counter to hug me. "Thank you, Charlotte."

I thought I heard tears in her voice as I hugged her back. She smelled like cookies. It felt good to have this young woman hug me so enthusiastically, and I relaxed in her arms, feeling like I was important to her.

Suzanne cleared her throat behind me, and I stepped out of Erin's arms, making eye contact with her. "I mean it, you call me!"

Erin nodded at me as we walked out the door. I fished my over-sized sunglasses out of my bag and then put them on to dim the afternoon Houston sun.

"How does The Rice Box sound to you? It's just around the corner," I asked.

"Perfect. And then you will tell me about... this?" She waved her hands toward the studio.

"Yes, I will tell you about… this." I laughed at her as I opened the door to my luxury SUV, stepped in, and buckled up.

I waited until she pulled her car out of the parking spot to follow me to the restaurant.

The Rice Box was neon-lit with lots of glass windows, had a few stools at the bar, and was just classy enough to make it a hipster place to be.

We settled in at the bar with our dinner: I had baby bok choy and orange-peel beef; Suzanne had Chinese eggplant with green beans.

"Talk," she said a little after our food was delivered.

I nodded at her and pointed at my mouth. She waited patiently until I finished chewing and took a drink of my tea.

"I started taking classes a few months ago. And Suzanne, I *love* it!" I looked heavenward and then back at her. "Sometimes I feel like it's the only place I can be me."

"What are you talking about? You've been you for a really long time. Mark adores you. *Everyone* adores you. You have the perfect house—that I sold you, of course." Her face had softened from the snooty face she used on Erin. "You're blessed, Charlie."

"That's just it, Suzanne, it's not perfect. I hate my job. I hate being there every day. Mark and I haven't had sex in weeks. My home is a museum…" I rushed on, putting my hand over hers so I wouldn't offend. "Don't get me wrong, it's beautiful. It just seems like every-thing after we graduated moved along like some checklist we were supposed to follow. What's next? Kids? A dog? A second home? A Peloton? A *second* Peloton?" I was starting to tear up, and she flipped her hand over to hold mine, squeezing my fingers tightly. "I just feel empty, Suzanne." The tears started to flow.

"And you thought stripping would fix it?" she whispered to me, sarcastically.

I laughed so hard that I snorted. The customers all turned their heads to us, and I lowered my voice to match hers. "It's not stripping; it's pole dancing."

"What's the difference?" She forked her dinner, taking a small bite.

"The difference is that I'm dancing in a studio with friends, feeling sexy and feeling uninhibited. I'm not in some lecherous club having creepy guys shove one-dollar bills in my panties." A handsome, sexy face entered my thoughts, and I inhaled sharply.

Suzanne paused her chewing, not missing the change in me. "What was that?"

"What was what?"

"You just got all flushed."

"My dinner is spicy."

"No." She tilted her head, tapping her finger on her lips. "Is there someone else?"

"No, Suzanne, there isn't anyone else." I pushed the thought of Paxton Crown out of my head and focused on my conversation. "There might be someone else for Mark, but I don't ask. I don't know if I care."

"Charlie, that makes me sad." She pouted.

"Don't be sad for me. I'll figure out what to do." I leaned back over to her and whispered, "There's a competition in three weeks. I'm thinking about entering."

She laughed and then said more quietly, "You're serious?"

"Yeah, sure, why not? They have instructors that can help me choreograph a routine. I pick music and an outfit." I waggled my eyebrows at her and shook my shoulders in a shimmy. "I get to be a real stripper."

I giggled, and then she laughed at me. "You're crazy, Charlie. But I support whatever you decide to do. I love you, and when you come out on the other side of this, I'll still be here for you."

Tilting my head to the side, I said, "Aww, I love you too. Thanks for not judging—too much."

She shook her head, and we finished our dinner in friendly conversation. For the party, we made plans to do our hair and makeup together on Saturday. Her fingers flurried across the keyboard of her phone, texting her contacts to make appointments. We talked about our dresses: mine was a gold brocade, off-the-shoulder mermaid gown, and hers was a ruby red, high-neck backless crepe ball-gown. Perfect for the bourgeois, elite crowd of Houston.

After we finished our dinner, we walked out into the humid Houston evening. The sun was setting and casting an orange glow against the glass of the high-rise buildings around us. A light breeze lifted my hair and blew it in front of me. I pushed it back behind my ear.

My phone rang. Reaching into my purse, I recognized the number to the dance studio. I let it go to voicemail, making a note to call Erin when I got in my car.

"You'll let me know what you decide about that stripper thing?" Suzanne feigned disinterest.

I smiled and responded matter-of-factly. "I will let you know about the pole dancing competition."

She chuckled as she got into her car. "Yeah, that."

Suzanne drove away, waving at me out of the top of her convertible.

I stood in the parking lot a moment longer, breathing in the night air and listening to the sounds of traffic rushing by on the freeway around the corner. I was startled from my trance by the shrill cry of my phone again.

I looked down to see an Arizona number light up the screen. I didn't recognize the number, but it could have been any number of people I knew. Suddenly, awareness shot through me, my phone felt like it was on fire, and I almost dropped it.

Calming myself, I clicked the green phone icon and said, "Hello?"

"Charlotte Chase?"

Oh, crap!

CHAPTER 4

THAT VOICE – the one that had propositioned me just hours before – washed over me like a warm shower. If I had been at home, I would have curled up on the couch, phone to my ear, and purred back.

Realization dawned on me that this was about the Facebook ad. "This is she."

"This is Paxton Crown."

"I'm sorry, who?"

A sardonic laugh came through the phone. And, in a tone that indicated he knew *I knew* exactly who he was, he said, "Paxton Crown. I own the Live Once Vertical Studio."

"Oh yes. How can I help you?"

Holding my breath, I sat down at one of the outside picnic tables and stared out at the cars passing by.

"It seems we owe you a reimbursement for the Facebook ad you placed."

"There's no need." I had crossed my right leg over my left and was swinging my foot back and forth.

"Yes, actually, there is. And how much will you need to charge us for your time today?"

I uncrossed my legs, and sat still. "Time for what?"

"For writing the campaign for her." Irritation laced his words and I suddenly panicked.

Oh no. I didn't want Erin to get in trouble. I had to focus on ensuring she kept her job.

"Mr. Crown —"

He cut me off. "Paxton."

His tone was softer, more intimate. I paused before continuing, allowing his name to settle between us.

"Paxton." Saying his name was unnerving, and I reverted back to formality. "Mr. Crown. I didn't write the campaign for her. She did it on her own. I'm in sales, and I simply acted as a thought partner for her today. She did all the work."

"What the fuck is a thought partner?" he asked abruptly in a boyishly annoyed tone.

"You don't need to be rude about it. Frankly, you should be a little kinder to your employees. Erin works hard for you and you might have asked her if she knew how to do a marketing campaign before expecting her to deliver one." I collected myself, feeling like I was on more solid ground, and said, "And a thought partner is someone you share ideas with, bounce your thoughts against, and try to come up with the best solution; A thought partner."

He inhaled deeply, apparently frustrated, and then said on an exhale. "I'm going to text you a phone number. Her name is Solara, she's our Chief Financial Officer. Please tell her you need to request reimbursement for an ad. She'll know what it's about."

The abrupt business-like tone was not what I expected to hear from him, and my emotions were zinging around inside me like a pinball machine. Sparks – respect – lust... they all hammered against the bumpers of my brain, demanding attention at rapid-fire speeds. One minute I was turned on by his voice. The next, it reminded me of being back in a boardroom.

"Mr. Crown – "

He repeated, "Paxton."

I once again settle into a comfortable lull from his voice, a sorcerer weaving his mystical spell on me. "Paxton."

I paused, then said in an almost pleading tone. "Paxton. She tried. She really did. I do sales campaigns and customer research for a living. I wanted to help her. Please don't fire her. She was really enthusiastic about what we came up with, and she's a good girl." He didn't immediately respond, and I said again with more closure, "She's a good girl."

He inhaled and then exhaled deeply. "I'm not going to fire her. Quite the opposite, actually. She said good things about you. She seems to admire you, and she expressed an interest in going back to school. I told her we'd pay for her first year of community college if she was interested. It's up to her now."

The person I was talking to was behaving entirely at odds with the man that had sparked in me a primitive need to be made love to. No, that wasn't what I needed from him. He was something else entirely.

Speaking softly, I thanked him. We both stayed on the phone for a moment longer, neither of us speaking. This afternoon's encounter played out in my mind until the quiet became awkward.

Breaking the silence, I asked him tentatively, in almost a whisper, "Is there anything else?"

He cleared his throat. "No. I'll send Sol's number right over."

"I'll call her tomorrow."

"Charlotte." His voice turned deep again, and I waited for him to continue. "It was nice to meet you today."

I inhaled sharply, and couldn't think fast enough to respond.

He saved us both. "Have a good-night," he said, and then hung up.

Sitting still, shocked and bewildered, I was jarred out of my thoughts when my phone chimed again, startling me.

"Christ!" I said out loud as I rolled my eyes heavenward and then down at the phone. A text. Solara's number. Nothing else. I saved both numbers to my phone. I would call Solara tomorrow.

The ride to my house was just a few short minutes and I clicked the automatic gate opener when I turned onto my street.

As I waited for the wrought iron gate to open inward, I stared pensively at the house. Upward lighting, planted in the yard in front, cast luminescence against the columns, making it appear larger, more statuesque. A wrought iron chandelier hung from the front porch and had been turned on by an automatic timer. It was a home worthy of a magazine spread, and yet, it looked…empty.

When the gates were fully open, I drove through and around back to the garage, parking my car under the portico and entering the house through the back door.

The lights were dim in the kitchen, and the rest of the house was dark.

Placing my bag on the granite countertop, I went to the fridge and pulled out a bottle of water. Drinking right from the bottle, I gulped down most of it before screwing the top back on and putting it back in the fridge. Glancing down the hall, a sliver of light shone from Mark's office and I walked down to talk to him.

He was at his desk, deep in thought, and I watched him from the doorway until he glanced up and noticed me.

"Hey, babe. How was your night?"

By all standards, he was genetically gifted. A perfect six feet tall. A perfect one hundred and eighty pounds. Perfect white teeth, courtesy of orthodontics. Perfect… just fill in the blanks. And, he was perfectly smart and driven.

For the first few years of dating, and eventually our engagement, we were surrounded by our college friends. We celebrated engagements and baby showers, weddings and baby's first birthdays. The last few years, we'd spent less and less time with our friends, and subsequently less and less time with each other. It's almost like we didn't really know who we were together, without our friends.

I sat down in the high back chair in front of his desk, slipping off my shoes, and tucking my feet underneath me. "It was good. Suzanne and I had dinner together, talked about the party Saturday night."

"Oh good! Are you excited?" He had gone back to work and his words felt obligatory. Like he wasn't really interested in my response.

"Mm-hmm." I continued watching him work. The line between his forehead deepened and I could tell he'd become engrossed in his work again, forgetting I was there.

I unfolded myself, picked up my heels by the back straps, and stood. "I'm going to head upstairs."

Absentmindedly, he responded, "Okay, babe."

Turning in the doorframe, I took one more look at him before heading back to the kitchen to grab my bag. I went around through our formal living room and headed towards the circular stairs in the front hall that would take me to the master bedroom.

Padding up the stairs, my feet sunk into the carpet, leaving impressions in the luxurious pile with every step.

When I reached the landing, I opened the French doors that led into our room, and crossed to my nightstand to plug in my phone. My bag went in the chair in front of my writing desk and I strolled into my walk-in closet.

The closet was the size of a small bedroom, and I put my shoes on a rotating rack that would fold in, only to reveal another row of shoes.

Gently, I took off my dress, and put it in a bin for dry cleaning.

As I stood in the middle of my closet, in only my underwear, I was struck with inspiration. Hurriedly, I opened the bottom drawer of the dresser in the center of the room and pulled out a sexy outfit I was saving for this weekend. The red and black bustier, with matching thong panties and garter, had been packed lovingly in a garment bag, with black silk stockings. Next to them in the drawer was a pair of black silk gloves that went past my elbows, and I gingerly pulled them out too.

I took my underwear off, and replaced them with the thong. The bustier was a little more complicated, and I had to leave it loosely tied. I sat down on my white cushioned bench and slowly slid on the stockings. Standing, I fastened them to the garter belt and went to find a pair of black stilettos.

Quietly, I walked back down the stairs to Mark's office, and sashayed over to his desk. He was once again totally engaged in his computer in front of him, so I rested a hip on the desk in front of him, pushing on his shoulder to get him to lean back in his chair.

"What are you doing, Charlie? I need to get this proposal response finished."

He had stopped his typing, and gave my outfit a cursory glance. His eyes dilated. He was affected by my seduction.

Leaning towards him, I unbuttoned the top button on his dress shirt and purred, "I thought you could take a break. Relax a little."

He grabbed my wrist, forcing me to look up from where my hands were caressing his now-exposed neck, into his eyes. "What brought this on, Charlie?"

A voice in my head said, *I don't fuck the dancers, but I could make an exception for you.*

I stood and straddled him in his chair, pressing down against him. Seductively leaning into his neck, I kissed him softly, whispering, "I want to make love with you."

His hands had raised to my hips and I ground down onto him, thinking my arousal was matching his.

Instead, he gently pushed me away. "I don't have time for this, Charlie."

Again, with the voice, *So, you don't want to fuck? I leave in an hour. There's time.*

Hot tears burned in my eyes, but I held it together. Doing my best to hide my embarrassment, I stood and laughed it off.

"No big deal. I just thought it would be fun. We haven't made love in a while, and I miss you."

"Soon, Charlie. But tonight, I really need to finish this project."

"I understand. I'm going to bed." I leaned down to kiss him and he kissed me chastely in return. I felt nothing.

He mumbled good-night, and as I went back up the stairs to bed, my tears started to fall.

When I reached my closet, I unceremoniously ripped off the garter and the bustier, not caring that I put a hole in the stockings and broke the strings. I shoved the garter back in the bag with less love than when I took them out. The stockings were next, and I threw them in the trash can under the bathroom sink.

My blue silk nightgown hung on the back of the bathroom door and I slid it on over my head. My tears were sporadic now, and I hiccupped as I brushed my teeth.

As I pulled back the covers on my bed and slid under the cool sheets, I reached for my phone on the nightstand. I pulled up my recent call log and stared at the last Arizona number. Turning off the phone, I set it back on the nightstand, reached up to turn off the lamp, and settled under the covers to sleep. Sleep came fitfully, tormented by dark eyes and a naughty voice.

CHAPTER 5

Locking myself in my office the next morning I made the call to Solara. I put my wireless earbuds in, clicked on the number Paxton had texted me last night, and tapped the call button.

After a few rings, she answered in an enthusiastic tone, "Solara Crown."

Expecting to hear a crisp business-like voice on the other end, I was shockingly surprised to hear a sultry, yet outgoing, woman. It was like bursts of light coming through the phone. And I would have giggled, if it hadn't been for her last name... it tripped me up. This wasn't his wife. Erin had told me she was in the hospital. Was this his sister?

My lack of immediate response had her asking, "Hello?"

I focused on the reason for my call and spoke efficiently, "Ms. Crown, this is Charlie Chase."

"Hi, how can I help you?"

"Mr. Crown said I was to call you about sending an invoice for my services yesterday." I almost bust out laughing thinking that if she didn't know why I was calling, she might wonder about what the dubious services might be.

She paused long enough to make me uncomfortable – that maybe she was thinking they were salacious services – so I hurriedly said, "The Facebook ad?"

It was her turn to laugh. And she did it robustly. "Right." Her voice took on the friendly tone she answered with. "Well, I'm so glad you called. The Facebook ad is still running, and it's getting a lot of hits. That was a fantastic idea, even if Paxton was annoyed that you paid for it yourself."

"Sorry about that." I responded a little sheepishly. "It just felt like the right thing to do at the time."

"Well, it worked. Why don't I send you a quick contract for marketing services, and when you get your final credit card bill, just send us the invoice."

This was a weird conversation. I rhythmically swiveled myself back and forth in my chair, and realized I didn't want reimbursement. Her no-nonsense delivery pulled me in. I wanted to be her friend. She reminded me of me, in a business sense, and I thought in another life we would be good friends.

"Ms. Chase? Are you still there?"

"Yes. Sorry." Christ! I was usually the professional one, and I was acting like a ditz. "You can call me Charlie."

She drawled slowly, "Okay…Charlie. Does my proposal work for you?"

"Yeah, sounds great." I rattled off my personal email address and then asked, "how long have you worked for the company?"

She laughed again, amused by me. "I was born into it. My parents started a small studio here in Phoenix when my brother was little. They now own twenty across the country."

"Paxton's your brother?" My question was intrusive for someone who was just…well, I don't even know what I was. But I didn't care. When she continued, she sounded curious, so I would need to tread lightly.

"He is…" She drew it out. "He's also the President of the company. I thought you met him."

I stopped my swiveling, and sat up straight in my chair. "Not officially, no. He was running out of the studio yesterday afternoon as I was coming in." I closed my eyes briefly and put my head back. I was getting all wrapped up in my lies.

"Huh." She paused, and then continued, in a conspiring tone. "We should go out to dinner when we're in town. I would love to meet you."

I needed to get off this call. Quickly. I snapped myself back into business mode and told her that sounded great. "Send me the contract, and you have my cell number now, so, just let me know about dinner."

She laughed again at my rambling, and we hung up.

Pulling out my earbuds, I threw them down on the desk next to my phone. I put my head back on my chair and let out a heavy sigh. "UGH!!! What am I doing?"

The rest of the day passed slowly, the clock hands on my watch moving like molasses. All I wanted was to get to my six o'clock class.

At five thirty, I shut down my computer, grabbed my pink bag and purse, and headed out to the studio.

Entering the lobby, I was greeted by a number of girls that had become regulars for the Tuesday night class. Erin jumped out from behind the reception desk and squeezed me tightly. "Charlotte! Oh my God! He *loved* our ideas! I had to tell him about the Facebook ad though. I had to give him your number. I knew he would know I couldn't have paid for it myself. I tried to call and warn you he would be calling."

"Yes, I know. He called last night."

She grimaced and apologized again. Her face crinkled up when she asked, "Was he nice to you?"

"He was…polite." '*What the fuck is a thought partner?*' His voice in my head almost made me laugh. I was saved by the instructor popping her head out of the studio telling us we had ten minutes. It was Dani from the other day, and I gave her a little wave before she went back in.

I spoke to Erin over my shoulder as I slipped off my shoes. "I need to get dressed. I'll talk with you after the class, okay?"

Erin went back to checking people in. I went to the back to change.

Once again, I selected a pole in the back, but Dani told me to move up front.

"You're really good Charlie. You should be up front. The others can follow you."

"Oh no, I'm good back here."

She picked up my water bottle and knee pads and brought them to the front of the room. "Yes. You should be up front."

Her tone was authoritative, so I didn't argue again.

While I stretched, she went to the music system and cued up her playlist. While we were waiting for the rest of the class, she started a conversation with me about the competition.

"Did you sign up?"

"No. I just found out about it yesterday. Do I have time? To put a program together?"

"Sure. We can choreograph something easy for you. Something basic, but sexy. You're better than you think, Charlie. Do you want me to work with you?"

In a fleeting moment, every reason why I shouldn't ran through my head: Mark, my reputation, my boss, how people perceived me, the stripper connotations, and Suzanne. Then I said emphatically, "Yes!" A giggle escaped me. "Yes! Yes!"

She laughed at my exuberance. "Wait after class so we can talk."

Class was exciting, and fast, and I was energized by Dani's confidence in me. As I moved, I started thinking about what a program would look like. What song would I pick? What would I wear? When the last song ended and Dani turned on the lights, we clapped for her and she threw up her hands at us. "Everyone have a great week! Stay sexy, stay strong."

I pulled a short wrap skirt out of my bag, tied it around my waist, and put my backless sweater back on over my head. Placing my bag over my shoulder, I approached Dani to ask her about choreography.

She was wiping her face with a towel, and she grinned at me as she threw it in a laundry basket.

"You really want to compete?"

"I do, actually. I love it here. And the timing seems right. It sounds like fun. Can you really do something for me in such a short time?"

"Sure. Let's start Thursday. I don't usually teach the night class; I'm filling in tonight. Can you come during the day?"

The slippery slope I was on just got a splash of olive oil. "Sure." And then the devil danced on my shoulder.

We agreed to Thursday and Friday after the noon class. I skipped, uncharacteristically, out into the lobby to have Erin sign me up for the event.

She was busy with a customer, so I shot off a text to Mark. *Can you meet me for dinner?*

His response came back right away. *8pm? Flemings?*

I looked down at my attire, knowing I was *not* appropriately dressed for Flemings, and texted back, *Sure*

While I waited for Erin, I flipped through the display rack of outfits thinking of what I would wear for my event. They all looked like bathing suits for the most part, but more mesh, and definitely with sparkles. A black one caught my attention and I pulled it off the rack to get a closer look. The bottoms were high on the hips, and dipped low below my belly button. The bra top had feathers across the top of the cups, which were jeweled with crystals. A layer of mesh lay between the straps in the front, and was covered in jewels that were made to look like a drape-choker necklace.

Caressing the material lovingly, I imagined that it wouldn't matter what music I selected, I had to have this outfit.

"You're so funny, Charlotte." I turned to find Erin leaning over the top of the counter, her chin in her hands, smiling at me.

I walked to the counter, placing the items on the desk as she sat up straight. "Why do you say that?"

"Because you so obviously love it here." She shrugged. "You're fun to watch."

"Thank you. I guess."

"Are you going to buy those?"

"Yes, and I need you to sign me up for the competition."

She paused and then a huge grin spread across her face, her full lips spreading wide, showing off her pretty teeth. "Really?"

I smiled, blushing. "Yes, really. Now ring up my clothes and sign me up for the competition."

Packaging my clothes gently in white and pink tissue paper, she placed them lovingly in a baby pink bag with a red heart sticker in the middle of it. The heart had the word LOVE in it.

"Aww, that's cute! LOVE, on the heart. I like it."

Erin had placed the bag on the counter and I was reaching for it when she responded. "Yeah, I always wondered if Mr. Crown did that on purpose, or if it was just a coincidence."

I put the bag over on the couch with my purse, and took out my wallet so I could pay for the registration and the outfit. As I crossed the room back to her, I asked, "What do you mean?"

"LOVE? The word? LOVE."

"Right. I know it's a word. What do you mean about it being a coincidence?"

"Live Once Vertical Enterprises? His company? He and his brother have a couple of businesses they manage. I don't really pay attention. Maybe I should. Do you think I should?"

I gazed at her in utter awe, and confusion. Was it really possible her life had been so sheltered, that she had no idea how to be part of a workforce? I didn't have the heart to tell her about my conversation with Paxton the night before, so I simply *suggested* that she may want to take a more avid interest in how things were managed around here. "You love it here; you should get more involved in the business. You might surprise yourself."

She handed me a form to fill out, and I entered as 'Entertainment Level 1.'

After entering all my personal details into the system, she handed me a packet with all of the information, including times and the location.

"So, you and Dani will need to arrive 45 minutes before your event time. Sometimes they run early. Once you decide on your music, you need to upload the mp3 file to the website listed in your packet. Your code is right here." She pointed at the packet where she had put a sticker with the studio name, phone number and the code she had written on with a sharpie.

"That's it?" I had expected it to be more thrilling.

"That's it. Now you just need a program." She laughed and smiled at me mischievously. "I can't wait to see what you and Dani come up with. She's amazing."

"Thanks, Erin. I'll see you tomorrow. I'm having dinner with my fiancé tonight and I don't want to be late."

We said our good-byes and I drove through the elite Houston neighborhoods to the restaurant. Mark was waiting in the bar for me, talking on his cell phone, a martini in front of him.

The barbie doll hostess greeted me and I pointed to Mark, indicating I would join him in the bar. She put the menus back in the hostess stand and told me to let her know when we were ready to be seated.

Waving me over, Mark put his finger to his mouth, indicating I should be quiet, while he finished his call. It struck me as rude and dismissive, since he was already in a bar filled with people.

I slowly, and quietly, maneuvered myself up onto the stool next to him and silently, almost just above a whisper, told the bartender that I would have a dry vodka martini.

Crossing my legs, I waited patiently for Mark to finish his call. I turned and watched him, twirling my finger up into the air, trying to tell him to wrap it up.

He looked at me, brows furrowed, and ran his finger through

the air from my calf to my neck, and twirled his finger around. He mouthed, "What is this?"

I laughed and almost choked on my drink. I mouthed back, "Get off the phone."

It was this kind of funny banter that I enjoyed with him. Feeling a little more lighthearted than I had this morning, I smiled at him and relaxed. Maybe our problems weren't too deep after all.

Ending the call, he put the phone on the bar, face up, and turned to greet me. I leaned in to give him a kiss and was greeted with a disapproving remark. "Seriously, Charlie, what are you wearing?"

I still had on my leg warmers and backless sweater. My wrap skirt was a little short, and had slid up the side of my thigh, revealing the hem of my boy shorts. Taken aback, I thought momentarily that they could have been mistaken for underwear, but his reaction was a little harsh and I told him so.

"Mark, they're just workout clothes."

"Could you have changed before you met me?"

"Actually, I have something I want to share with you. And before you react, just know that I'm really happy about it, and I hope you will be too."

"Please don't tell me you're pregnant. We talked about this, Charlie. We agreed we would wait another year or two, when things settled down for you at work."

A knot lodged in my throat, and I struggled to keep it down.

"Uhm…actually no, that's not what I was going to say." I took another sip of my drink, hoping to keep the tears back. His words felt like a slap, and I wasn't even sure I wanted to stay for dinner now.

He waved to the hostess that we were ready for our table.

"Hold that thought, babe." He asked the bartender to bring our drinks to our table, and we followed the hostess through the restaurant to a booth in the back.

The surroundings were blurred from the rise of my unshed tears as I walked behind him. My steps were heavy.

Once seated, he asked, "What was it you wanted to tell me?" With manicured hands, he unbuttoned his sleeves and rolled them up on his forearms.

I blurted out, "I've been taking pole dancing classes."

He paused his rolling, "As in stripping?"

"Not stripping. Pole dancing."

"Stripping. Is that what this get-up is about?"

My face flushed, and my anger rose. "It's dancing, Mark! And I really like it. It's harder than you would imagine, and, in case you haven't noticed, I'm in better shape than I've been in a long time."

"It's still stripping, Charlie. Put a pretty name on it, but it's for trash." Not making eye contact with me, his eyes scanned the menu.

I inhaled sharply, and felt sick to my stomach. When had he become such an ass?

"I signed up for a competition."

He slowly lowered the menu to the table. He squinted, and looked me in the eye. "I'm not following you, Charlie."

I rushed on, "It's in two weeks. I'm doing a beginner program and I would really like it if you would come."

"No."

"No, you won't come?"

"No, you aren't doing it."

"Why would you say that?"

"It's embarrassing, Charlie. And I won't have my future wife doing something that's beneath us."

"You mean beneath you?" I asked him sardonically.

"Beneath us, Charlie. We've worked hard to get where we are. I won't have you risking some scandalous story because you want to play sorority girl."

Words wouldn't come to me. I sat in shock, staring at the man I no longer knew. I would never have expected him to be so closed minded, and my anger simmered. Not wanting to say anything I might regret, I slid out of the booth, grabbed my bag, and stood to leave.

Quietly I said, "I'm going to head home. We can talk about this later."

"You don't want to stay for dinner?" His obtuseness almost made me laugh.

"I'll get Taco Bell."

I walked quickly to my car before my tears could fall.

CHAPTER 6

"SUZANNE, I'M TELLING you, I don't know if I can go through with it."
I was walking quickly across the parking lot, my heels clicking on the
concrete. Cradling my cell phone between my ear and my shoulder as
I opened my car door, I threw my bag onto the passenger seat. It was
Friday and the office building garage was already empty.

For the past two days I had been working with Dani on a dance
routine, and I was already feeling really good about it. Confident and
sexy. Every time I returned to my *real* life, the burden to keep up a
facade felt heavier and heavier.

Dani and I had settled on Demi Lovato's "Confident." Dani loved
my outfit and every day I was getting more and more excited about
the competition. The looming engagement and celebration party
was starting to feel more and more like a roadblock to my personal
happiness.

Mark had called Suzanne the day after I ran out on our dinner,
and now she was acting as a go-between. It pissed me off that he
would use her to talk to me. I was pulling farther and farther away
from him.

Her voice interrupted my thoughts. "He's invited everyone, and
I mean everyone, that the two of you know. You can't back out now."
She paused, and then continued almost accusingly. "Unless...are you
completely backing out?"

I pushed the start button on my car and the phone switched to Bluetooth.

"Charlie, are you there?"

"Yes, I'm here, I was just turning on the car. And no, I'm not *completely* backing out." I drove out of the garage, heading home to meet the caterers and party rental company. "I don't think," I said as an afterthought.

"I'm on my way over to your house. I have your dress, and we can talk more then."

I started to tell her I wanted to be alone tonight, but she hung up and the Bluetooth disconnected.

After the dinner with Mark earlier this week, I'd called Solara. I loved Suzanne. She was my closest friend. But Solara felt...bold, alive, and vivacious. And non-judgmental. I told her I'd signed up for the competition and asked if she had been serious about meeting for dinner. Her response? An enthusiastic "Yes!"

The competition would run until 7 p.m., so it would be a late dinner, but I didn't care. I needed something to ground me, to give me something to look forward to.

Suzanne's car was in my driveway when I arrived.

Mark was nowhere to be seen, and honestly, I was grateful. We'd been tip-toeing around each other this week and he'd been sleeping in the guest room.

Elegantly, Suzanne stepped out of her car as I approached her.

"Were you sitting here when you called me?" I asked.

"No, but I was around the corner showing a house."

Three white party trucks were parked alongside the curb, and one of the drivers ran up the driveway when he saw me pull in.

"Mrs. Kingsley?"

Suzanne crossed her arms and smirked at me as if to say, *How are you going to respond to that?*

I frowned at her and said to the driver, "Yes. Are you bringing the tables and chairs?"

"Yes, ma'am. And we have the tent and serving ware too."

I turned back to Suzanne. "Can you direct him, please? While I go change?"

With saccharine sweetness, she replied, "Of course, Mrs. Kingsley, I would be happy to." Then she turned on her heel, telling the men to follow her.

I knew Suzanne would direct them to set up the party with the utmost perfection, and I left her to the details.

The day of the party, I woke to a brilliant bouquet of red roses and a note on my dresser:

To Charlie,
My life just wouldn't be the same without you in it.
Mark

With a heavy sigh, I put on my bathrobe, grabbed the vase, and went downstairs to get my morning coffee. Caterers, and florists, were already bustling around. An ivory and gold garland twisted around the banister, and oversized vases sat at the foot of the stairs.

The caterers had returned to set up lights and a dance floor in the backyard. Surprisingly, the weather was cool, almost wintery for Texas, but the sky was clear and blue. Heat lamps were placed close to the seating area and would be turned on later this evening.

Mark was sitting at the kitchen bar drinking coffee and reading the news on his laptop.

He raised his eyes to me and smiled tentatively. "Good morning."

I set the vase gently on the counter. "Thank you for the flowers."

"You're welcome."

We were wary around each other. More and more frequently our conversations were stilted and forced.

I crossed my arms in front of me, smiled, and nodded out towards the back yard. "It looks nice out there. It should be a beautiful party tonight."

Ignoring my attempt at banalities, he said, "Charlie, about the other night…"

I dropped my arms and stepped between his legs. Hooking my hands behind his neck, I cut him off. "You don't need to apologize, Mark. I should have told you sooner."

He reached around his neck and unclasped my hands, "I wasn't going to apologize."

Stepping back from him I crossed my arms again. "Then what were you going to say?"

He exhaled and looked me directly in the eye. I really didn't want to get into this again with him. I was exhausted.

"Nothing. Nothing at all." A forced smile spread across his face. "What time are you and Suzanne getting your hair done?"

I walked to the other side of the kitchen and pulled down a mug. Pouring the coffee, I responded, "She should be here to get me in about an hour."

He moved behind me, and I put my mug back down on the counter. His arms wrapped around my middle and he buried his face in my neck. "I don't want to fight with you, Charlie."

Placing my hands over his forearms, I rested my head back against his shoulder and whispered, "I don't want to fight with you, either."

"Tonight is going to be beautiful. And you are beautiful. And we are going to have a beautiful life together."

I tilted my head to him for a kiss, and he pressed his lips gently against mine, breathing in for just a moment and then releasing me. "I have some work to do and then I'll see you this afternoon, alright?"

I nodded. He grabbed his laptop and coffee and headed back to his office down the hall.

Taking my coffee upstairs with me, I changed into a button-down shirt and jeans. Suzanne arrived a short while later, and the rest of the day passed in a blur. She carted me from one appointment to the next, and by the time we returned to my house, all I really wanted was a nap.

Promptly at six-thirty, Mark knocked on our bedroom door. Applying one last swipe of lip color, I grabbed my shoes and went to open it.

He swallowed visibly. His throat moved as his eyes scanned me from head to toe and back up again.

"Charlie, you look so lovely."

His custom tuxedo made him appear almost regal, and I couldn't disagree that he was an incredibly handsome man.

I curtsied and thanked him for the compliment. He held out his hand and walked me down the stairs. At the bottom of the stairs, I slipped into my shoes and we prepared ourselves to meet our guests.

Despite my reticence, I enjoyed the evening. Our friends arrived in glamourous fashion in their Mercedes and Bentleys.

Mark was the ever-gracious host, never far from my side as we walked through the rooms and greeted everyone.

Dinner was served in the backyard under the large party tent. Oversized glass candelabras with flameless candles acted as center-pieces, and I couldn't help but think that had been a bad decision. I couldn't see the guests across from me, and at one point that made me laugh. The entire evening felt like frosting on a sugarless cake.

Servers passed behind me, taking my plate. My wine glass was filled from over my shoulder. Silverware clinked on the china and the sound of high-pitched laughter merged with the conversations carrying on all around me. I could see mouths moving, and I smiled and nodded, but I couldn't hear the words. I started to sweat.

Mark reached out to grab my hand under the table and I glanced at him, smiling the frozen smile I had mastered so well. I pressed my other hand against my stomach and turned to whisper to Mark that I needed a minute.

"Not yet. I was just going to make a toast."

He pulled his hand from mine and stood, clinking his knife against his glass.

"Good evening, everyone." He waited until the murmurs of conversation died down. "Hello. Good evening. Welcome everyone to this beautiful night. We are certainly having a beautiful spring in Houston, are we not?"

Everyone murmured their agreement, smiling and clapping.

Mark droned on and on about what a lovely job the caterers had done and the beauty of the evening. I smiled and clapped at the requisite times. He congratulated me on my promotion, and I smiled appreciatively at our sophisticated guests when they clapped.

When he reached down to take my hand, I gave it to him, and he gently pulled me up out of my chair.

"Ladies and Gentlemen, the reason for our party tonight. My lovely bride-to-be, Charlotte Chase."

Everyone around us stood and clapped. Mark wrapped his arm around me and leaned in for a kiss. We were handed champagne flutes and I raised my glass to everyone in gratitude.

I nodded, smiled, and put my arm around him to steady myself. My stomach churned. Mark continued with his speech, letting everyone know the band would start soon.

I leaned up to Mark's ear, telling him I would be right back.

"Okay. Don't be long. There are a lot of people here for you."

"I won't be."

I weaved through the tables and made it into the house before I was intercepted by my boss's wife. "Charlotte! What a divine party." She took my hands and tugged gently on them with each word.

Leaning down to kiss her cheeks, I responded. "Thank you, Marjorie. I am so glad you could make it."

"You know, Richard says the most wonderful things about you. 'A rising star, that Charlotte, a rising star.'"

"Well, thank you so much! If you could just excuse me for a moment, I was on my way to the den to get something for Mark."

She didn't let go of my hands. "You look a little thin dear, are you feeling alright?"

With a tight smile, I responded, "Yes, actually, I've been working out more often. Trying to get back in shape, you know."

"Oh goodness, yes. I tried running once. Bad for my knees. What have you been doing?"

"Dancing."

"How fun! Is it a Zumba class? I understand all the young girls are taking Zumba these days."

"No, it's more of a specific style of dancing."

"It's not that awful hip-hop stuff, is it? You're too old for that kind of nonsense."

My blood pressure was rising. My shoulders tense. I took a deep breath and tried to calm down but the words just came out. "No, Marjorie. I've actually been taking pole dancing classes."

"Pole dancing?" she nearly shouted.

"Yes, it's actually incredibly difficult."

"Isn't that for strippers?"

Mark came through the back door at just that moment. His face contorted with fury. "Charlie, can I see you for a minute, please?" He lightly but firmly grabbed my elbow and steered me towards the home office.

When the door was shut behind us, he turned on me. "What the hell, Charlie? Now you're sharing your little escapade with your boss's wife?"

I shook off his hand from my arm. "She didn't seem all that upset by it. If you hadn't dragged me off, I might have had an interesting conversation."

Pacing the room, he shook his head in disbelief and then let out an audible sigh. The fight left him and he softly said, "Charlie, seriously, are you ok?"

Sitting gingerly on the edge of the couch, I resigned myself to the conversation. "I'm fine, and I'm having a really difficult time understanding why this is such a big deal. It's just another form of exercise and I enjoy it."

"It's not just that, though. It's everything about you lately. You seem really disconnected and I'm starting to wonder if maybe we rushed things buying this house. Did we move too fast? I feel like you aren't in this with me."

I stood and went to him. Standing directly in front of him I did my best to make eye contact. I reached for him and spoke softly. "I am in this with you. I do feel a little suffocated, but – "

He blew up. "Suffocated?!"

My head jerked back in surprise.

The door to the office opened and my boss walked in, his eyes darting back and forth between us. Shutting the door gently behind him, he said, "Everything alright in here?"

"Hi, Richard. Yes, everything's fine."

"Marjorie said you appeared a little distraught."

I smiled and assured him everything was okay. Mark loosened his tie and poured himself a drink from the side table.

Richard entered the room in a cautious manner and addressed Mark. "Do you mind if I talk to Charlie alone for a moment?"

He raised his glass in a mock salute. "Be my guest."

Tossing back the drink, he left us alone.

When the door shut behind him, Richard stuck his hands in his pockets and rocked back on his heels. "You seem a little stressed tonight, Charlotte."

"Mark and I are a little..." I searched for the right word, "... disconnected, lately."

"That happens with couples. The two of you are getting ready to embark on a big commitment. With your promotion, and the plans for the wedding, I can see how that might happen."

I didn't like where this was going. I flushed, my hands clammy as I clasped them together. My world was slipping out of control.

He took his hands out of his pockets and crossed his arms over his chest. "Why don't you take a leave of absence? At least enough time to get ready for the wedding. You've worked hard and you need a little time to yourself."

And there it was. *Slip.*

Desperation laced my words. "Richard, I don't need any time off."

"Nonetheless, I'm giving it to you." His look was pointed. It was the look he used when he wanted the recipient of his decision to stop talking.

I opened my mouth to argue, and he raised his gray brows questioningly at me.

I tried to inhale deeply to relax, but my dress was restricting me. "Thank you, Richard. A little time off will be wonderful."

"Great! Then it's settled. I'll have Peggy send out an email and bring you your things on Monday."

"Monday?" I was met with silence. "Monday will be fine, sir."

"Very well." He turned to head back out to the party. "Lovely party, Charlotte. Lovely party."

CHAPTER 7

"I THINK YOU'RE ready Charlie."

My daily private lesson had just finished. I was sliding down the pole from the top, cleaning as I went.

"I think so too. I'm nervous, but ready."

"Maybe taking time off was good for you."

My feet had just touched the ground and I looked at Dani skeptically. "Maybe. But not so good for my career."

Taking my hands in hers, she looked me in the eye. "Things happen for a reason, Charlie. Whatever it is you need, you'll find. It just doesn't always arrive in the package you expect."

"That sounds very wise," I teased her.

She laughed heartily. "I've been where you are."

It suddenly occurred to me that we had been working closely together for a little over two weeks and I didn't know anything about her.

After the weekend of my so-called engagement party, I started training with Dani every day. The first few days I was so sore, every muscle in my body had ached. I'd thought I was ready for a competition, but she put in so many moves and transitions that I hobbled home every afternoon like an old woman.

Mark worked late almost every day. The only evidence of him being home was his coffee mug in the sink.

Despite all the time with Dani, I was ashamed that I just assumed she'd always been a dancer.

"What do you mean, 'Where I am?'"

She laughed at my naivete. "I was a financial analyst for the Federal Reserve Bank."

"Seriously? The one down the street?"

"Yes. I went for a run on the bayou after work one day and ran past the studio. I'd had a bad day, as we all do, and found myself inside, signing up for a class. That was twelve years ago."

"Maybe I should become an instructor."

She chuckled under her breath as she packed up her bag. "Maybe you should."

We cleaned up the studio together. "I'll see you tomorrow for the exhibition. Thanks for your help cleaning up."

"You're welcome. I'll see you tomorrow."

As I entered the lobby, Erin was busy and stressed, trying to get everyone checked in for the class that was about to start.

"Erin, can I help you?"

I'd had so much free time over the past two weeks, I'd spent most of it here. Erin had been showing me all the programs and classes and information about the company. I almost felt as if I *did* work there.

With the look of a deer caught in the headlights of a car, she said, "Paxton and Solara are arriving tonight and the studio's a mess."

I glanced around. It looked clean to me.

"You really need to stop stressing out when they come to town. They're just people, just like you and me."

"I know, but they make me nervous."

"How can I help?"

She paused, putting one finger to her mouth. Abruptly she jumped off the stool and walked around the desk towards the studio door. "Okay. The exhibition is tomorrow and we need to set up one half of the studio with all the chairs and the table for refreshments."

"How many people are coming?"

A young lady interrupted us. "Can I check in?"

Erin looked at me in frustration.

I squeezed her hand. "Okay, never mind, I'll take care of it." I went back into the studio and closed the partition doors to separate the next class from where I was setting up.

Folding tables were located in the back room. I carried them out into the studio, stumbling along with the weight of them. *Maybe I should get some help*, I thought to myself.

I unfolded the tables I'd brought out and lined them up against the back wall. The folding metal chairs were stacked up against the wall and I started setting them up in rows.

"Do I need to pay you for this, too?"

The deep, baritone voice startled me. When I turned, I backed into the stack of folding chairs, tripping and clattering to the floor with them.

"Oh, Christ! Are you okay?" He ran to me and knelt down as I rolled myself up to a sitting position.

"For God's sake, Paxton. Don't sneak up on people."

"What happened to 'Mr. Crown?'" His eyes crinkled at the corners in a small smile.

Before I could respond, I heard the robust, teasing voice of who could only be Solara. "What on Earth?"

Paxton stood, holding out a hand to me. "I startled her."

Reluctantly I took his hand, and he pulled me up off the floor. The warmth and strength of his hand caused me to inhale sharply, confusion and desire in his eyes, reflecting back at me.

With enthusiasm, Solara crossed the room. "You must be Charlie. I'm Solara. It's so nice to meet you."

I reached out my hand to her and she enveloped me in a hug. She was curvy. Her lush body made me think of what it must be like to be smothered by a mother hen. As she pulled back, she held onto my shoulders, her eyes scanning my face.

"She's not average. She's gorgeous." She glanced scornfully at her brother.

"I didn't say she was average. I said she was ordinary."

"WOW! Right here!"

Solara took me in another hug. "Apologies for my brother. He's going through a rough time and doesn't know how to be normal."

Paxton started picking up the chairs and stacking them neatly back up against the wall. He didn't look at me again, only commenting, "I think we need to put her on the payroll."

Solara piped in with a grin on her face, "Oh yes! Let's do that."

"No, really, I have a job. I was just helping Erin get ready for the exhibition tomorrow night."

Announcing that he was going to the back office to get the schedule ready for the weekend, Paxton disappeared through the door in the back of the studio. I found myself staring after him.

Solara cleared her throat and said, "Soooooo, are you ready for this weekend?"

Snapping out of my haze, I responded. "I am. I'm a little nervous, but excited too."

"It's going to be a blast! I never get tired of events. They are long and exhausting, but some of the moves the masters make are just sick!"

She scrunched up her face and I couldn't help but laugh at her.

She grabbed me by the arm. "C'mon, you don't need to do this. We have a crew that will come in and do it after the last class."

"Erin was really worried about having it set up."

"Paxton makes her nervous. She doesn't need to worry about this. I'll talk to her later. Let's go next door and get a drink."

Allowing her to pull me along beside her, I grabbed my gym bag and my purse and put both in my car before we walked next door.

"I'm so happy to meet you. You sounded so nice on the phone, and when Paxton told me you were going to call me, I was excited to see who had him all twisted up."

I slowed my walk. "I think you have it wrong. He was actually quite rude to me."

"Yeah, he said that too. His ex-wife was a bit of a tramp, so he doesn't think too highly of dancers right now."

"She was a dancer?"

Solara smiled knowingly at me. "I'll let him tell you."

"Solara, I'm engaged to be married. I don't know if you knew that or not, but I'm not interested in Paxton."

She stopped at the front door of the Irish bar and smiled at me, her hand on the door handle. "Well, then you and I will be friends."

Her nonchalance made me laugh, and I followed her into the bar. It was already crowded with people arriving after work. Music blared from the speakers in the corners, and we wiggled our way further inside.

Leaning up against the bar, she flagged down the bartender and ordered two Guinnesses. A man on the barstool next to us stood to leave and I sat down in his place.

The bartender placed the mugs on the bar with a smile. Solara handed him a twenty-dollar bill. "Keep it."

He smiled at her. A sexy grin spread across her face – that looked like a, 'Sure, I'll go home with you later,' smile.

Making small talk, I asked her, "You live in Arizona?"

"Phoenix. It's where we have our flagship studio. I love coming to Houston though. The humidity is so good for my skin. It's so dry in Arizona that I feel like my skin is cracking."

"I understand. I grew up in Scottsdale."

"No way!" She practically jumped out of her skin.

"Yes. I went to ASU and then my fiancé got a job offer here after graduation. I came out a few months later. It's home."

Paxton and a couple of the instructors came through the front door. The girls waved down Solara and she shouted, "I'll be right over."

Paxton leaned on the bar behind Solara, waved at the bartender, and circled his finger above us for another round.

"Here, take my seat, Paxton. I'm going to talk with the girls. I'll be right back."

She jumped up off the stool and headed over to a table. My eyes shifted and my heart raced. I didn't want to be alone with him. I glanced around the bar looking for an escape. When my eyes settled back on him, he was watching me with a knowing grin on his face.

"I won't bite."

"You sure about that?" I snapped a little too quickly.

"Is that an invitation?"

I stood to leave and he placed a hand on my arm. "Sit down. I'm just playing."

I huffed out a breath and relaxed on my stool.

"Let's start over."

Eyeing him warily, I introduced myself. "I'm Charlotte Chase."

"Paxton Crown."

"It's nice to meet you."

"You as well."

The smile on my face grew.

He leaned into me. "Do you come here often?"

"Oh my God! Is that your pickup line?"

He laughed heartily, and winked. "No, I can do better than that."

I took a sip of my beer and side-eyed him.

His feet were resting on my barstool, caging me in, and he'd turned to face me.

Leaning towards him a bit, I said, "I think you owe me an apology."

He whispered back, "I thought we were starting over."

I raised my brows at him.

Sighing heavily, he said sarcastically, "Charlotte, please forgive my behavior when last we met. I found you extremely attractive and was overcome with a carnal need to kiss you."

"That's an apology?"

He smiled over the top of his glass. "The best I can give." And he took a drink.

"I forgive you."

"Mighty kind."

His eyes crinkled at the corners. His mouth turned up slightly in a grin. We sat in charged silence a moment longer. I felt his stare on me and turned to find him scanning my body, pointedly looking at my engagement ring. His eyes met mine and he smiled.

"Do you want to go join your sister?"

"No."

For lack of much to talk about, I asked him, "How are you enjoying Houston?"

"When are you getting married?"

"I, uhm, well, we haven't set a date yet." I wanted to ask about his wife, but then I didn't want Erin to get in trouble.

"What does he think of you doing a competition?"

His eyes were boring into mine.

"Why do I feel like you already know the answer to that question?"

He shrugged.

Looking down into my beer I ran my thumb and forefinger up and down on the glass, removing the condensation.

"Actually, he's not very happy about it."

Softly, almost understandingly, he asked, "How come?"

His questions were making me uncomfortable, and I shifted on my barstool to leave. "I think I might go join Solara."

He nodded knowingly at me, slowly removed his feet from the rungs, and stood to allow me room to get past him. I had to squeeze by. I could feel the warmth coming off his chest and it was all I could do not to push myself up against him. My breath came short and shallow. I looked up just in time to see him glance down at my mouth.

When I had a safe distance between us, I turned and thanked him for the beer.

He nodded. "I'll see you tomorrow."

I nodded back and weaved my way through the tables over to the girls.

Paxton didn't leave the barstool, and I tried not to glance his way. It was so difficult. He was so brooding, and sexy, and raw.

Solara and the girls kept me entertained with their silly, sexy innuendoes about the guys in the bar, and misconceptions about dancers. I sipped more slowly on my drink, knowing I had to drive home soon.

At one point, I gave a sideways glance back at the bar and noticed Paxton was no longer where I had left him. My heart sank, and I realized that I, too, no longer wanted to be there.

Excusing myself from the table, I told Solara I would see her tomorrow and snuck out the side door into the parking lot.

The humid night air enveloped me. When I reached my car, I looked to the upper outside deck of the bar and saw Paxton leaning up against the railing, a chesty blonde pushed up close against him. Apparently, he hadn't left.

He saw me as I stepped into my car. When he caught my eyes, he turned back to the blond, running his hands down her back and grinning broadly down into her face.

Asshole.

CHAPTER 8

I WOKE EARLIER than usual for a Saturday morning. Enthusiasm and excitement had me up before the sun.

Rolling to my side, Mark was sleeping peacefully beside me. I reached out my hand to push the hair back from his forehead. Then I stopped, returning my hand back under my cheek, wondering where things had started going wrong. I thought back to the start of our relationship, letting myself get lost in my memories of how we'd gotten to where we were now...

When I met Mark in Cozumel my senior year in college, I thought he was funny and smart. For some reason, I also thought he still had a thing for Suzanne, so I steered clear. Mark and three of his college friends had rented the condo next to ours, which, as I found out later, Suzanne had recommended. Her father was a developer, and this was one of his properties.

Mark was polite and I enjoyed his company. It wasn't until the last night of our trip that he asked me out.

We'd all gone to the bar on the beach, just in front of the hotel. A ceramic fire pit surrounded by Adirondack chairs was set up a safe distance from the deck stairs. I'd been sitting serenely, enjoying the fire, watching the glass beads flickering and sparkling in the night, when he walked up behind me and handed me a beer over my shoulder.

"Mind if I join you?"

Glancing over my shoulder, I reached for the beer. I smiled up at him and tipped the neck of the bottle towards the chair next to me. "Please."

We'd never talked just the two of us. His presence felt soothing and comfortable, like someone who would protect me. I smiled at him as I took a drink.

The golden fire illuminated his tanned skin, his blue eyes almost glowing in contrast. "Did you enjoy your vacation?"

"I did, thank you. And you?"

He leaned back in the chair. "Yeah. It was a nice break. I didn't see much of you, though."

"Yeah, I'm not really big on zip-lining and hiking. I stayed here and did the spa thing. Spent some time on the beach."

He shifted a bit in his seat and crossed one ankle over his other knee. "I was kind of hoping we could have talked more."

I stilled.

He rushed on. "I mean, you're Suzanne's best friend and it would have been nice to get to know you better."

"Oh. Of course. You and Suzanne."

"No." He repeated, "No. That's not what I meant." He dropped his head, shook it side to side, and laughed. "I'm getting this all messed up."

"I'm not really following you."

"I would like to take you out when we get back to Arizona."

"Out?"

"On a date. Dinner. Coffee, whatever."

"Uhm, aren't you and Suzanne a thing or something?" Lord, now I was mucking this up.

He laughed. "No, Suzanne and I are just really good friends. We went to prom together in high school, and our dads are friends. We dated for a bit, but just never clicked like we should have."

"Oh, well, sure, I'd like that." Butterflies danced in my stomach, as the smile grew on his face.

We continued to talk until the others drunkenly joined us on the beach. Suzanne sat on my lap, her black hair swirling around in the wind. I was worried it would catch on fire. We all sang and joked and celebrated our last night of vacation before heading back to Arizona.

The next morning, Suzanne was still passed out, a satin cover on her eyes and a bottle of aspirin on the nightstand. Quietly and methodically, I packed our things while she slept.

The sheets ruffled and a groan came from under a pillow. I sat down next to her on the mattress and held a bottle of water out to her. "You're alive."

She pushed the pillow off her face and lifted the eye cover up on her forehead, bunching her hair. Mascara-smudged eyes looked at me in shame. "Did I do anything last night I need to make amends for today?"

"No. You were perfectly gorgeous and delightful."

"Ugh." She took the water and sipped on it slowly.

When she handed it back to me, she laid back on the bed and asked, "What time is it?"

"Time for you to get up and shower. I called for a taxi. It'll be here in an hour."

She threw her forearm over her eyes. "My God! I think I might be dead."

I wanted to tell her about Mark before she saw him this morning. This wasn't the ideal time, but it would have to do.

"Mark told me he's on the same plane as us."

"That's nice." She sat up again slowly. Swinging her feet out from under the covers and placing them on the floor, she rested her head in her hands, elbows on her knees.

"He asked me out."

She dropped one hand and turned sideways to glance at me, her head resting in the other. "He did?"

"Yes."

When I failed to elaborate, she raised her brows questioningly at me.

"I thought you two, well, I thought you still had a thing. But when I asked him, he said you didn't. So... I said yes."

"Huh."

"Do you still have a thing?"

"Oh, God, no!"

"You're okay if I go out with him?"

"Sure. We weren't that serious. He's a good guy." She slowly stood and made her way to the bathroom.

"Why don't you sound convincing?"

She raised her hand, and said, "Shhhh. My head."

I followed her. "Are you sure you don't mind?"

She stopped in front of the sink and I met her eyes in the mirror. "I'm positive. You guys are actually kind of cute together."

I leaned against the wall and crossed my arms, watching as she put toothpaste on her toothbrush. "How so?"

Before putting the toothbrush in her mouth, she said, "You know. Perfect."

And perfect we had been…until now.

Light snores were coming from his mouth as I slowly rolled out of bed. I slipped my feet into my slippers and reached for my robe at the foot of the bed.

Padding down the steps into the kitchen, I put on a pot of coffee. As I waited for it to brew, I opened my iPad and pulled up my to-do list for the day.

My event was at four-thirty. Dani had suggested I get there a few hours early to watch the early competitors and get myself ready. She'd also told me I could stay after for free and watch the championship levels and the exotics.

I needed to pack a change of clothes for dinner after the show with Solara, my outfit for the event, a bathrobe and the makeup kit I'd purchased from a theatre company earlier this week.

The coffee pot beeped and I poured myself a cup, taking it to the white fabric-covered couches in my family room just off the kitchen.

Setting my cup on the coffee table, I fluffed the pillows on the couch and lay down, staring up at the ceiling. I had so much time today before the event and nothing to fill it with.

The next thing I knew, a noise came from the kitchen. Opening my eyes, I squinted and blinked at the brightness coming through the windows. Mark came around the corner and took a seat in the oversized chair at the end of the table.

I stretched and looked around. "What time is it?"

"Good morning."

I smiled. "Good morning."

"It's ten-thirty."

"Oh goodness, I must have fallen back asleep."

He tentatively sipped his coffee. "What time did you get up?"

"I don't know. It was still dark."

I sat up, took my mug to the sink, emptied the now cold coffee, and poured myself another cup.

He said loudly from the other room. "What time is your thing today?"

I took a deep breath to calm my nerves. His tone was casual, but it was his use of the word *thing* that had me gritting my teeth.

Sitting back down on the couch, I tucked my feet under me and sipped my coffee. "It's at four-thirty but I think I might go early to watch the other competitors."

He nodded solemnly, sipping on his coffee. The air was thick with tension. "I think I might play golf today."

His tone was so dismissive, it was all I could do not to throw a pillow at him. I smiled instead, determined not to let him ruin my day. "That sounds like a great way to spend the day."

The silence stretched between us, turning awkward. He pulled out his phone and started scrolling through it.

The birds chirped outside, sitting on the edge of the birdbath.

Not able to take the silence any longer, I stood to leave. "I'm going to get ready and head out."

I had taken a few steps back toward the kitchen when he called my name. "Charlie."

Stopping, I turned back towards him and waited.

"Good luck today."

My shoulders relaxed; my hands lowered. "Thank you."

He nodded and went back to his phone.

After showering, I gathered up my travel bag, my dress, and all the things I would need for the day. When I went downstairs, Mark was already gone. The house: silent.

It didn't take me long to get to the small theatre that was hosting the event. When I pulled into the parking lot, I was surprised by the number of cars that had already filled the lot.

It looked like a warehouse from the outside, but when I entered the front doors, I was met with palatial, gilded-age décor.

The carpet was a deep turquoise, the walls: the color of melted butter. Dark gold brocade curtains, pulled back by thick, gold rope, hung over each of the entry points to the theatre.

A small concession stand offered sodas and candy. Throughout the lobby, vendors were strategically placed to catch your attention as you passed by on your way to the restrooms or concessions.

Glancing around looking for someone I knew, I saw Dani and a number of other girls working behind a long folding table. A black tablecloth was draped over it, with the L.O.V.E. logo emblazoned on the front.

A line was forming at the table. Girls loaded down with dress bags and makeup kits chatted enthusiastically with each other. Oddly, many of them were dressed in sweatpants and slippers.

"Hey, Charlotte."

I jumped at the sound of my name and turned to see Paxton coming out of one of the side offices. He was wearing a similar outfit to the one he'd had on the first time we met. Only this time, he also had a headset draped around his neck, and a wireless radio box that was attached to a clip on his belt.

"Hey… Paxton."

He grinned wide. I wasn't surprised to see sharp canines. I *was* surprised to see such a beautiful smile.

"Do you need to check in?"

"Do I?"

He laughed. "C'mon." He took my bag and placed his hand at the small of my back, lightly touching me and guiding me towards the table.

Over the heads of the other girls in line, he called for Dani. "Charlotte's here."

A large hanging rack stood at the side of the table and he hung my bag on it. He whispered to me. "Good luck today."

I was going to thank him, when Dani squealed and ran around the table to hug me. "You're here! Oh my God! Are you excited?"

I was squished in her embrace and smiled broadly, laughing at her enthusiasm. "I am. I'm really nervous though." On the other side of the room, Paxton headed off in the direction of a set of stairs.

She stepped back from me, and went around the table. "You'll be fine. Let me get you checked in, and then I'll show you where to go."

Reaching under the table, she handed me a gift bag and a lanyard with the word COMPETITOR printed on the badge.

All the girls behind the desk were dressed in black leggings, soft shoes, and black T-shirts emblazoned with the L.O.V.E logo.

"Come with me, Charlie," she said with a wink.

I laughed nervously. "You sound like you're leading me into a den of sin."

With a nod of her head, and a quick laugh, she gestured for me to follow. "Hardly." She paused. "But then, I guess if that helps you dance better."

I grabbed my dress bag from the rack and followed her as she headed towards a side door, opened it, and gestured me through. "This is where you can get ready. There are dressing rooms down this hall, bathrooms to the right, and the entrance to the stage is at the end of this hall."

Now that I was back-stage, the butterflies in my stomach were getting worse.

I tugged on Dani's arm and whispered, "Dani, I'm feeling really nervous."

Her eyes met mine and she took both my hands in hers. "You are going to be amazing. You can totally do this. Just forget about everyone else and do your thing. Erin and Solara and I are all here for you."

I exhaled dramatically. "I can do this."

She nodded. "You can do this. Now, let me show you where to put your things."

Leading me to the dressing room, she walked me to one of the empty vanity tables.

"Put your makeup here, and hang your dress on the hook on the back of the mirror."

Girls were fluttering about all around me. Sexy, sparkling costumes hung from racks and doorways. Everywhere I looked was color and shine. Everyone was laughing like they knew each other. After hanging up my outfit, Dani pulled me back out into the hallway and down towards the stage entrance.

From the brightly lit hall, we stepped into the darkness of the wings, and I had to blink a moment, allowing my eyes to adjust. The only lights came from the stage in front of us.

To my right were four girls in black L.O.V.E T-shirts and black booty shorts. They were barefoot, and Dani whispered in my ear, "Those are the pole cleaners."

"What do you mean, 'the pole cleaners?'"

"After every dancer, two of the cleaners will go out onto the stage and clean the poles. One takes the static pole, the other, the spin pole. They climb to the top, just like you do in class and clean top to bottom."

"So, I don't need to clean the poles afterward?"

She smiled sweetly at me. "No, darlin'. You're the star today."

That made me laugh. She continued telling me how the event would work. "You'll check in with Erin, and tell her what position you want to start in. When you go out on stage, she'll wait until you're in that position, and then she'll use her microphone to tell the soundstage to cue your music."

My eyes had adjusted to the darkness, and it was then that I noticed Erin behind one of the curtains. Three dancers were waiting to talk to her, so I just gave her a little wave. She smiled back at me and pointed to her clipboard.

Dani was still talking. By the time I refocused my attention on her, all I heard her say was… "and then you just… dance."

"Okay. Got it." Shit, no I don't.

"I'm going to leave you here. I need to go back up front and check people in. You'll be fine, Charlie. You'll be fine."

I nodded at her and watched her walk away. The light from the hall momentarily blinded me. I blinked my eyes a few times after the door shut, adjusting once again to the darkness backstage.

On the stage was a steel frame with two poles mounted from the top. One was the static pole. The other was a spinner.

Stage lights hung from the top and were mounted on the side of the structure, strategically placed to highlight the moves and the glinting steel of the poles.

I looked around in fascination at the other dancers, dressed in outfits ranging from pink and sassy to black dominatrix.

When Erin finished with the other girls, she came straight to me and told me I needed to go get dressed.

"How much time do I have?"

She looked down at her clipboard. "Maybe an hour? You can warm up on that pole over there." She jerked her chin towards a pole I hadn't seen when I came in.

"Okay. I'm going to watch for just a few more minutes, then I'll go get dressed."

When I'd seen enough to give me an idea of how this worked, I went back to the dressing room and sat down at the vanity mirror where I'd left my things.

I took my time flat ironing my hair, making sure it was as long and sleek as I could get it. Then I braided two small sections starting from my forehead, tying them together at the back of my head with a small rubber-band.

I applied heavy makeup with lots of contour since the lights were so bright. My eyes were lined with heavy black eyeliner and I applied thick silver glitter eyeshadow.

When I was satisfied with my makeup, I took my outfit to a dressing closet and changed. The top sparkled like a mirror ball. The feathers ruffled softly.

My black platform shoes with the clear acrylic heels laced up to my calf and stayed in place with black leather buckles just under my knees. When I stood, I was over six feet tall.

I had just placed my duffle bag back under my vanity table when I heard my name.

"Charlotte?"

I turned to see Suzanne standing in the door frame.

"Suzanne? I'm so glad you made it. How did you get back here?"

Approaching me cautiously, her eyes were wide as she looked me up and down. Stuttering a bit, she responded, "I, uhm…WOW! This is you!"

"This is me." I twirled in front of her, smiling.

"Charlie, you look phenomenal."

"Thank you. But who let you in?"

"Oh, some huge beast of a man. Looked annoyed when I asked about you."

"Paxton."

"Who's Paxton?"

"He's the owner of the studio. I think annoyed is his general state of being. C'mon. Let me show you the backstage area, and then I'll walk you out. You can watch from the theatre seats."

She followed behind me to the backstage area. I explained to her what Dani had told me, and then took her back out to the lobby.

Before I opened the doors, she put her hand on my arm. I had to look down to her. She was much shorter from this height.

"Charlie, I'm really proud of you. I know it sounded like I scoffed at this, but it takes a lot of courage to perform. Just know that I'm proud of you."

I leaned down to hug her, careful not to get makeup on her beautiful peach silk blouse.

"Thank you, Suzanne. I needed to hear that. And thank you for being here."

We walked through the doors and I took her directly to the ticket office. Before I could get there, Paxton stopped me.

"Charlotte."

I turned. His eyes roved slowly over my body, and I held my head high, not wanting him to affect me. It didn't work. My lips parted on a breath, and my body flushed. I was almost eye to eye with him. Not backing away from him, I held my head high, almost challenging him to say something snarky.

When he spoke, his voice was gravelly. "You don't need a ticket for your friend. You get one free guest. I'll take her to a seat for you."

Trying to act unaffected, I looked to Suzanne. "Suzanne, Paxton Crown. Paxton, my friend Suzanne."

Suzanne extended her small hand politely and he looked at it, almost disdainfully, before quickly shaking it and then turning towards the theatre. "It's this way."

Before she followed him, she whispered so only I would hear, "Did he just eye fuck you?"

"Suzanne!"

"He did. Christ almighty. We need to talk."

"Not now. Go!" I pushed her gently on her way and she looked at me pointedly. "Later. I promise."

Paxton efficiently directed her towards the theatre and pointed to a row of seats. Then I ran as quick as my platforms could carry me to the entrance to the competitor's area.

I took one last minute to swipe on a bit more lip gloss and then went backstage.

Erin saw me and waved me over. "What's your starting position, Charlotte?"

My head started to swim. I thought to myself, *Breathe, Charlie, breathe.* "Okay, uhm. I'll be to the left of the static pole, my back to the audience, feet apart, my left hip cocked. My right arm will be extended above me and wrapped around the pole; my left hand will be on my hip."

She scribbled furiously on the pad of paper. When she looked up she was smiling. "Okay, one more and then you're next."

She left me to help the girl after me and I stepped over to the side curtain, watching the current girl on the pole. I swayed back and forth on my platforms, trying to work out the nerves.

The lights were giving off so much heat. I started to sweat.

The current performer finished her routine and I backed up to the practice pole to warm up. After a few turns and some visualization of my program, I went back to the curtain to wait. Adrenaline pumped through me. I pulled one of the curtains back and peeked out to the audience. Suzanne sat a few rows back from the stage.

The music ended and claps and cheers came from the audience. Then a flurry of pole cleaners went out to prepare the stage for me. Hugs and laughter swirled around me, and I wiped my palms on my legs.

Erin came up beside me and smiled. "Are you ready, Charlie?"

It was now or never. Taking a few deep breaths, I responded, "Ready."

Erin clicked her microphone and spoke into her headset. "Charlotte's ready."

Solara's voice announced over the speakers, "She represents the Live Once Vertical Studio, please welcome Charlotte Chase."

And I stepped out onto the stage.

CHAPTER 9

I WAS NO more than five years old when I had my very first ballet recital. The tiny studio in Scottsdale was just down the street from my house in a fashionable strip mall. Tucked in between a dog grooming business and a kick-boxing studio, it was the 'in' place to send your children.

The morning of that recital, my mom had slicked back my hair, yanking and brushing it up into a tight bun. Sitting prettily with the other girls in folding chairs alongside the back wall, I nervously picked at my pink tights. Across the room, my instructor, holding a skinny, dark-haired boy close to her, talked with my mom.

He was maybe eight years old, and when he caught me staring at them, he bugged his eyes out at me, as if to say, *What are you looking at?*

Pulling my chin to my chest, I tried not to cry at the boy's unfriendly gesture as I waited for my program to start. When the parents were all seated and the program began, I forgot all about the stupid boy and lost myself in the dance.

In my mind I was a beautiful fairy, twirling and flitting from tree to tree. My arms extended above my head, I held my chin high, smiling and dancing to the classical music.

I was little - girl-perfection in my pink tutu. As the program ended, I knew I was destined to be the next great prima ballerina.

Bowing with a grand gesture, I grinned ear-to-ear as my parents stood and clapped for me.

We left the stage single file and I skipped joyously towards my parents. Before I could get to them, I tripped and fell, landing on my hands and knees.

The boy appeared to help me up, and I thanked him. I thought he would be kind to me. Instead, as I looked up into his chocolate brown eyes, he said, "You're the horriblest ballerina."

My chin began to quiver, and I raised my chin. "Well, you're a stupid boy."

He laughed at me – a knowing laugh, too old for what I imagined were his eight years.

Both our moms had rushed over, and my instructor had asked me if I was okay. I nodded and tucked myself into my mom's side.

Looking down into her son's face, my instructor held his chin. "Paxton Michael Crown, you apologize to Charlotte."

He mumbled a weak apology and then ran from the room.

Addressing my mom, my instructor said, "I'm so sorry. I remarried a few years ago and we just had a baby. Paxton is still having a difficult time adjusting to a step-brother and a baby girl in the house." She looked down at me. "And I know he's really sorry for saying that to you. I hope you'll forgive him."

That was my last recital. I'd never wanted to go back.

The memory of that day came rushing out of my subconscious. Before I could process the truth of it, the music started and I had to perform. All my emotions were getting tangled up in my head with the actions my body was supposed to take.

Step around the pole, back up against it… Paxton… step forward, lower myself… Michael… lift my heels, grind my hips… fucking… slide one leg out, run my hand down my thigh… Crown!

Doing my best to push those thoughts out of my head, I finished the program, my body glistening from the exertion, and I left the stage.

Girls I didn't know hugged me. The pole cleaners high-fived me. Someone handed me a bottle of water.

Erin squealed. "You did it!"

Despite my recent realization, I was incredibly happy. What a strange experience. I felt empowered and confident.

I stood backstage for a few minutes longer, watching the next dancer and catching my breath.

What was I supposed to do now? I didn't know where to go after my performance, or what to do about my realization. There was no way Paxton would remember me.

When the next dancer was on the stage, Erin came to tell me about dinner. "Wait in the lobby for me. I need a ride, and then I'll Uber home." She looked at her watch. "We should be finished in about an hour."

I nodded my agreement and headed back towards the dressing room.

This moment was surreal. It just ended. All that work and stress, the fights with Mark, the leave of absence from work... over.

Changing into high-waisted, burgundy palazzo pants; a sleeveless, high-neck blouse; and a pair of ballet flats, I packed up my belongings. I waved a quick good-bye to the girls remaining in the dressing room, and headed out.

I was on my way to my car to store my things, but Suzanne caught me outside the dressing room door and gave me a huge hug. "Charlie! That was amazing!"

Her praise was a welcome gesture and my eyes watered. "Thank you."

"Are you crying?" She pulled me to the side and whispered, "Why are you crying?"

"I don't know. These past few weeks have just been so emotional, and now it's over."

"Oh, sweetie. You were so beautiful. I'm so impressed, and I'm sorry I ever made fun of you."

I pretended to be shocked, putting my hand to my chest. "You made fun of me?"

"Well, you know…" her voice trailed off and we both laughed. "Seriously, I hope you're really proud of yourself."

"Thank you." I said again and hitched my bag higher on my shoulder. I wiped the tears away from under my eyes.

"Do you want to grab some dinner?"

"I can't tonight. Solara asked me to join her and some of the girls after the show."

"And that man?" she said in a sly tone, smiling mischievously. I gave her a look from under my brow, and she laughed again. I was just about to disclose everything when she grabbed my elbow and said, "C'mon, walk me to my car."

When we stepped outside, the sun was setting and the air was still warm and balmy and thick with humidity. We walked to her car and she mentioned we should have lunch the next week.

"That sounds great! I'll call you tomorrow!"

She hugged me again, smiling broadly. "I really am so proud of you."

Then she got in her car and drove off.

After watching her drive out of the lot, I went to my own car and put my bags in the trunk.

I had just closed the back hatch when I heard yelling from a few cars over. Not wanting to intrude, I lowered my head and tried to walk by.

As I passed by the large SUV, I saw Paxton standing next to it, screaming into a cell phone. He caught my eye and I froze in place.

Speaking more quietly to the person on the other end, I heard him say, "I'll call you back." He snapped his phone case shut, and slid it into his back pocket. The headset from the microphone was resting around his neck, still attached to the clip on his buckle.

He approached me cautiously, staring me down, not breaking eye contact, until he was just a few feet in front of me. Without my heels on, he towered over me. I inhaled sharply at all his sexy tallness. Then he scanned me from head to toe and back up again.

"Would you please stop doing that?" I said with just a hint of annoyance.

"Apologies. You're just somethin' to look at." He didn't seem apologetic, but then his tone changed to one of genuine kindness. "You look pretty."

His words were soft and sweet, and they made me nervous. So, I lashed out. "Don't you have a wife?"

I instantly regretted the words.

His eyes went dark, and the easy banter was replaced with hostility. "Had."

I shuffled uneasily, realizing I should probably continue back into the theatre.

Then he spoke again. "Have. Kind of. It's complicated." He dropped his eyes to the ground, lost in thought.

I wasn't ready to tell him I remembered him. This was a really weird place to have that conversation. It was all weird, actually.

Trying to bring the conversation back to a safe place, I asked, "Are you joining us girls for dinner?"

"I think it's more like you're joining us for dinner."

"How can you go from being nice to being an ass so fast?"

"Language, Charlotte!" He laughed at me.

I pushed past him and headed back to the theatre.

He called after me. "See you at dinner!"

The rest of the show wrapped up quickly and I helped Solara, Erin, and another girl named Story from the Phoenix location, box up the gift bags.

"What happens with the rest of the stuff?" I asked Solara as she stacked boxes onto a flat pushcart.

"A crew will come in tomorrow and pack everything into a rig. Then they move on to the next location."

"The next location?"

Solara paused and smiled at me sweetly. "We do these events all around the country. This season just started and it will finish Labor Day Weekend. Our world championship event is in Irvine, California."

"I'm so impressed, Solara. I had no idea."

"We'll tell you all about it over dinner. You ready to go?"

I nodded that I was, and waited with her while Erin and Story gathered up their things. Erin looped her arm through mine and we followed Solara and Story out into the parking lot.

Paxton had pulled the black SUV up front. He jumped out of the driver's side when he saw us and held the passenger door open. Erin announced, "I'm going to ride with Charlotte."

Solara stepped up into the passenger seat, and before Paxton could shut the door for her, she told me to follow them. Story stepped into the backseat without a backward glance, and Erin cringed.

Addressing me, Paxton said, "I'll wait until you pull up before I drive away."

His voice was more kind. I couldn't breathe. His presence was everywhere, and the gentler Paxton was someone I did not have the strength to resist. So, I just nodded and steered Erin to my car.

When Erin and I had buckled up and I pulled out to follow Paxton, she let out a bellow. "UGH! I hate that girl!"

"What? Who? Solara?" Her outburst shocked me.

"Gah! No. Story. She's such a tramp."

Oh no. This was not something I wanted to get in the middle of.

Paxton had waited for us. When he made eye contact with me in his side mirror, I nodded and he turned out towards downtown.

Erin's phone chimed and she looked at the incoming text. Saved by the bell.

"Solara said we are going to Brenner's on the Bayou, in case Paxton loses you."

I nodded and stayed close to the SUV.

Erin continued with her rant. "She was friends with Paxton's ex-wife, or something, and she keeps trying to console him. It makes me want to vomit."

Her head was resting back against the headrest, eyes closed. She looked like she was nodding off.

The adrenaline from earlier in the day was gone, and I was suddenly incredibly tired myself. The quiet was a welcome reprieve from the music and the hustle of the dressing room. I relaxed in my seat and followed Paxton at an easy pace, until Erin came back full force with her thoughts.

"She started about the same time as Myla. I think they both worked in the same strip club. Myla was apparently the sweeter of the two, or more deceptive. But both of them had a thing for Paxton. I think."

I tried to cut her off. "Erin, it sounds like you don't really know the whole story. You do this often. You really shouldn't gossip if you don't know. How *do* you know all this?"

She had the decency to look somewhat embarrassed. "You're right."

I side-eyed her, indicating I knew she was avoiding the question.

"Fine. I just heard things," she pouted. "And she's never been very nice to me anyway. So, for that reason alone I don't like her."

Paxton turned into a driveway that led to the restaurant and stopped in front of a valet stand.

I stopped my car and said to Erin before we got out, "Just ignore her. It isn't worth getting all worked up over someone who doesn't even live here."

The valet opened my door and I unbuckled my seat belt. "Now c'mon. I'm hungry and I need a glass of wine."

Solara and Story had walked ahead. Erin walked in front of me, and Paxton placed his hand at the small of my back, escorting me in.

My emotions were pinging around again. I couldn't decide if I should stop abruptly so he would walk into me, or if I should speed up so I could breathe.

When we reached the entrance, he stepped quickly ahead of all of us, and held the door open. Solara was oblivious to his gesture. He smiled down at me as I went through.

While we waited for a table, Paxton stood unnecessarily close behind me. I crossed my arms in front of me defensively. The restaurant was loud with late dinner and bar patrons.

"Have you been here before, Charlotte?" He spoke softly so only I could hear.

Glancing over my shoulder at him, I was eye level with his chin and had to raise my eyes. "A few times."

"Anything you recommend?"

The hostess approached us and directed us to our table. As we walked, I said, "The quail is really good. It's wrapped in bacon."

He chuckled behind me. "Well, yeah, it's bacon. You could wrap a piece of cardboard in bacon and it would be good."

Solara reached the round table first and indicated I should sit in the chair next to her. Erin sat to my right, and Story sat down next to Solara. I guess the negative feelings were mutual.

Paxton held my chair for me and waited until I was seated before taking the seat between the two frenemies.

The conversation before dinner was mostly technical. I learned that not only was Story a friend of theirs, she was their Operations Director. She coordinated all the events, arranged lighting and sound, made all the hotel and airline reservations... Essentially, she did everything.

Every now and then she would reach over and touch Paxton's arm or his thigh. She would laugh robustly in a forced way, and I could feel Erin tensing up next to me.

Sliding my foot over towards her, I gently pressed my toes to the side of her foot. She visibly relaxed.

Paxton ordered my recommendation and he smiled at me as the waiter took away his menu. Nervously I sipped my wine. He had looked at me in that same knowing way the day I watched him step into the limousine.

Dinner was served and the conversation turned to the talent at the competition.

"Did you see Cheeky Warbler today? She was *sick!*" Solara was so enthusiastic, it was hard not to smile at her. "She was talking about entering an exotic competition for Irvine."

"What's an exotic?" I asked her.

Paxton was still grinning at me. Story was not.

Solara leaned over her chair-arm towards me. Up close I noticed she had the same sprinkling of golden freckles as Paxton and I almost missed what she was saying.

"What you did today was more fitness pole. It's technical and fun but not quite... naughty." She said the last word in a conspiratorial tone, and then she laughed.

"And exotic is...?"

Paxton finished my sentence from across the table. "...naughty." And then he leaned back in his chair and smiled smugly.

I clenched my sex and squirmed in my seat. Good lord, I needed to get away from him.

Raising her glass of wine, Solara gently tapped her knife against the base. "If I could... please raise your glass to our new friend, and no longer a virgin pole competitor... Charlotte Chase."

I blushed at her words, and heard Erin giggle next to me. "To Charlotte."

Even Story smiled thinly and toasted.

And Paxton grinned his knowing grin and raised his glass to me. "To Charlotte."

The waiter appeared to clear our plates, and Solara ordered another bottle of wine.

"Seriously, Charlotte. You did great today. You really should do another event. Challenge yourself." Solara would have made a great cheerleader and I told her so.

"HA! My mother would never let me cheer in school."

Feeling suddenly guilty, I almost told them that I took dance at their mom's studio, but Solara continued before I had a chance.

"You really should do more events. Dani can do so much more for you."

"Maybe. This was fun, but I really need to focus on my job. Get back to my real life."

She looked confused and a little hurt. "Real life?"

"I'm sorry. I don't mean it in a bad way. It's just... Well, I don't have a lot of time to do another program."

She smiled sweetly in understanding. "I get it, I do. But you should think about it." She looked at Erin for confirmation. "Right, Erin? She should dance more."

Erin hugged me. "Of course, you should. What would I do without you?"

Paxton glanced at her, and smirked in a teasing way.

Solara addressed her brother. "What do you think, Paxton? She did great today, didn't she?"

He shrugged. "Enh, it was cute."

My stomach dropped, a deep knot clutching my insides.

"Cute? She was amazing."

"What do you want me to say, Sol? It was Demi Lovato. It was cute."

My face flushed and I took a drink of water. No longer able to look him in the eye, I fidgeted with my napkin and looked at my lap.

Solara took up my defense. "Don't tease her. This was a big deal for her."

They went back and forth about the reasons that people dance, and what do you know about it, and he's just a stupid boy, and she's always taking in strays...

No longer able to sit and listen to them arguing, I put my napkin on the table and slowly stood to leave, saying quietly, "If you guys will excuse me, I think it's time I headed out."

Solara stood to hug me. "I'm so sorry for my asshole brother. I think you're incredible, and I would love to see you dance again."

"Thank you." My eyes burned from holding back the tears.

Erin started to rise. "I'll go with you."

I put my hand on her shoulder to keep her down. I didn't want a witness to my crying. "No, stay. Enjoy the rest of your evening. I'll see you next week."

Paxton stood from his seat, a flash of remorse in his eyes. Not able to look directly at him, I nodded in his direction, said my goodnights, and walked quickly out of the restaurant.

The valet took my ticket, and I hugged my arms tight around me. I choked and the tears started to fall. I'm so stupid, I thought to myself. Out loud I said, "Stupid, stupid, stupid."

"Charlotte."

I looked behind me, startled, and saw Paxton coming down the walk. I turned back to wait for my car, wiping away the tears on my cheek. "What do you want, Paxton?"

"I'm sorry."

"Well, good. Now go away."

My car pulled up against the curb, and the valet came around the front to give me my keys.

Paxton gently grabbed my elbow and addressed him. "She'll be right back."

He gently steered me down the path around the side of the building. When we were out of sight from the front of the restaurant, he moved us into the shadows of the sycamore trees. Illuminated by the up-lights in the landscaped area, we were surrounded by soft lighting.

I shook off his arm and he stepped back from me. Stoically, I stood waiting for whatever he had to say to me.

"I..." he started. I waited. "I really am sorry, Charlotte. My behavior has been... unlike me lately, and I'm sorry."

His admission gave me strength to tell him how I really felt. "You have been the horriblest person to me since the first time I met you."

"Horriblest isn't a word, Charlotte."

I turned to leave and he gently held my elbow again.

"Don't run off."

I stopped and waited.

"You're just so… stunning. You should dance more. You're good."

I leaned into him. His head dipped lower towards me and he whispered. "Next time, though, you should dance like you want to fuck."

Shaken, I pulled my head back, raised my hand, and slapped him. "You're disgusting."

His head went to the side and he put his palm to his cheek, rubbing out the sting. His eyes took on an amused look, and he said, "Then dance like you want to fuck me."

I raised my hand to slap him again and he caught my wrist, turning it behind my back and pulling me close up against him. My chest rose and fell, and I wanted nothing more than for him to put his mouth to mine. Adrenaline rushed through my body and I almost wept with need when his lips hovered over mine.

He spoke slowly, and softly. "The next time you slap me, you better mean it."

We stood pressed against each other, both of us trying to calm down. He slowly released his hold on my wrist, his fingers lingering softly as he stepped back from me.

For a moment, we both just stared at each other – my eyes wide.

He trailed his fingers to my hand. "C'mon. I'll walk you back to your car."

I cautiously took his hand, and he helped me back onto the path.

When we reached my car, he took the keys from the valet, tipped him, and escorted me around to the driver's side.

He cupped my cheek and rubbed his thumb across my bottom lip. I stared at him wide-eyed and felt him reach behind me, opening my door. Speechless, I stepped in and buckled up.

He spoke so softly when he said, "Goodnight, Charlotte."

CHAPTER 10

I WOKE THE next morning, staring at the ceiling fan spinning around. A tremendous feeling of loss was consuming my thoughts.

It was just another Sunday, yet it wasn't. I was changed. But I didn't know what to do with the differences. There was no place for me in the pole world—no place for me in my old world. So, I sat in the middle. Confused.

"Good morning, beautiful."

Rolling my head to the side, I smiled at Mark's pretty, perfect face. "Good morning."

He scooted over the bed, buried his face in my neck, and started kissing me. "You smell so good."

Giggling, I whispered, "What are you doing?"

"I'm kissing you."

I closed my eyes. "Mmm, that feels nice."

His lips made their way down to my collarbone, and he pulled the spaghetti strap of my tank down off my shoulder. I closed my eyes and relaxed into his gentle kisses. "You have the prettiest skin."

Dark eyes teased me. *'You look pretty.'*

God bless! He was everywhere. I opened my eyes and scooted over onto my side, facing Mark and forcing him to stop kissing me.

He frowned. "You okay?"

I ran my finger between his brows, smoothing out the wrinkle. "Yeah, just a little tired still."

Propping himself up on his elbow, he suggested we go to brunch. "That sounds nice," I said.

"We haven't done that in a while, and, well, I'd like to spend some time with you. Just the two of us."

"I'd like that, Mark." I tucked my hands under my cheek and smiled at him sweetly. He pushed the hair off my face.

With tenderness, he kissed the tip of my nose. "Get up then, lazy. I'm hungry."

I took my time getting ready, blowing out my hair and picking out the perfect outfit.

As I applied lotion, I noticed all the bruises on my upper arms and thighs from gripping the pole. I wouldn't be wearing a sundress.

Instead, I dressed in a lemon-yellow jumpsuit, culotte-style, with long billowing sleeves. I felt pretty and feminine and was rewarded with a low whistle from Mark as I descended the staircase.

When I reached the bottom step, he enveloped me in a hug, and I relaxed into him. "Ready?"

I nodded my response. He held my hand as we went out the back door to the garage.

The ride to the restaurant was peaceful. Mark was his former adoring self, and I thought that maybe he had come around regarding my dancing.

My phone pinged with an incoming message. I ignored it.

"You can check that if you like."

"I'll get it later. It's probably not important."

We rode in silence for another mile or so, and he reached over to take my hand. Raising it to his lips, he kissed the back, and then said, "You know, we should start planning the wedding now that you have some free time."

I tensed and had to force myself to relax. "Yes. Yes, we should."

"We also have that gala we volunteered to host. Remember? The one in September for the American Cancer Association? Suzanne is organizing the auction, and—"

He kept talking.

Meaningless noise.

Same words, different year.

The world we'd built was so predictable. I retreated into my shell, nodding as needed and smiling when appropriate.

We arrived at the restaurant, and he jumped out to run around to my side of the car. Helping me out, he tucked me into his side and escorted me in.

The restaurant was tucked into the woods. This was rare for Houston: a hidden gem in the busy city. Made of logs, it had a rustic and romantic feel about it.

Tiered decks were cut into the bayou embankment, and the hostess seated us in a cozy corner looking out over the creek below.

The waitress brought us mimosas, and Mark toasted us. "To our bright future. I love you, Charlie."

I raised my glass. "To our bright future."

We went through the brunch buffet, and I loaded my plate with fresh fruit, scrambled egg whites with vegetables, and mini blueberry muffins.

Mark commented that I needed to eat more, so I grabbed a chocolate truffle and shoved the whole thing in my mouth, causing him to laugh.

When we were seated at the table, he mentioned that he talked to my boss the day before, and I stiffened.

"He said you could go back whenever you were ready. I thought since your thing was over, you might be ready to go back. I told him you would call him Monday morning." He forked a bite of omelet into his mouth, and I took a sip of coffee, giving me time to gather my thoughts.

My phone pinged again, and we both glanced at my small handbag, neither of us saying anything.

"Actually, I've kind of been enjoying my time away. I thought I might go visit my parents."

"Oh." His tone was surprised.

I was surprised myself, but as soon as the words left my mouth, they felt right. "I haven't seen them since Christmas. Maybe my mom can give me some ideas about the wedding."

He reached his hand across the table and squeezed my fingers. "That sounds like a great idea, Charlie." His voice was light and cheerful.

We finished our brunch, enjoying companionable conversation. Not once did he bring up my *thing*.

My comment to Solara last night about getting back to my real life, heard in the light of day, sounded so dismissive of her world. I needed to talk with her; I owed her an apology.

When we returned home, Mark pulled into the driveway and left the car running.

I shifted in the passenger seat so I could see him better. "Are you going somewhere?"

"I'm going to play a round of golf. I'll be home after dinner. Go ahead and eat without me."

Resting his arm behind me across the seat, he leaned into me, gently pressing his lips to mine. "Thank you for having brunch with me."

I reached up to touch his cheek. "Of course, I'll see you tonight."

The house was quiet when I entered through the front door. I slipped off my shoes and went up the stairs to my room. Placing my shoes on the floor, I spoke into my phone, "Hey, Siri. Play 'Gasoline.'"

My speaker responded, "'Gasoline' by Halsey. Now playing."

The haunting, evocative music began to play, and I closed my eyes, swaying and moving to the dark words. I slowly started undoing the buttons on the front of my jumpsuit, shimmying it down my body.

When my clothes fell to the floor, I put my hands on the post on the bed. I ran through my dance from yesterday. This time, I heard Paxton's words: *'Dance like you want to fuck'*. The dance took on an entirely different feel.

I was lost in the moves and the music, swinging my hips out and around. I became a seductress—dropping to my bedroom floor and practicing the body slide (which was difficult to do on carpet) and then a forward crawl.

I flipped my hair, lifted my legs, clicked my heels, and then dropped my legs to the ground as the song ended.

As I lay there catching my breath, I giggled and then pulled myself into a sitting position.

Mark was standing in the doorway. Reproach and desire swept over his face, warring with each other.

I wanted to make love with him, and so I sat there, watching him. Waiting.

"I forgot my club card."

He crossed the room into the closet with long, quick strides. Emerging a few moments later, he tucked his wallet into the back pocket of his pants. His eyes flitted down me, and then he continued out of our room, saying over his shoulder, "I'll see you tonight."

I sat there speechless in the middle of the floor.

Then I started to laugh—uncontrollable, enthusiastic laughter that had tears falling from my eyes.

I stood and threw myself onto the bed on my back, smiling as I scrolled through my texts. I read the one from Solara first: *It was so good to meet you – Remember, you aren't strong because you pole dance, you pole dance because you are strong. Hugs, Sol*

I could imagine her laugh. I texted her back: *Good to meet you too. Thank you for the support*

The one from Erin was a little more cryptic: *Monday noon class – need to talk to you.*

I sent her back a question mark.

The next text was to my mom. I made arrangements to fly out on Thursday and stay the weekend.

The rest of the day passed quietly. I spent most of it listening to music and watching YouTube videos on pole dancing.

I made a light salad for dinner, and then I sat out on the back deck enjoying the humid summer night air with a glass of white wine. A soft breeze stirred the pool water, and the lights reflected up into the trees, creating shadow waves.

I kept my phone close. Waiting. For what, I couldn't admit.

Mark still wasn't home when I went to bed, and he had left early for work when I woke up.

I took myself to the studio a little before noon and was greeted with an enthusiastic hug from Erin.

"Oh, my God! I'm so happy to see you!" She pulled me to the couch and launched into what was so important.

"After you left the restaurant the other night, Solara told Story that you would be perfect for their event coordinator position. Story needs help, and they are trying to hire someone."

"Are you going to apply?"

She slapped my arm playfully. "No, silly. You are!"

"But I have a job, Erin. And I live here."

My words didn't deter her from enthusiastically pleading for me to join their team. "But you hate your job. And honestly, I think you hate your fiancé."

"Erin!" I stood from the couch. "My relationship is none of your business."

She blushed and sank low in the seat. "I'm sorry. You just always seem so unhappy when someone brings it up. And you were so *happy* this weekend."

Inhaling and exhaling loudly, I sat down next to her. "How are you so young and yet so observant?"

She shrugged. "You feel like a big sister to me. I like you, and you seem happy here."

I reached out to hug her, this dichotomy of a girl. Grown but childlike. Naïve yet wise. "I am happy here. For now, tell me more about the exotics."

She lit up and started telling me how it was much more fluid and sexier. "They use lights and strobes, and the music is much more erotic and darker. There is way more floor work, and you can kind of dance... like, well... you touch yourself more."

It was my turn to blush. She looked at her watch. "C'mon, we have time before class starts. I'll show you."

She took me into the studio and put some music on. Climbing the pole when the music started, she swung herself around, hooked to the pole behind her knee, and then swung up and hooked her ankles. After that, she dropped her head down and then slowly slid herself headfirst to the ground.

When she reached the floor, she slithered away from the pole, pushing her butt up in the air like an inchworm and then rolling over to her back. Then, she spread her legs, swiveling her right knee and running her hand down between her legs and her inner thighs.

Popping herself up on both knees, she ran her hands up and over her breasts, swinging her hair around and pushing her knees out and then back in, as if she was having sex on top. After a few ups and downs, she jumped up into a standing position, grabbed onto the pole, hooked her knee around it, and swung fast. As her free arm and leg swung out far, she leaned her head back until she slowly slid herself back down to the floor and came to a stop.

I stood, staring at her, speechless.

She smiled at me, her skin glistening from the exertion. "Something like that." Then she laughed. "What? Why are you just staring at me?"

"I just—" I paused. "I just didn't know you could do that."

She waved me off. "Enh, it just takes practice."

Dani opened the studio door. "Erin, there are people out there that need to check in for the noon class."

Erin wiped her face with a towel. "I'll be right out. Charlotte wants to do an Exotic."

It was then that Dani noticed me standing in the corner. "Oh, hey, Charlotte. Sure, we can do that. Are you staying for the noon class?"

I was still in awe of Erin's performance. I simply nodded and may have muttered an "Uh-huh." Erin left the studio to help the girls in the lobby, and I went in the back to change.

Dani was her usual exuberant, engaging self during class, but I was distracted. I had felt really sexy when I did my performance. Watching Erin, though, I could almost understand why Paxton had said my dance was 'cute.'

I went through the class's motions, but I kept thinking about how I could do it better. Sexier. When I was packed up and ready to leave for the day, I told Erin I was going to be gone for a few days.

"Oh, where are you going?"

"I'm going to visit my parents."

"In Arizona?"

"Scottsdale."

She practically jumped out of her chair. "You should go to Phoenix and see the studio. It will blow. Your. Mind." She made an exploding sound and released balled fists into spread fingers.

I hitched my bag over my shoulder and stepped back into my shoes. "Maybe. My mom and I are going to plan some wedding stuff, so I might not have time to run down there."

"Ugh, boring, but okay." She smiled at me and hugged me tightly. "I'll see you when you get back. And I want to know all about it."

She smiled knowingly; she knew I would go to the studio. Even I knew I would go to the studio.

CHAPTER 11

"SO WHY ARE you really here, honey?" My mom was painting her most recent ceramic plate and getting ready to fire it in her kiln.

She was an artist. My dad? A vice president with US Airways. They were a cute and quirky couple, and I was their only child.

They still lived in the rambler style house I grew up in, which was part of an upscale Scottsdale neighborhood. My dad had built her a studio for her pottery when I was in junior high. I still loved to hang out with her and watch her work. The earthy smell of clay always reminded me of her.

My flight had arrived late last night. After the Uber driver had dropped me off, my mom had greeted me at the door, kissed me on the cheek, and strolled back to her room to go back to bed. I'd gone right to my old room and fallen fast asleep.

This morning, I was sitting on a barstool watching her work.

In response to her question, I shrugged my shoulders. Picking at the dried clay chunks on the worktable, I said (a little too nonchalantly), "I thought you could help me plan the wedding. Mark has been bugging me about setting a date, and we did just buy that house. So, I don't know. I thought you could help me."

"I'll only say this because you aren't married yet, and then I'll keep my peace. But honey, seriously—Mark is so uptight you could put a piece of coal up his ass, and two weeks later, you'd find a diamond. Are you sure you want to marry him?"

"Mom, stop it! He's just focused; he wants to be successful."

She shrugged her shoulders and then went back to painting. The silence stretched between us. She wiped her brow with her forearm, and I shifted on the stool.

"I took a leave of absence from work."

That got her attention, and she stopped painting. "Why?"

I paused, wondering how much to tell her, and then the words just came flowing out of my mouth. "A few months ago, I started taking pole dancing classes. I wanted Mark to be supportive, but all he did was chastise me and make me feel bad about it."

She raised her eyebrows and tilted her head. I could practically hear her thinking, *See, I told you, coal to diamonds.*

"Let me finish."

Putting her thumb and forefinger together, she pretended to zip her lips and then tossed the imaginary key in front of her.

"The more involved in dancing I became, the more distant he became. I've been really stressed at work, and dancing helped me relax."

She waited patiently for me to go on.

"Then I started kind of spacing out at work. I could get by with doing what I already knew how to do, but I wasn't giving much more than that. Richard expressed his concern that maybe I was getting distracted trying to plan a wedding, but I told him I was fine. When Mark wanted to show off the house and our engagement a few weeks ago at our housewarming party, I mentioned to Marjorie, Richard's wife, that I'd been taking pole dancing classes. She didn't seem too put off by it, but Mark overheard me, dragged me into the den, and proceeded to rip into me."

My mom tried to hold back a smile.

"Richard followed us in. He told me to take a leave of absence so I could think clearly, get the wedding planned, and then come back when I was ready."

After sharing this with my mom, a huge sense of relief washed over me.

"What about the dancing?" She asked.

"That's the other thing. Mark thinks I got it out of my system, but Mom, honestly, I feel even more drawn to it. I love it. I love the girls and the dancing and the sexiness of it all. And it isn't even about sex. I just feel so... I feel so... strong."

Her eyes sparkled, and then she started to laugh. And laugh. And laugh.

"It's not that funny, Mom."

When she could catch her breath, she said, "Yes, actually, it is."

"Why?"

"I always thought you were so much like your father: serious, focused, determined to advance. You made vice president so fast, I kind of worried that you hadn't really figured out who you were. Now I'm seeing that you do have a little bit of me in you."

I pretended to be hurt, but a smile was forming on my face. "It's still not funny."

"Ironic then, how's that?" She continued looking at me with love in her eyes. "You look really pretty, sweetie. You look happy. Softer."

"Thank you."

I stayed with her a little while longer, telling her about the dancing, the music, Solara, Erin, and finally, that I would probably go visit Solara the next day.

"That sounds like a nice visit." Her words were bland, but she looked at me and smiled slyly.

I stood to leave. "Are you going to be out here all day?"

"Most likely. I have a yoga class later today, and then I thought you and your dad and I could have a nice dinner tonight. Maybe grill on the patio?"

"Sounds great. Can I borrow your car? I might go for a drive. Maybe go to the club and swim for a bit. I'll be back in time for you to go to yoga."

I hugged her from behind, careful not to get clay on me. She told me to be careful, and I kissed her on the cheek before taking myself back to the house.

The weather was so hot and dry. Different from Houston. I closed my eyes, inhaled deeply, and took in the smell of the desert: cinnamon and pine. I had missed this.

Palm trees and cacti lined the winding drive through the valley, which wound down into the suburbs and strip malls. At the bottom of the hill, I stopped to get an iced coffee at the coffee shop. The shop was filled with students and stay-at-home moms.

This *not working thing* was starting to grow on me. But then my mortgage payment—dollar signs dancing in the air—came into my mind, and I pushed that thought away and focused on enjoying this poorly initiated so-called vacation.

Taking my drink, I continued my drive. Eventually, I found myself parked in front of my childhood ballet studio. I was surprised it was still there. It looked exactly the same: the same cactus out front and the same gravel landscaping. Small succulent plants thrived in planter boxes at the head of each parking space.

Stepping out of my car, I stared up at the sign, struck by how similar the font and color schemes were to the L.O.V.E. studio logos. The desert wind blew my hair, and I reached up to hold it back as I looked around.

It was quiet here. I glanced around the parking lot, noticing only two small sports cars and a larger SUV.

Glancing one more time at the front door, I turned to leave. I was reaching for my door handle when two men came lazily out the front door. One in a suit, the other in cargo shorts and a T-shirt. Their conversation was easy, and laughter flowed between them.

The dark-haired one reached out to hug the blond one, commenting that he would see him in a few weeks.

The blond in the suit responded, "I love you, man. You'll be okay."

They hugged again, and then the dark-haired man saw me.

Confusion—then delight, then more confusion—crossed his face. "Charlotte?"

It was too late to run.

"Hey, Paxton." I set my drink on the hood of my car, wiped my palm on the front of my shorts, and reached out to shake his hand.

He took it and chuckled under his breath.

The blond stepped closer to us and put out his hand to me. "Max Crown."

I glanced quickly between the two of them. I must have looked confused because Paxton responded, "My brother."

"Max and Pax?" I couldn't hide the amusement from my question.

Max laughed good-naturedly. "You're not that clever. We've lived with that our entire lives. Well, most of our lives." He smiled at his brother fondly and slapped him on the back. "I've got a plane to catch. You take care. I'll see you soon."

They hugged one last time, and then Max stepped into one of the sports cars, honked his horn, and drove off.

I stared after the car for as long as I possibly could, not wanting to explain to Paxton why I was there.

"Charlotte?"

I turned back to him, my face blushing slightly. "Hey."

"Hey?" He laughed. "That's what I get? A 'hey.'"

"I—" I stuttered. "I, I'm not really sure what I'm doing here."

Stepping a bit closer to me, he looked down into my face. He ran his thumb thoughtfully across his lower lip. "That's, uh... that's funny. Because I don't know either."

I shifted uneasily. "I used to dance here. When I was little."

"Interesting." He stepped closer.

"I came to visit my parents this weekend and thought I would drive by. See if it was still here."

He reached up with one hand and gently held my face. His calloused thumb, still damp from his lip, brushed my cheekbone. I was forced to look up at him. Dark hooded eyes bore into mine and then dropped to my mouth.

"I'm going to kiss you, Charlotte." His words sounded like a wish.

All I could do was squeak. My lips parted on a gasp, and his lips slowly descended. When they hovered ever so lightly on mine, I lifted myself onto my toes so I could press against him.

His lips were so soft, yet firm against mine. We just stood like that, pressing against each other, breathing each other in. Softly, he pulled on my lower lip with his lips, and I sighed. His hand went around the back of my neck, holding me firm, and he maneuvered his mouth so he could run his tongue along the seam of my lips.

I moaned and stepped back slowly from him, raising my fingers to my mouth, eyeing him warily.

His hand dropped slowly back to his side, and he grinned at me mischievously. "Are you going to slap me again?"

I shook my head and whispered, "No."

Pulling his lips together and raising his eyebrows, he asked me again what I was doing there.

"I really used to dance here when I was little. I had a memory of it, and I wanted to see if it had been real."

"And is it?"

"You don't remember me, do you?"

It was his turn to look confused. "Help me out, Charlotte. I'm a little poleaxed here and, quite frankly, I just want to fuck you on the hood of your car."

"Jesus, Paxton. I don't know if I'm comforted or disturbed to know I get the same Pax regardless of the city I'm in." I crossed my arms in front of me.

The door to the studio swung open. An older lady—who looked *exactly* like Solara but with shorter hair and a smaller frame—came out, hitching a large tote bag over her shoulder.

"Oh, Paxton, you're still here. Good, good." She reached in her bag and pulled out a large manila folder. "This is from your attorney. I forgot to give it to you earlier today."

She paused when she saw me. "Oh. Hello." Then she glanced up at Paxton, expecting an introduction.

"Charlotte, this is my mom, Olivia. Mom, this is Charlotte Chase."

"*The* Charlotte?" She took my hand in both of hers. "It's nice to meet you. Paxton told me nothing about you, but Solara said wonderful things. Are you visiting?"

Paxton prevented me from answering her. "Mom, Charlotte and I were just going to get lunch. Thank you for giving this to me."

She patted his cheek gently. "Fine."

She glanced back at me and walked to the other sports car in the parking lot, speaking loudly over her shoulder. "I hope I see you again, Charlotte."

"Nice to meet you, Olivia."

She drove off, and it was just Paxton and me.

"No one else is going to come out of that door, are they?"

He glanced over his shoulder at the door and then back to me. "Nope, that's about it."

A gentle breeze had picked up, and I had to tuck my hair back behind my ear. His eyes ran the length of my body, and he smiled at me sweetly.

"I guess I should get going." I walked backward toward my car.

Standing in place, hands on his hips, he asked, "Do you want to get lunch?"

Butterflies danced in my stomach. "I really shouldn't."

"I'll drive."

I paused, feeling light and happy. "I'll follow."

His grin grew.

CHAPTER 12

I FOLLOWED THE black SUV and laughed to myself when he pulled into TopGolf. He waited until I parked next to him, and then we walked up the stairs together.

"I thought you meant food."

"We can eat here."

He held the door for me. I waited in the lobby while he got us a golf bay. The hostess checked us in and then walked us to the top floor, directly across from an extended bar and a private patio.

I sat on the couch and watched as she showed us how to use the system. She left some menus on the low table after Paxton ordered us two iced teas.

"Unsweetened okay?"

I shrugged my shoulders and nodded.

Now that we were here, I felt awkward. I fidgeted with the hem of my shorts. Paxton took a club out of the bin and handed it to me.

I stood abruptly. "Paxton, listen, this is weird. I don't even really know you. I don't know what I'm doing here. I'm getting married soon, and, well… I think this is a bad idea."

He grinned his big bad wolf grin, looking even more devilish with a few days of scruff on his jaw; it looked like he hadn't shaved since last weekend.

"I agree it's a bit weird, but not that it's a bad idea. And I can't help you with the marriage part, but I'm not the one that showed up at my mom's studio. Why don't you start with that, and we'll figure out the rest as we go?"

"You aren't supposed to be so rational."

He held out the golf club again. "You're up. And what did you expect? I'm not an uncouth beast all the time." I stood warily gauging him, and he extended the club. "C'mon, it's golf. Knock out your frustration."

"I'm not frustrated."

"Well, I am. So hurry up." He winked at me, and I took the club from him, stepping up to the tee box and tapping the ball release.

I hit the ball hard, and it went flying out toward the back net.

"Are you grifting me?"

I turned and saw him leaning back against the couch cushions, arms crossed over his chest, one ankle crossed over his other knee. He was smiling. His cargo shorts showed off his thick thighs and didn't do anything to lessen my attraction to him.

"I play with my dad. Played. I haven't golfed in a really long time."

Extending the club to him, I expected him to take it. Instead, he scooted over on the couch and patted the cushion next to him.

"What should I remember about you?"

Taking a deep breath, I sat down next to him, pulling one knee up onto the couch so I could face him. He didn't move.

I told him about the ballet recital and what he'd said to me. He shifted in his seat, turning so he could face me.

When I was finished, he reached out and tucked some of my hair behind my ear. His thickly-lashed eyes roamed my face, my hair, and finally—my mouth.

He whispered, "It seems I've been a shit for as long as you've known me."

"A fair assessment."

The waitress interrupted us, placing our drinks on the table. Paxton ordered fajitas for two. He asked me, "Is that okay?"

"That's fine, yes."

When she left, he turned back to me. "But that doesn't answer why you were there today."

His gaze was piercing mine. My chest felt tight. "I… I don't really know."

"You're a coward, Charlotte." He said on a short laugh. His words felt like a slap.

"Why are you always such an ass?"

I stood to leave, and he reached out for my wrist, holding me in place. "I'm sorry, please stay."

Inhaling, I whispered sharply, "You have been nothing but rude, and crass, and… well, just everything deplorable in a human being since I met you. Then you kiss me and act like a gentleman. Kind of. I think I could like you and then you call me names."

He held me in place, but his grip softened. "Charlotte, my actions toward you have never been anything but truthful. If you could step back for just a minute, you might see that it's your actions you're doubting. I've made no pretense that I want you."

"No, you've made no pretense that you want to fuck me." I frowned at him.

"Well, you have me there." He was placating me. Pointing out that he was married would just add fuel to the fire, so I chose not to bring it up.

He took the club from the table where I'd left it, went to the tee box, and set up to hit a ball. He hit a few while I simply sat there watching him.

My own motivation in coming here wasn't something I was willing to dwell on.

"Tell me about your brother."

"He's more your type, huh?"

"If you mean personable, friendly, and kind, then yes, I guess he's my type."

He placed the golf club back in the holder, grabbed another one, and hit another couple of balls before sitting back down beside me. He stared out at the driving range, and I took this time to look at his profile.

His golden freckles were more pronounced in the sun. His eyes were contemplative. His jaw was tense, and I could almost see the wheels turning in his head.

Our food arrived. We continued to sit in silence, each of us arranging the tortillas and meat on the small plates.

I took small bites of my lunch; he inhaled three fajitas. When he was finished, he wiped his hands, took a sip of tea, and turned to face me.

"My mom was a ballerina. When she was younger, she was prima with the Phoenix dance company. Unwisely, she had an affair with the director, got pregnant, and was kicked out. He was married and refused to accept that the child was his."

"You?"

He nodded and cleared his throat. "Ballerinas aren't paid much to begin with, and now she didn't have a paycheck at all. She moved into a not-so-nice apartment complex and made friends with the other girls that lived there. They happened to be strippers and suggested she try dancing. She was young, and now she had a baby. It was a way to make money."

"But she has a successful studio." It was both a comment and a question.

"She does now." He took a drink of his tea. "She wanted to go to college, so she would leave me with the girls during the day and dance at night."

"Oh, my goodness. You really have been in this business your entire life. You were like their little doll."

He laughed. "I guess. But I'm not in the strip club business, Charlotte."

"I didn't mean it like that."

"That's kind of the perception, though, isn't it? Pole dancers? Strippers? It's difficult to separate the two."

He was right. I had been angry with Mark for exactly the same thing. "How did she get back to ballet?"

"One night, my dad"—he paused— "Max's dad... One night Max's dad came into the club with some of his business partners. He'd lost his wife, Max's mom, to breast cancer a few years prior, and they wanted to get him out of his funk. They came here for a convention and showed up at the club where she worked."

"Poor Max. How old was he when his mom died?"

He looked like he was doing math in his head before he responded. "Um, maybe three or four? He and I are the same age. Same grade. Not the same disposition."

I shook my head. "Go on."

"He was instantly taken with her, but she didn't want anything to do with him. He tried to get her attention, but she was focused on school and me. Or so she says." He laughed at himself. "This is my mom's version of the story, of course.

"Why did she agree to go out with him?"

"He would come to the club during the day, waiting for her, so he could ask her out on a real date."

"That's kind of creepy." I crossed my arms.

"You mean like showing up at someone's place of business?" He looked at me pointedly, putting me in my place.

I raised my chin. "I thought that was your mother's place of business. I didn't expect to see you."

He smiled knowingly and leaned forward. "But you didn't expect *not* to see me?"

I blushed and looked back out at the driving range.

The waitress arrived with our check. "Your bay reservation ends in fifteen minutes."

Paxton took out his wallet, pulled out his credit card, and handed it to her with the check. "Thank you for reminding us."

We waited until she left, then I commented, "Obviously, she eventually said yes."

"Obviously."

"You and Max seem really close."

"We are. We weren't always, though."

He left it at that.

"Do you want to hit a few more balls?"

Raising his eyebrows at me, he asked, "Do *you*?"

"I should probably get going."

He stood, extending his hand to me. "I'll walk you out."

I took his hand, and he didn't let go as we walked back out into the parking lot. When we reached my car, I leaned against the door. He put his hands on the frame of the car, caging me in.

I licked my lips, hoping he would kiss me again. "You didn't finish your story."

"Are you asking me out?"

He was so close to me. All I had to do was push off the side of the car, and I would be pressed up against him.

"No, just making small talk."

He laughed and pushed himself away from me, reaching into his shorts pocket and pulling out his keys.

"You should go see Sol tomorrow." He paused. "If you're still here."

"Maybe."

"She teaches a group beginner floor class at noon. I'm sure she'd love to see you."

"Solara teaches?"

He was backing up toward his SUV. "Go see her."

I was left staring after him, more intrigued than ever. I watched as he drove out of the parking lot before I took myself back to my parents.

CHAPTER 13

A TEXT: *COME dressed for class.* And a smiley face.

The hot Arizona sun was rising across the desert. Stretching languidly in bed, I smiled at how well I had slept as I stared out at the rugged landscape of my parent's backyard.

Paxton must have told Solara I was here. I was curious to find out how that conversation happened, and I was hoping she would finish his story for me.

Yesterday had been an unexpected—yet pleasant—surprise. The layers of the man were slowly being pulled back, and I didn't have much time to figure out... figure out, what? I shoved that question away and got myself out of bed.

My parents were on the covered back deck, drinking their morning coffee before the heat became unbearable. I joined them with my own mug. A palm frond fan whirred softly above them, stirring the heavy air with a light breeze.

I tucked my feet underneath me on the lounge chair, sipping my coffee and enjoying their companionable silence. My mother was on her iPhone; my father was old school and still read the newspaper.

"What are you guys doing today?"

My dad lowered the newspaper, peeking at me over the top rim of his readers. "I have a tee time at eleven, and your mother and I have an art show to attend tonight. You're welcome to join us if you like."

"That sounds fun. I'd like that. Mom, what are you doing?"

"Nothing. Absolutely nothing." She smiled at my dad, and he chuckled as he picked up the paper and started to read again. Their inside joke was that she never did 'absolutely nothing.'

Turning her attention to me, she asked, "What do you have planned for the day?"

"Remember that thing I told you about yesterday? That dance studio?"

She smiled and shot a covert glance at my dad before responding, "The friend from Houston?"

"Yes. She texted me this morning, so I think I'll go meet her."

"Sounds like an interesting day." She gave her attention back to her phone, a small knowing smile on her lips. It wasn't that I was trying to hide it from my dad; it was that he was a need-to-know kind of guy. Knowing how much he loved my mother, I wasn't remotely worried that he would judge me for the dancing.

I texted Solara: *What time? No clothes. Can I buy something there?*

Her response: *Noon—come early, I'll show you around, yes*

Invigorated with a sense of purpose for the day, I quickly showered, dressed, and grabbed some breakfast. My dad had left for his golf game, and since my mom wasn't going anywhere, I took her car.

The drive to the studio was shorter than I'd thought it would be. Located on the north side of Phoenix in a more suburban area, it didn't take me long to get there.

Following the directions from Google Maps, I pulled into an elegantly landscaped suburban shopping area. Tall palm trees lined the entrance and, colorful desert flowers were planted strategically along the sidewalk.

Standing apart from the strip of shops was a two-story stucco building. On the front was the L.O.V.E. logo. I was struck speechless by its size and opulence.

Awe kept me in my seat, staring at the front of the building. The building's size was intimidating, but curiosity, and my desire to see Solara, forced me from my car.

Hitching my bag over my shoulder, I pulled open the double doors and entered a lavish lobby. The front area was carpeted in white, and the black and chrome counter was emblazoned with the L.O.V.E. logo.

On the back wall was a waterfall. The water ran down clear glass through multi-colored lights. On the other side of the fall, I could see a long hallway that led to the back of the building.

A young girl with feathered, strawberry-blonde hair greeted me enthusiastically. "Hi, welcome to LOVE. Can I help you?"

Her eagerness reminded me of Erin, but they had completely different looks.

"I'm here to see Solara."

"Solara Crown?"

I wanted to snap, *"Who else?"* but held my tongue, remembering that she had no idea who I was. My thoughts of self-importance caused me to chuckle when I responded. "Yes, Solara Crown."

"She's just finishing a class. I'll send her a message. Who should I tell her is here?"

"Charlotte."

She raised her eyebrows at me questioningly.

"Chase. Charlotte Chase."

She pulled a phone from her hip and sent off a quick text.

She pointed to a white leather couch, similar to the ones at the studio back home, and said, "You can wait over there if you like. She should be finished in about five minutes. Can I get you a bottle of water?"

I looked at my watch. It was almost eleven thirty. "No, thank you. I'm fine."

As I waited, I looked through the clothes that were tastefully displayed in one corner of the lobby: bikini tops, short shorts, leggings, shoes, and knee-pads. Everything a dancer needed to ensure she—or he—was free to do what they needed to do.

A few girls entered the building and scanned a card over a black box on the counter. The strawberry-blonde greeted most of them by name before they disappeared down the hallway.

Covertly, I watched them enter, trying to disguise my anxiety (and excitement) at seeing the rest of the studio.

Settling on a pair of black, wet-look leggings and a so-called pole position cross-back tank, I took the items to the counter to purchase.

As the girl was placing the clothes in a paper bag with tissue, Solara descended the circular stairs.

"Charlotte, you made it!" She leaped off the bottom step and enveloped me in a huge hug.

I held up my bag. "I did. And I bought clothes."

"Excellent! I can show you around, and then you can take my noon class."

Stuttering a bit, I looked at her in awe. "I didn't know you taught as well."

"Of course, I do." She smirked at me.

"It's just... well, you're so..." I faltered. She had struck me as the back-office type.

"Fat?"

I just about choked. She was curvy but by no means overweight. "Oh, my God, Solara, no! That's not what I meant. I just thought you were the office type. I'm sorry, I should stop." I pulled myself together and said, "I'm excited to take your class, Solara."

She laughed and pulled me along beside her. "C'mon, let me show you where you can put your things."

Hooking her elbow in mine, she took me down the hall I'd watched the others disappear down.

"The men's and women's dressing rooms are on the left, and there are four entrances to the gym—one from outside that can be accessed by key code, one from the hall at the end, and one from each dressing room."

"You have a gym?" My eyes darted around, trying to take everything in.

"We're the training center for the Phoenix ballet. They like to workout at odd hours, so we have an outside entrance for them." She smiled at me.

"I had no idea."

"It's okay. Why would you?"

She walked me into the women's dressing room and showed me to a row of lockers. "The ballerinas all have their own lockers, and they are marked. You can take any of the others that are open. Do you know how to use the combination locks?

I nodded and told her I did.

"Great. Leave your stuff here while I show you around. Then you can come back and change.

She waited while I got settled and then briefly showed me the gym. It was equipped with all the standard cardio equipment and free weights. Nothing special or out of the ordinary. Then she took me up a set of stairs in the back that led to a loft that looked down into the lobby.

Crossing the open area, she opened a door and took me into a string of offices. "This is where Paxton and I work. Max has an office, too, but he lives in California." She looked at me knowingly. "You remember, my brother you met yesterday?"

I blushed slightly. "Can we talk about that later?"

She laughed and ushered me into the larger of the two. "This is Paxton's office."

"Huh." I tried to hide my curiosity.

Her phone beeped at her side, and she glanced at the incoming number. "Give me a minute. I'll be right back."

She left me standing in the middle of his unoccupied office. It was very sterile with floor-to-ceiling windows that looked out toward the mountains.

My feet settled into expensive, gray carpet, and I glanced around at the black and chrome office furniture, thinking that the coldness of it suited him. An oversized black leather chair sat on the other side of the desk, but what caught my attention was a hand-carved, wooden train that held a number of pens and highlighters in the smokestack.

I gently picked it up and admired the craftsmanship. It was small but solid, and there was an engraving on the side—*Charlie*. I sucked in my breath.

"Find what you were looking for?"

I dropped the train on the desk, pens spilling everywhere. "Christ, Paxton! What are you doing here?"

"That's a question for you, really, since this is *my* office."

He crossed the room efficiently, placing his messenger bag on his desk, scooping up the pens, and putting them back in the train.

"Solara left me here. She had a call. She'll be right back."

He was back in his usual black jeans and T-shirt, and he was putting his laptop and files into his bag.

When he was finished, he came back around the desk and gently grabbed my arm. "Huh. Well, how about if I take you to *her* office and you can wait for her there?"

He tried to usher me out. I shook his hand off my elbow. "Who's Charlie?"

"None of your business." His eyes sharpened on me.

I stood my ground, not backing away from his stare.

He looked away from me and turned to leave his office. "Fine. Stay here. I have a plane to catch."

I followed after him. "Who's Charlie? And where are you going?" I sounded desperate and was slightly embarrassed by my behavior. I could feel pain washing off of him. I wanted him to let me in.

When he turned back to me, his laugh was almost cruel. Slowly stalking toward me, he palmed my cheek, brushing my lower lip with his thumb. "Oh, Charlotte, you do want me. Shame I have to leave. I've dreamt of nothing but turning you inside out and upside down. You haunt me, but I don't have time for games."

He looked me up and down, the top of his head almost hitting my forehead, and he growled. "Maybe one for the road." And he bent his head and kissed me, taking everything from me. Pulling my tongue into his mouth and devouring me. I fought for control of my emotions, but I was losing. My knees weakened, and I let go.

Reaching out to him, I tucked my fingers into the waistband of his jeans so I could pull him closer. As soon as I did, he abruptly released me and stepped back.

Confusion crossed his face for an instant and was gone just as quickly. He dismissed me and headed toward the circular stairs that led back into the lobby, saying over his shoulder, "Have a safe flight home, Charlotte."

I walked over to the railing to watch him leave. Solara stopped him on her way back up, and he handed her the folder from his bag. She took it from him, gave him a hug, and a pinch on his cheek before continuing her way back to me.

"I'm so sorry. We have an event in Denver next weekend, and I have to do all the coordinating. It's making me crazy. Let me finish showing you upstairs, and then I'll show you the downstairs pole room. You can change for class."

She walked toward a studio that spanned the length of the building with windows looking outside. "This is where we do hip-hop and pole class. The poles unscrew from the ceiling and floor, and we store them in the back room over there."

She pointed to a closet long enough to keep the poles stacked. Similar to the ballet room, the pole studio had floor-to-ceiling mirrors on one wall. Because of the windows, it was bright and cheery.

I only slightly heard her words, my lips still tingling from Paxton's kiss. I tried to act engaged and asked, "Who teaches hip-hop?"

In a self-deprecating tone, she said, "Not me."

"Paxton?" I asked hesitantly.

"Oh, my God, you are *not* serious." She laughed out loud. "He could—but it would be under threat of cutting off his penis." She laughed again. "No. We have a few instructors who have been with us for years. Most of them have full-time jobs or are students at Arizona State University."

She turned off the lights, and we headed down via the back stair. She pointed toward the dressing rooms, told me to get changed, and then meet her in the pole studio across the hall.

"Do I need shoes? I didn't bring any."

"I have extra. What size?"

"Nine."

She nodded and disappeared through the studio room door. The girls I'd seen arrive earlier were in the changing room, stretching and pulling on their leg warmers.

I changed as quickly as I could, noticing the time on the clock tick toward noon. Walking across the hall from the changing rooms to the studio, I was struck with surprise as I stepped into the room.

This was not the hip-hop room from upstairs. This was magnificence, and sexiness, and all things shiny.

The wood floors shone, polished and glossy. There were no windows in this room, and mirrors lined the front wall from corner to corner.

Red and purple paint swirled decoratively between the mirrors and the ceiling. The back wall was painted purple with flecks of gold that sparkled under the mirror ball spinning from the ceiling. The ceilings were painted black. Low, recessed lights shone down on the floor.

This room was sin and seduction; I was almost brought to my knees in wonder.

I noticed that the other girls had pulled mats from the sidewall and set themselves up next to individual poles. I followed their lead and sat myself down at a pole near the back corner. Spaced six feet apart, there was enough room between the poles for almost full leg extension.

Solara was standing near a stereo system, poking at her iPhone. When the music started, she strutted over to the front of the room, gave me a big grin, and introduced me to the girls in the room.

"Everyone, this is Charlotte. She's from our studio in Houston. Charlotte, everyone. Take a minute after class to say hi to her."

She sat herself down on her mat cross-legged, put her hands on her knees, and started to roll her head around on her shoulders. Eyes closed, she looked ethereal. I found myself closing my own eyes and following her verbal instructions.

The sexy techno beat had me swaying and stretching, rolling my shoulders and extending my hands down to my feet. When she instructed us to spread our legs in a "V" and slide down on our left leg, I opened my eyes. She and the other girls were seductively sliding their hands down their legs to their feet, resting their chests on their thighs. To the music's tune, they slid themselves back up and repeated it on the other leg.

When the warm-up was finished, Solara told everyone they could get their shoes if they wanted.

"Charlotte, I have a pair for you." She handed me the six-inch platforms and then put hers on.

"This is a floor class, so no pole today. Charlotte, you okay with that?"

I nodded dumbly and then sat with my ankles crossed, hands back as instructed.

For the next 30 minutes, Solara walked us through the elements of a floor routine. She talked us through the mechanics of each move, showing us the transitions.

"The transitions are just as important as each move. Make the viewer follow your fluidity. Entrance them."

She walked the room every now and then, helping us get our legs and butts into position. I struggled a little with one move that required me to keep my shoulders on the ground while lifting my butt and pivoting myself in the opposite direction.

I laughed when I rolled over like an egg, and Solara said, "You'll get it. Use your hands to propel your lower back off the ground."

I followed along better than I thought I would and found myself actually sweating.

When she was finished with the instruction, she said, "We're going to run through the full routine. If you want to record yourself, now is the time to set up your phones."

A couple of the girls set their phones on yoga blocks up against the mirror. The music started, and Solara got herself back into position on the floor, ankles crossed, her platform heels shining in the mirror. Her hands were braced behind her, her chest was pushed out, and a small smile was on her face.

"Ready?" She looked around the room, and the music began.

Sliding my right leg out, my left knee fell to the floor of its own accord, and I found it easy to follow the routine. I closed my eyes. My knowledge and training with Dani took over from there, and I simply followed the music's beat. Hips, thrust. Legs, extend. Chest, undulate. Hair, flip. Lips, part. The music was lulling me, erotic and wanton.

I was lost in the routine and forgot all about the other girls in the room. At one point, I opened my eyes to make sure I was doing the right move and saw Solara lost in her own world. I was captivated. She was a master. Eyes closed, she rolled her head, and her body undulated. A goddess; completely confident with her sexual power. My chest felt tight. She was love incarnate and unabashedly unashamed. I would have never called her fat, but I would never have imagined that her stout and sturdy body was capable of this level of exquisite movement.

I was momentarily frightened. I had stepped so far out of my real life… I didn't know how I could go back. Feelings of sorrow welled up in me, and I pushed them back down. I didn't need to think about that today. I needed to be here—in this moment, in this world.

CHAPTER 14

"GREAT CLASS, EVERYONE!" Solara was standing now, clapping and giving kudos to most of the girls.

A few of them stopped and said hello. I tried to remember their names, but it was difficult for me to keep up in the flurry of smiles and hugs.

When the room emptied, I laid back down on my mat, crossed my arms over my stomach, and stared up at the ceiling—exhausted. I let my eyes drift closed.

Solara's voice came from above me. "Are you dead?"

Opening one eye, her pretty face was staring down at me, smiling, a towel around her neck.

"There is a high probability."

She chuckled. "Stay right there. I'll get a mat and join you. I need to stretch some more."

Pulling one knee to my chest, I rolled my ankle and then did the same on the other side. Solara turned the music down and placed her mat next to mine. Rolling my head to the side, I asked, "Are you finished for the day?"

"I am. I only do the two on Saturdays. During the week, I do the chair classes on Tuesdays and Thursdays. I'm too busy to teach more."

"I thought you were the chief financial officer."

"I am. But we're a family business, so I travel for events, and teach, and do whatever else is necessary."

"What does Max do?"

She giggled a little and responded, "He's in sales. He works for my dad in California."

I lifted myself to a sitting position. "Solara, I'm going to be perfectly honest. I am—" I looked heavenward, searching for the right words. "I am overwhelmed and blown away, and my head is just spinning with questions."

She sat up, spread her legs in a "V" to keep stretching, and then lowered her forehead to the ground. Her voice was muffled when she asked, "What do you want to know?"

"How did your mom… your mom too, right?"

She looked up and smiled, "Yes."

"How did your mom go from being a ballerina to a pole dancer to a business mogul?"

Scooting herself backward, she leaned against a pole, pulled her heels to her bottom, and then wrapped her hands around her knees.

"I told you I was born into this. I really don't know any different. Paxton and Max… they're the ones that carry the most memories. He likes you, you know?"

"Max?"

She frowned at me.

I lowered my eyes to my mat. "I'm engaged, Solara. I told you."

My comment was met with silence, and I looked up to find her staring at me pensively.

She shrugged. "Anyway. From what I've been told, my dad—Max's dad—wanted my mom to have everything. When he finally convinced her to go out with him, he wouldn't let her go. He bought her the small ballet studio so she could teach, get away from pole dancing, and do things her way. And then, just because he could, he built this studio and started offering ballet, pole dance, and then hip-hop."

"How did you end up being the training facility for the Phoenix ballet?"

"I think that my dad did that as an eff you to the ballet company. Because he could."

"What happened to Paxton's dad?"

"He died in a car accident in France with his new wife. Olivia's replacement."

I covered my mouth with my hand. "Oh, my God!"

"Paxton never knew him. As far as we're concerned, we're family."

"When I met Max yesterday, they seemed really close."

She nodded and smiled. "They are. My dad adopted Paxton and never treated him any differently. Although, my mom will tell you Max and Paxton used to fight and beat each other up. Max is so blond, and Paxton looks like the devil himself. I think he was probably jealous of what Max had."

"But Max's mom died."

"Doesn't matter. To Paxton, it was what you could see on the outside that bothered him. He was essentially raised by strippers, and Max was raised in Southern California, the son of a wealthy businessman."

"Paxton still seems to carry a chip on his shoulder," I commented.

"Not anymore. Not about family." She was looking directly at me, challenging me almost. "He would do anything for us. And Max is his best friend."

I was silent and did a few more stretches. "Do you have studios in California?"

She laughed at my attempt to change the subject. "No. My dad sells fitness equipment, ballet bars—" She paused. "And poles."

"Really?!"

"Yes."

"So, you really were born into it."

"I really was born into it."

My sweat was starting to dry, and I got a chill. I stood and grabbed my sweatshirt from the bench, pulling it on over my head. "I guess I should get going."

Solara had turned the stereo off and was walking toward me, a water bottle in her hand. She said softly, "How come you haven't asked me about the job?"

I sat myself down on the bench, blankly staring up at her. Her stare was patient. Knowing.

"I'm…" I cleared my throat. "I'm having a hard time lately."

"I gathered."

I chuckled. "Is it obvious?"

"Women, especially executives, don't just throw their careers and fiancés away to start pole dancing. Unless something is shifting."

My eyes watered, and I swiped away a tear from the outside corner, lowering my chin.

"And they certainly don't cry over it." She sat down next to me and pushed me gently with her shoulder.

"I haven't thrown either away."

Her eyebrows raised, and she chuckled. "Are you going to?"

My tears leaked out. "Solara, how do I compartmentalize these two worlds?"

"I don't know. I've never had to do it. But I have been judged. And dumped. And heartbroken."

"I wish he supported me more."

"Do you?"

"Of course!"

"Why?"

"What do you mean 'why'?"

She had the sense to look somewhat embarrassed. "I'm sorry. It's just—Paxton was different when he came back from his last trip to Houston. He walked faster. He smiled more. He seemed… I don't know… hopeful."

I chortled, "How can you possibly get hopeful from his deplorable behavior toward me?"

"I can't make excuses for him. I know how he can be. But it's been a few years since he's been truly happy, and it was fun to see him a little uncomfortable around you."

"He was hardly uncomfortable."

"I can see why you would think that, not knowing any different, but he was."

"Are you going to tell me why?"

"Why what?"

"Why he hasn't been happy."

"I can't."

"Who's Charlie?" I took this window of opportunity to press for more.

"That's his story to tell, Charlotte. But I can't help feeling that if you were here, he might... I don't know. He might be the Paxton he was."

I teased her. "So, purely selfish motivation?"

"Do you want to know about the job?"

I shook my head.

"Would it make a difference if I told you it was only for two months, then you could go back to your—" She made air quotes. "real life."

Laughingly, I shrugged. "Maybe."

"Let's go upstairs. I'll show you everything."

After leading me up the back stairs, we settled in a large conference room between Solara and Paxton's offices. It looked more like a war room.

A map of the United States was on one wall, with pins pushed into cities and dates scribbled to the side. On the other wall was a bulletin board with checklists and assignments for everyone.

She sat down at the head of the table, picked up the phone, and pushed a button. After a brief pause, she spoke into the receiver, "Story, can you get some lunch for Charlotte and me?" She covered the mouthpiece and mouthed, "Is chicken salad okay?"

I nodded.

"Two chicken salads and two iced teas."

She replaced the phone and looked around the room. "What do you think?"

"Story's here?"

"She is. She's trying to get everything ready for the Denver show. They don't have enough volunteers to work the show, so she's frantically trying to get organized. She'll leave Monday."

"Is that where Max was going?"

"No, Max was going back to California."

She waited, knowing I desperately wanted to ask where Paxton was going. I didn't.

"What's all this?" I crossed my arms in front of me and looked at all the pins on the map.

She laughed and went to the map of the United States. "These are all of the cities we have events in for the next few months. This is our busiest time of the year. We travel a lot. We don't sleep much. And we have a shit-ton of fun!"

Her excitement made me laugh, and I turned to see her grinning at me. I followed the red arrows drawn on the map. They ended at Irvine.

I touched the map and looked at her questioningly. "This is the last show?"

"It is, and we always have a big party in Laguna Beach. Paxton rents us all rooms at the Pacific Edge Hotel, and we have a huge celebration. During October, I go to Mexico. I am usually spent." She smiled at me.

I noticed the last event was the week before the gala that Mark and I were hosting. Flickers of excitement fluttered through me. Maybe I could do this. Wandering over to the other side of the room, I nodded my head at the wall. "And this?"

"These are all the competition schedules. It helps Story if she can see how many competitors have signed up: their times and their events. Then she knows how many volunteers to ask for. Some events have two stages running at the same time, and it gets really chaotic."

Story came in backward through the conference room, carrying a drink tray and balancing a to-go pack in her fingers.

"Lunch is here. Hi, Charlotte." She grinned at me. An unusual response judging from the last time I had seen her.

"Hi, Story. Thank you for lunch."

"Of course. I was told you're going to be working with us for the next few months." She seemed genuinely happy to see me. It was such a change from our first encounter at the competition in Houston that I was curious about why she was behaving so differently now. But maybe I had just misjudged her or been more influenced by Erin's gossip than I'd wanted to admit.

I glanced quickly to Solara, and she grimaced, a sheepish expression on her face. She raised her hands in surrender, pretending she had nothing to do with it. I should have felt ambushed. Instead, I felt wanted.

"Not sure yet. I have some things I need to work out first."

"Well, I would love to have the help. And Erin and Dani said amazing things about you."

"Solara was just telling me about how it works."

The two of them tag-teamed each other with the job requirements. I had never been recruited so hard for any executive position. They were good; Solara was good. She would have made an excellent chief executive officer. Then again, that was Paxton's job, so I guess that position wasn't available.

My head was spinning with all the things they were telling me. The job didn't sound easy, and I could imagine why Solara would take off for a month at the end of the season.

"You can have any two days off during the week that you want. On the weekends, you would travel, and during the week, you would work the front desk and any other administrative things that need handling."

"Do we travel every weekend?" I was exhausted just listening to them.

"No, there are a few when we are here. We also have a Phoenix competition, so that's nice. We can stay home."

I looked up at the map. Denver was next weekend, and the Phoenix show the week after that.

"Well, that sounds intriguing. I'll need to think about it."

"Do you want to know what it pays?" Story asked me.

I said with a laugh, "No."

Solara laughed, too, knowing that it would be nowhere near my current salary. The pay wouldn't be the draw to this job, and she knew that.

Story balled up her sandwich bag and threw it in the trash. "Think about it. I could really use the help."

I nodded at her and watched as she turned to Solara. "Did I see Paxton's truck this morning?"

"Yeah, he came by here to pick up some files."

"I thought he was flying out yesterday."

Solara turned back to me, raising her eyebrows as if to say, *See, I told you.*

She turned her attention back to Story. "He had an important meeting yesterday afternoon. Missed the flight."

"Damn! I had some outfits I wanted him to take to Denver. Oh, well, I can pack them. I just really didn't want to check bags this trip."

"Do you want me to bring them? I leave on Wednesday."

"That would be fantastic. Thank you!" She was leaving out the conference room door, and I gave her a little wave good-bye. "Charlotte, I hope I see you in Denver. I would love to have your help."

"Thanks. We'll see."

She left the room. Solara and I sat in silence. I frequently used her silent treatment technique: wait the person out, and eventually, they would talk.

I gave her what she wanted. "You ambushed me," I said with just a hint of accusation.

She leaped over to me, almost childlike. "Charlotte, there is something in you. I feel it. It's like you're ready to crack. I didn't mean to ambush you, and if you don't want the job, I totally understand."

My tears were leaking out again. I wiped at them.

She reached out for my hands and said, "I just feel like, like I'm witnessing a butterfly being born, and I want to be part of it."

I laughed and choked on a tear. "Oh, my God! That is so silly."

She laughed at herself. "Fine, it's silly. But I like you, and I think you like it here. I won't pressure you anymore. You can let me know on your own time if you want the job."

"Thank you."

"Just let me know by Monday because I need to make flight reservations for you."

I chuckled again at her. "No pressure?"

"No pressure."

We finished our lunch, and I told her about my parents and growing up in Scottsdale. Paxton never came up again, and we steered clear of anything serious.

I had to admit, I did like the feel of this conference room. And the view of the mountains was pretty extraordinary.

"When are you flying home?"

Solara's words jolted me from my daydreaming.

"Tomorrow morning. First thing."

"I'm really glad you came by today."

"Me too."

There was nothing left to talk about until I made a decision.

She excused herself to get back to planning, and I told her I would see myself out.

Hugging me, she said, "Have a safe flight home. Let me know what you decide."

Leaving me alone in the conference room, I stared vacantly out the window. Cars rushed along the main road out front: flashes of silver, red, and black moved along with such importance. Business people were having lunch at local restaurants. Stay-at-home moms were taking yoga classes.

Life was just moving along. People doing their things, whatever those were. And yet, here I stood, stuck in the middle of a decision, doing nothing. If I closed my eyes, maybe I would wake up and find that this was all a dream. Home was so far away.

I waited. Processing my decisions. Waiting for inspiration. Something to tell me what to do. Anything. A feeling. A movement. A sign. I looked at my phone in my hand, willing it to ring with an answer.

Solara peeked her head back into the conference room. "9:00 a.m. out of Houston to Denver on Wednesday. Should I book it?"

My smile grew. Bless her heart.

"Book it."

CHAPTER 15

"I can't believe I'm doing this."

My mom was driving me to the airport to catch my flight home to Houston, and I was actually giddy with anticipation. Giddy.

Solara and I had immediately started making arrangements for the next weekend. We scheduled my flight to arrive in Denver at the same time as hers, so we could ride to the hotel together. I'd told her I had no idea what I was doing, and she'd assured me I would figure it out.

Maneuvering her way to the passenger drop-off, my mom just laughed at me. "I can believe it. You seem so happy right now, and I'm so glad you'll be staying with us for a while. It'll be nice to have you around."

When she came to a stop at the curb, she popped the trunk, and I took my bag out of the back.

"Okay. Now, I arrive back here late Sunday night, so I'll just Uber home. Don't worry about me; I'll text you from Denver." I hugged her tightly and said again, "Oh, my God, I can't believe I'm doing this."

"Have you told Mark yet?"

"Don't bring me down, Mom. I have a whole flight to think about how I'm going to do that."

"Fair enough." She grabbed my cheeks and looked at me lovingly. "I love you so much. You be careful. I'll see you in a week."

"A week. Wow! Yes, a week."

"Go. You're gonna miss your flight."

"Okay, I'm going." I leaned down to kiss her again. "I'm going." I blew kisses at her as I went backward through the automatic doors into the airport. They closed behind me, and I made my way to the check-in counter.

My flight home was uneventful, but the farther away I got from Phoenix, the more doubt started creeping in. I practiced my speech to Mark, and it sounded crazy even to me. Resting my head back on the seat, I tried to take a nap, but my brain wouldn't shut off. I'd felt so confident standing in that conference room. Now I was conflicted.

By the time the flight landed, I had emotionally wrung myself out. I texted Mark: *Just landed. Will Uber home.*

His response came quickly: *Great! Can't wait to see you. Suzanne is here. We're planning the gala.*

I groaned out loud and waited for my luggage.

The Uber driver pulled into my driveway, and I clicked the automatic gate opener in my purse, allowing the driver to let me out close to the back door.

I stood in the driveway and watched as he drove away, steeling myself for the next few hours of party planning. I had really wanted to be alone with Mark tonight. That wasn't going to happen now.

Suzanne threw open the back door and squealed. "You're back!"

"I'm back!" I mimicked her enthusiasm.

"Mark, get her bag." She ushered me into the kitchen, looping her elbow with mine. "We have the best idea for the gala." She stopped to make sure I would hear her, and with dramatic flair, she said, "*Gatsby.* Don't you love it?"

"Love it."

Mark had kissed me swiftly on the lips before stepping outside and getting my suitcase. "We were talking about classic movies, and it was either *Breakfast at Tiffany's* or *The Great Gatsby.* It's not breakfast, so that went out the window. And not the old *Gatsby*—the Leonardo DiCaprio *Gatsby*—with a retro theme."

What was wrong with the two of them? They were both skittish and talking really fast; they were exhausting me.

"Can I get a glass of wine? I had a really long flight, and I'm kind of hungry. Did you guys eat?"

Suzanne talked as she went into the kitchen. "We had takeout. I'll bring you a plate and a glass of wine. Just sit and relax. Let Mark show you what we've come up with."

Sitting down at the dining room table, I finally let my eyes settle on Mark. He stopped talking, and we simply stared at each other in the quiet.

His eyes were kind, and now that Suzanne was out of the room, he visibly relaxed. He whispered, "Did you have a good visit with your parents?"

"I did."

"I'm glad you're back, Charlie." I must have flinched because he suddenly asked, "What is it? Are you okay?"

I reached out and took his hand. "I'm fine. Just a long flight and I wasn't really prepared for company tonight—even if it is just Suzanne."

He squeezed my fingers.

"Here you go." With a flourish, Suzanne reappeared and set a plate in front of me. She placed a glass to the right of the plate, grabbed a napkin and fork from the hutch, and then poured me a glass of wine from the bottle on the table.

"Mark, a little more?"

"Sure."

When our glasses were filled, Suzanne raised her glass to us. "Welcome home, Charlie."

Her nervous gestures and hovering were making me uncomfortable. I pressed my forefinger and thumb to the sides of my forehead, trying to rub away the pounding behind my temples.

The two of them proceeded to share their ideas: How the house would be decorated. What the color scheme would be. And, wouldn't it be great if we could get fireworks?

My head was spinning. I just nodded obligingly and gave words of agreement and appreciation as required. It was becoming too easy to just fake my way through these kinds of moments.

Abruptly, I stood and grabbed my plate. "If you guys will excuse me, I am exhausted. And now that I've eaten, I just really need to lie down. You've done a great job; I think the gala is going to be beautiful."

Suzanne stood and said she would help me with my bag. Their treatment of me was annoying, as if I was frail or delicate in some way—breakable.

I took my plate to the sink and told Suzanne I would call her in the morning.

"Do you want to meet for lunch?"

I nodded and said pleasantly, "That sounds great."

Tilting my head toward Mark, I said, "See you in a bit?"

"I'll be up in a little while."

It was a burden to drag myself up the stairs: the heavy weight of sorrow slowed my steps. It was all I could do to brush my teeth and change into my pajamas. Even knowing what I had to look forward to in Arizona didn't ease the guilt and sadness that hung on my heart at ending my relationship.

A few hours later, the mattress dipped with Mark's weight.

He whispered my name as he rolled on top of me. Kissing my face reverently, he slid my nightdress up around my waist and then gently stroked my breasts.

What I had been trying so hard to get from him for weeks now left me feeling hollow and sad.

"Is this what you want, baby?"

I was torn—*one for the road*. I choked out a yes, and he slid into me. It was fast and unemotional. Mechanical and unfeeling. I was so ashamed. I just lay there, biding my time until he finished.

When he let out a deep grunt, I rubbed his back and waited for him to roll off of me.

"Oh, man. That was good. Why has it been so long?" He stepped out of bed and went to the bathroom.

I rolled over on my side and silently wept.

The next morning, I was woken by the fresh, bold scent of coffee. When I rolled to my side, a fresh cup was on my nightstand. Mark was sitting in my vanity chair.

He smiled tentatively at me. "Good morning."

I slowly sat up and leaned back against the headboard. "Good morning."

"I have a long day today, but I was hoping we could have dinner tonight, talk about wedding plans, and discuss when you might want to go back to work."

"Actually, I do need to call Richard. And we need to talk."

He apprehensively got out of the chair and sat down on the edge of the bed. Reaching out, he brushed my hair off my face, tucking it behind my ear.

"I've been a real ass to you lately, Charlie. I hope I can make it up to you. I hope… well, I hope we can move forward."

I swallowed the lump in my throat and simply nodded.

"Good. I'll see you tonight? I'll have someone bring dinner over, so you don't have to cook. We'll have a quiet night in." He leaned over and kissed me on the cheek, and then he stood and left.

Taking my coffee mug, I went to shower and get ready for the day. I called Peggy to see if Richard could see me today, and she scheduled me for a 10:30 a.m. meeting. Then I called Suzanne and asked her to meet me at the Italian restaurant just behind my office.

Wanting armor, I pulled out my best suit: a chocolate brown pantsuit with a salmon-colored shirt—and three-inch leather heels. Brushing my hair up into a French twist, I pulled a few strands out to soften the severity of the sleek style.

I went to my office building before lunch, parked in the visitor parking and used the main entrance. Just like any other day, I swiped my badge at the security desk and went through into the marble-walled lobby and gold elevator bays. Nothing had changed. No one looked at me differently. No one really even saw me. I was just another suit starting my day.

The elevator doors opened, and I stepped inside, smiling kindly to another rider. The floors zoomed past until we arrived at Richard's floor.

I took a deep breath and put my practiced smile on my face. Pulling open the doors, I stepped into the hallway that led past all the executive offices to Peggy's desk.

I said her name tentatively, and she jumped up out of her chair. "Oh, darlin'! You're back."

She squeezed me tightly. I would have found this inappropriate with someone else, but not with her. She was like a grandmother to me, and she knew my secrets.

"Kind of. Is Richard ready for me?"

"Just like you. Get right to the point."

I found that an odd observation, since I had felt like anything *but* direct these past few weeks. "Yep, that's me."

"Let me buzz him for you. Your office is empty if you want to wait in there."

"I'm fine out here."

She nodded at me, smiling ear to ear. I wandered away from her desk. Not too far that she couldn't see me, but far enough to give her privacy on the phone.

My office door was open, so I peeked inside. The lights were off, and it looked sad and dark. The ghost of who I was appeared in my mind. I was apprehensive about the conversation I was about to have with Richard. Asking for an extended leave was not usually done at this level. I was hoping Richard would be somewhat understanding.

"Charlotte, welcome back." Richard's booming voice jolted me out of my daydream. I put my hand to my chest, trying to still my heart.

"Hello, Richard. Yes, it's so good to see you."

"You're looking fit and healthy. Ready to come back to work?"

He ushered me into his office, gently clicking the door closed behind me. It sounded like a prison door clanging, and I visibly stumbled.

Walking around the edge of his desk, he gestured for me to sit. He waited until I had adjusted my legs underneath me before starting.

"You've had some time to clear your head? Plan the wedding?"

"Actually, Richard," I cleared my throat and started over. "Actually, Richard, I have had some time to clear my head, and I wanted to talk with you about extending my leave. Maybe another couple of months. There are things I would like to do, and I could use the time to do them."

He leaned back in his chair, crossing his hands over his middle. "Did you and Mark settle on a wedding date?"

"Actually, no, not yet. We might be postponing it for a while."

"Do you have a family emergency?"

I started to feel uncomfortable. This was not the friendly, mentoring relationship I'd thought we had. His tone was one of displeasure.

"No," I drawled. "It's personal."

That didn't seem to satisfy him. "You have a big job, Charlotte. A big job that needs doing. I offered the leave so you could plan your wedding."

This man across from me was formidable, and a creepy sense of finality was washing over me.

"Yes, sir, you did."

"I'll be honest, Charlie, it concerns me that you feel you need more time off."

The chopping block was being prepped. The decision rested with me.

"You're right, sir. I don't need any more time off."

Jubilantly, he smiled and slapped his desk. "I'm happy to hear that, Charlotte. We're ready to have you back." He reached for his phone to call Peggy, but I extended my hand to cover his, gently putting the phone back in the cradle.

Confusion crossed his face, along with mild irritation at my touching him.

I reached behind my neck, pulling the badge up and over my head. "I don't need more time off because I'm resigning.

I stood and placed my badge on his desk. "I will email you a formal resignation letter and work with Peggy on processing out."

He looked like a guppy with his mouth hanging open.

"I'm sorry to leave like this. I enjoyed working for you very much. I'll ask Peggy to walk me out."

My hands were shaking as I left his office. What had I just done? My head was spinning with possible consequences. This was the longest career I'd ever had, and I was quite positive Richard would not be giving me a good reference.

"Peggy, I left my badge with Richard. Can I call you later?"

I faltered in my step and paused briefly. "Actually, I think you need to walk me out."

I started walking again toward the elevator, and Peggy scrambled to catch up. I pushed through the glass doors into the elevator hall and hit the down button.

Peggy came rushing through the glass doors just as the elevator opened, and I stepped inside. She skipped in next to me before the doors shut.

"Charlie, what on Earth?" Her eyes were wide, almost frightened.

Crossing my arms, I responded, "No clue, Peggy, no clue. No, that's not right. Lots of clues. I just finally pieced them together." I started laughing. Almost maniacally. "Do you think I'll regret this? No. I won't regret this. I have plenty of savings. I can get another job later, maybe. Holy shit! I just quit."

I realized I was having a singular conversation and laughed some more.

Peggy looked so concerned. "Charlie, are you okay?"

I suddenly realized I was frightening her. Taking a deep breath to calm myself down, I said, "I am, Peggy. I am okay. Or, at least, I will be."

The elevator doors opened, and she walked with me to the security gate. She stopped me before I went through the badge gate, placing her hand gently on my forearm. "I won't pretend to understand what is happening for you, but know this: if you need me, I'm here for you."

"I'll call you later. I promise. I have other things to take care of today, but when things have settled down, I will call and explain everything."

She leaned up to kiss me on the cheek. Then she told the guard to open the gate for her.

He looked at her questioningly, and she spoke more sternly. "Please."

The guard opened the gate, and I went to my car, still shaking and a little dazed. Looking at my watch, I saw I still had some time before meeting Suzanne for lunch. I decided to stop in at the studio.

Erin sat behind the desk and looked up when she heard the door chime. "Hi, welcome to L.O.V.E. Can I help you?"

"Erin, it's me, Charlie."

"Good lord! What are you wearing?"

"I do have a job, you know."

"Sorry. I just can't quite connect that"—she pointed her finger up and down me— "with you."

"Don't judge."

"Sorry." But she didn't look sorry. Then she realized that I was back from Arizona, and she jumped out of her seat. "How was Arizona? Is that place just sick or what?"

"I was a little intimidated. It's a beautiful building and such a well-run business. They've done a really good job."

"And?" She bounced up and down on the balls of her feet.

"And I saw Story."

"Enh, whatever. What else?"

"And I met Max."

"Aww, he's so sweet." She mooned over him for a minute and then asked, "Anything else?"

I knew what she was getting at, and I waited just a moment, drawing out her suspense as her eyebrows climbed her forehead in anticipation. Finally, I ended her torment, blurting out, "I took the job."

"Yes, I knew it. I knew you would take it. I am so jealous and so excited for you!"

Her enthusiasm had me laughing. I knew I'd made the right decision. Wherever it took me, this was the path I wanted to be on.

"I leave Wednesday, and I need to pack still, so I probably won't be in a class today or tomorrow."

"Don't worry about me. I will miss you, but I'll see you soon." She hugged me tightly. "I am so happy for you."

"I can't breathe."

She backed up. "You look happy."

"Thank you."

"But don't wear those clothes."

CHAPTER 16

SUZANNE'S FACE WAS void of emotion—as if she was being told the sun was the moon and the moon was Mars. Then she started to laugh. And laugh.

"Oh, Charlie, that is so funny. I'm sure Mark didn't find it funny, but—oh, my God! You really did it?"

My laugh was slow to come. My smile grew only because I thought she was overreacting. "Mark doesn't know yet."

Then she laughed even harder, almost choking.

She wiped at the corners of her eyes, her laughter slowing and then speeding back up. "I can't, I can't stop laughing. I'm sorry. I know it's not that funny."

"I didn't intend to quit. I just wanted to take some additional time off to go work the events for the next two months."

"You couldn't have possibly imagined that Richard would be okay with that. You're a vice president."

I looked into my iced tea and stirred the spoon around and around, making little vortices. "Maybe it's for the best."

When I looked up, Suzanne was looking at me in wonder. Softly she said, "That took a lot of courage, Charlie."

"Hmm. Maybe. Or I'm really stupid."

"You can do anything now. And you're talented. Who knows, you could start your own marketing firm. Be a consultant."

Our lunch was delivered, and we both took a few bites before continuing our conversation.

"There's something else I need to tell you." I waited until she put her fork down. My heart was racing like a jackrabbit.

She looked at me with concern. "Are you dying? Is that what this is about?"

I chuckled. "No." Her seriousness helped me relax, so I jumped in. "I'm leaving Mark."

Her eyes bored into mine, assessing whether I was serious or not. Calmly, she asked, "Have you told him?"

"No."

We stared at each other. I fidgeted with the napkin on my lap, and she spun her wine glass between her fingers.

"Are you sure about this, Charlie?"

"Yes."

A few more moments of silence stretched between us.

Then she said softly (her laughter gone), "I was always kind of jealous of you."

My eyes opened wider in surprise. "Why?"

"You were always so calm, so focused, so... content."

I reached across the table. "Suzanne, you have been my best friend since college. Why did you never say anything?"

"There was nothing to say. You're my best friend, too, but it doesn't mean I didn't kind of wish I had what you had."

Her eyes didn't waver from my face.

"Mark? But you said... you said that day in Mexico that you were fine with it."

"And I was. We were friends. I didn't think anything of it until you moved to Houston and your relationship with each other got really serious. I felt like I was losing two best friends. And now you're moving back, and I'm left here."

She swiped at a tear.

I reached out to take her hand. "Oh, Suzanne, I thought you were so happy."

"I am happy. You're just upsetting the apple cart, and now what I thought was seemingly perfect no longer exists."

"No one is perfect, Suzanne."

She snapped herself out of her melancholy. "Well, after the shit-storm that I expect to happen tonight, you are welcome to stay with me if you need a place. Who knows, maybe I'll pack up and leave too."

"Don't rush that decision. I may not stay. It's only for two months."

She raised her glass to me. "Here's to new beginnings."

"And old friends."

I clinked my glass to hers, and we finished our meal in a stereotypically girlish way: loudly and with lots of laughter. She walked me to my car and told me (again) that I could stay with her tonight if I needed a place to stay.

The drive back to my house was short. Not nearly enough time for me to gather my thoughts and my courage. I'd left most of it back in Richard's office.

Sitting in my car in my driveway, I thought through what this meant for the house. Then I laughed because I didn't really want the house. Then I panicked because I thought, *Do I need to buy him out? Wait, no, I don't think so. We aren't married yet—but my name was on the loan.* My stomach dropped; it was possible I was going to throw up. What a debacle.

The house was so quiet. I had a few hours before Mark was home from work, so I went to my closet to start packing for Denver and Phoenix.

I changed into leggings and an oversized T-shirt, pulled the pins from my hair, and let it hang loose. The twist had made my scalp hurt. I rubbed my head to ease away the tension.

I started pulling out most of my comfortable clothes, athletic wear, and casual outfits. Taking everything into the guest room down the hall, I laid all the clothes out neatly on the queen-size bed so I could see what I had.

Back and forth, I went with my clothes. Back and forth, I went with my shoes, luggage, and toiletries.

Hours had passed when the beep of the house alarm alerted me to a door being opened. It echoed through the house—Mark was home.

Shoeless, I ran down the stairs and into the kitchen to meet him. He had just put his bag down on the kitchen counter and was rubbing his hands up and down his face.

When he stopped, he opened his eyes and saw me standing in the doorway. "Hey, you look cozy."

He walked toward me and enveloped me in a hug. My heart squeezed, and I steeled myself against the tears that were forming in my eyes.

"How was your day?" I asked him as I went to the wine cooler and pulled out a Chardonnay.

"Long. Exhausting. I'm glad we're staying in tonight." He took the glass I poured him and went to sit on the couch in the attached family room.

A container of cashews sat on the counter, and I put some in a small dish. I poured myself a glass of wine, took a long drink of it, filled it back up, and went to join him on the couch.

His legs were stretched out in front of him, feet on the coffee table. I placed the nuts on the table and curled up fawnlike at the end of the couch with my feet under me.

I rested my glass on the side of my knee and waited for him to talk.

He started talking about a new project and a new team member, and his words all just rolled together—noise in my head.

"Charlie, did you?"

Oh, crap! "I'm sorry, did I what?"

He rolled his head over on the back of the couch to look at me. "Did you talk to Richard today?"

"I did."

Mark put his feet down and reached out to get some cashews from the snack dish on the table. "And? When did he say you can come back?"

I shifted uncomfortably. *I can't believe I'm doing this.* "Um, I resigned."

"That's funny, Charlie. Really, when are you going back?"

Nothing I could say would make this any better, so I just waited until he realized I was serious.

He leaped up from the couch and erupted. "What the fuck, Charlie? Are you out of your *fucking* mind?"

I flinched. That word coming out of his mouth was so harsh and offensive. He rarely said it, and I cringed.

"Please sit down, Mark. There's more, and I need you to be calm."

He was pacing in front of the unlit fireplace. Stopping, he put his hands on his hips and shook his head at me. "What else could there possibly be?"

"I took a job in Arizona; I'll be gone for a few months."

He was shaking his head from side to side and pacing again. "I don't understand, Charlie. I don't understand."

"It's an operations job. I'll be traveling most of the time to different cities."

I was embarrassed that I couldn't tell him exactly *what* I'd be doing. I was ashamed that I wouldn't take ownership of it. I was no better than him for judging, but I also knew it would just make things worse.

He stopped pacing. "Who are you? What happened to our plans?"

His words sliced me open, and the tears I'd been holding back all day let loose. "What plans? *We* didn't have plans. *You* had plans, and I followed along."

"I thought you wanted the same things. We fit so perfectly. We never fought—until recently. We like the same foods and movies. What happened, Charlie?"

"I don't know, Mark. What I do know is that I'm not happy

anymore." I reached for the hem of my T-shirt and wiped the tears from my eyes.

Mark walked away and went to the half bath, returning with a tissue box. "Here."

"Thank you."

I blew my nose, and he sat down next to me.

"Are you coming back?"

"I think so. I don't know."

"Are we pushing out the wedding date?

My tears formed again, and my lip quivered.

He nodded tersely. "I see."

I started to sob. "I'm so sorry, Mark. I'm so sorry."

He didn't comfort me. He didn't say anything. Just sat there staring at the fireplace while I cried.

His voice was cold when he said, "We're hosting the fundraising gala in a few months. Will you be here for that?

The lack of emotion in his words was like a deluge of ice water, and my tears abruptly stopped. I responded that I would.

"When do you leave?"

"Wednesday."

He clenched his jaw and took a deep breath. Turning to me, he said, "I love you, Charlie. I would like for you to give us some thought while you're away. I can't pretend to understand what's happened to you, but I know I love you."

These were the words I'd needed to hear weeks ago. I was already emotionally out the door, so his thought that something had happened to *me* made me bristle.

He continued. "I want us to be together. I want us to build a life together. And if it looks different than what I imagined, then I can work with that."

I was emotionally exhausted, so I just nodded.

As he stood, he said he was going back to his office. "I'll sleep there tonight. Do you need a ride to the airport Wednesday morning?"

This cold, monotone Mark scared me a little bit. I don't think he fully understood what I'd told him.

"No, I'll Uber."

He nodded gravely at me and then took off down the hall.

Sitting numbly on the couch, I waited for him to return. A few minutes later, he came back through the family room with an overnight bag.

"Please text me when you land." He looked so sad and heartbroken. But I couldn't change things, and I couldn't go back. I was numb.

I simply nodded and watched as he went out the back door, locking it behind him. The engine's soft purr grew quieter as he left the driveway, and then it was silent.

This had been the longest day *ever*!

When I knew he was gone, I sat back down on the couch and wept—not the racking sobs from earlier, but tears of loss and grief. I don't know how long I lay there and cried. My tears turned to shallow breaths and then shudders as I wore myself out.

My phone pinged with an incoming text from Suzanne: *You okay?*

I texted back: *No, but I will be.*

The phone rang, startling me. I answered, "Hi."

"Do you want me to come over?"

"No, I need to be alone."

We were silent. I knew she wanted to ask about what had happened.

"Charlotte, honey, are you sure this is what you want?"

My heart was so heavy, my eyes swollen and sore. I lay back down on the couch, closing my eyes and holding the phone to my ear. "Yes. Maybe. I don't know. Everything happened so fast, and yet it didn't really. It's been building for months, maybe even the past year. I just—" I started to cry again. "I just didn't think it would hurt this much."

"I'm coming over."

I sat up. "No!" Then, less emphatically, "No, I'm fine. I just need a good night's sleep."

"How about if I stay tomorrow night and take you to the airport in the morning?"

I cried again and tried to speak. My throat had closed, and I had to swallow so I could get the words out. "I'd like that."

"I'll be there around six? I'll bring Chinese."

"Thank you, Suzanne."

"You're welcome, sweetie."

I fell asleep on the couch, waking a little after two in the morning. I trudged slowly up the stairs to my bed—my beautiful king-size bed with 1200 thread count, Egyptian cotton sheets. I cried all over again.

Tuesday was a whirlwind day. I ran errands, finished my packing, and arranged for the cleaning lady to be paid while I was gone.

Solara had emailed me a huge file of paperwork to fill out for employment, as well as instructions for the event. She wrote in her email: *Text me when you land, and we'll ride together to the hotel.*

I printed everything out and put it in my carry-on bag to review on the plane. I could have downloaded it all to my phone or a tablet, but I was old-fashioned in some ways and still liked holding paper in my hands sometimes.

Suzanne arrived right on time. We took our dinner out onto the back deck to enjoy by the pool.

"You really want to give all this up?"

She was laughing at me, I knew, but still, I responded, "This doesn't mean anything to me, Suzanne."

"I know it doesn't. But it sure is a beautiful house."

"Maybe Mark will let you move in."

She chortled, "Oh, please no."

After a moment of silence, I told her I was tired and ready for bed. "The guest room is all made for you."

"I want to sleep with you. Like when we were in college."

That made me laugh. "All right."

"You go up. I'll clean up here and be there in a minute."

When I reached my room, I saw it for what it was: just a room.

My suitcases were packed and set at the top of the stairs. My carry-on bag sat on the ottoman at the foot of the bed. My purse was on the vanity chair.

The only room I'd ever loved in this house was my room, but I would have another room. Another house. Another life. Somewhere.

For now, with fresh, rested eyes, I knew I was making the right decision. I was all cried out, and I was free.

Suzanne took me to the airport in the morning. She cried.

"Stop! No crying. Come visit me if you want or go visit your parents, for goodness sake."

"Will you text me and tell me where you are, what city you're in, and when you're back in Phoenix?"

She pulled up to the curb and hugged me tightly. I'd hardly had time to breathe in the last seventy-two hours.

"Yes, I will. And I'll be fine."

"I know you will. You always are."

I hugged her back, squeezing her one last time. "I'm really happy, Suzanne. This is the right thing for me."

She got back in her car and waited until I was inside before driving away. My grin grew bigger, my steps were lighter, and my heart was less heavy the closer I got to security.

I was doing the right thing.

CHAPTER 17

"Where's Solara?"

Paxton was unceremoniously throwing my luggage into the back of a rented SUV. "She missed her flight."

My plane had landed in Denver just before noon, and when my phone could be turned on, I'd seen a text from her: *Meet Paxton outside level 4, black SUV, grumpy face.*

"What do you mean 'she missed her flight'?"

Paxton pushed the button to automatically shut the hatch and turned to me, squinting his eyes. "I know you're a smart girl, Charlotte."

Then he turned and went around to the driver's side, getting in while I scurried to catch up. I opened the passenger door to get into the oversized vehicle. I'd barely shut the door and put my seatbelt on before he pulled away from the curb, following the signs to the airport exit.

"I mean, I know what it means to miss a flight, but I could've taken an Uber."

"We have things to do today, and we need to get you ready for tomorrow. The show starts at four, and then it will run all day Friday and Saturday. We'll fly back to Phoenix on Sunday morning."

"Are all the shows this long?"

"Not usually, but there aren't a whole lot of cities up in this part of the States that can support more than one show. We make this one regional, and we run it longer than the others."

His driving was erratic but controlled. It made me a little nervous when he took his eyes off the road to stare at me.

"Can you slow down just a little? And keep your eyes on the road." I put my hand on the dash when we abruptly came to a red light just outside the airport.

Now that we were stopped, he rested his arm over the steering wheel and turned to me. "Solara is incredibly good at math, and she's a semi-good instructor. But she is *horrible* at time management." He rolled his eyes heavenward as he spoke. "Honestly, I was a little surprised she had the two of you on such early flights. Solara seems to show up when she wants to."

I blushed, thinking maybe Solara had done it intentionally.

"Why are you turning pink?"

I glanced out the window, grateful that the light turned green so he would stop looking at me. Then, a little too haughtily, I responded, "A gentleman wouldn't call a lady out on that."

"I've never pretended to be a gentleman."

I noticed, and was oddly flattered, that he didn't correct my comment about being a lady. I tried to steer the conversation to safer ground: business. "What's the plan for the day?"

As we drove from the airport into downtown Denver, he shared that we were going directly to the venue, where he would walk me through my job.

"I apologize that you won't have any kind of formal training. But you've already competed, so you know how the first-timers will feel. You've also seen how backstage works, so really, you're already halfway there. When we get back to Phoenix, Story will walk you through everything in more detail. We have an event next weekend in Phoenix, so you'll have a little time to breathe and get settled."

"Thank you. This all happened so fast. I, I'm not really sure what I'm doing." I blushed again, realizing my mistake in admitting this when he briefly glanced at my engagement ring.

"What does your fiancé think of you running off for a couple of months?" He was staring out the front window, but his knuckles were white on the steering wheel.

I couldn't look at him when I responded, "He's not happy."

I twisted the ring on my finger. It felt wrong to remove it so soon after I told Mark it was over—and I needed armor around Paxton. I didn't intend to lie to him; I just didn't want to tell him the truth about calling off the wedding—yet. Paxton was too much. Too big, too sexy, too invasive. And he was now my boss.

All he did was grunt under his breath.

Maneuvering his way through the downtown streets, he parked in a lot across from the Paramount Theatre , paid the attendant, and then guided me across the street.

"This is a lot fancier than the Houston location."

"Like I said, two and a half days, and a regional competition."

He held the front door to the theatre open and ushered me through with his hand at my back.

A portly man with a handlebar mustache greeted us in the lobby. With his hand extended, he exuded joviality and western graciousness. "Mr. Crown, Ms. Crown. Nice to meet you. I'm here to get you settled for your pole dancing event this weekend."

Paxton winced at the gentleman's lecherous enthusiasm, but he shook his hand anyway. "Thank you, sir. And this is Ms. Chase. Ms. Crown will be here tomorrow."

With a southern drawl that even I, coming from Texas, didn't have, he said, "Well, it's nice to meet you, and welcome to Denver. Let me show you around the stage, and then we'll get you settled in one of our conference rooms."

Pulling my lips in between my teeth, I tried not to laugh. Paxton looked at me in warning.

Following the gentleman through a side stage door, we went down a dimly lit hall. He showed us the dressing rooms and how we could access the side stage.

While he was showing Paxton the back entrance where we could bring in the rigging, lights, and poles, I wandered out onto the stage. When I stepped out from behind the curtain, I gasped and then let out a breath.

The theatre was exquisite, and thoughts of performing in it raced through my mind. I wouldn't be, of course, but just pretending felt magical. The red velvet seats and the gold leafing on the walls reminded me of the roaring 1920s and old burlesque shows.

I struck a coquettish pose and put my hand to my chest as if to say, *Who? Me?* I giggled and did a pirouette across the stage. Then, practicing a move Dani had taught me, I stopped, bent over at the waist, and seductively trailed my hand up my leg. Flipping my hair, I winked at the fictional audience.

"Let's go."

I stood abruptly, this time putting my hand to my chest to calm my heart. "Christ, Paxton! Do you ever *not* announce yourself like a drill sergeant?"

He gave me a sweet smile. "C'mon, Gypsy Rose, you can dance later. We have work to do."

He walked off, and I had to run to catch up with him. We walked back down the hall and up a flight of stairs to the offices.

Our lascivious host left us at the entrance to a large conference room. He told us to find him when we were ready to leave, so he could let us out.

Paxton entered first and put his bag down at the head of the table. His commanding presence was fascinating; he assumed that place at a table so comfortably. He was so unlike my previous employer in outward appearances, yet the authoritative role was exactly the same.

He looked up and caught me staring at him. "What?"

"Nothing." It was difficult not to smile at him.

Slowing his movements, he removed his hands from the files he'd put on the table and stood to his full height. His eyes never wavered from mine. Stepping around the chair, he took a few steps closer to me.

My lips parted. He glanced at them, briefly licked his, and then let out a heavy sigh.

"Charlotte." He said my name on a low growl. "Solara and Story are glad you're here," He paused. "but I can't touch you now."

He lowered his head, so his mouth was inches from my cheek. "I can't kiss you or touch you, and it's making me crazy." His breath was on my cheek, warm and feather-soft. I closed my eyes, allowing his words to flow over me. "You've made this really difficult for us, and—as much as I want to—I can't make love with you now."

"Why not?" I couldn't believe the breathy voice that came out of my mouth was actually mine.

He stood straight and stepped back a foot. With both hands, he reached up and clasped his fingers behind his head. Lowering his head, he rubbed the back of his head and then dropped his arms. "Because you work for me."

His hair was now mussed.

He had just turned back toward his chair when I said, "Just say something cheeky, like 'I don't usually fuck my employees, but I could make an exception for you.'"

Anger flashed in his eyes, and he came back toward me, grabbing me by the arm and pulling me up close to him. "Don't tempt me, Charlotte. You have no idea what you're saying."

"Paxton, you're hurting me." He wasn't really, but something needed to be said to diffuse the tension between us. And I was embarrassed that I'd actually repeated his words back to him. I'd turned it into a joke. I could see now that it wasn't funny.

The tension on my arm lessened. When he stepped back, he groaned, rubbing his hands over his face. "Gah, this is such a bad idea."

He shook his head and put his hands down on the table. "Charlotte, there are things—

He paused and continued without looking up at me. "There are things you don't know."

"I understand."

He laughed sardonically. "No, you don't. But I appreciate you saying that."

"No, you're right, I don't. But… but I do work for you. And I can appreciate that." I swallowed my pride with my next words and shifted uncomfortably. "This is a new industry for me, and I wouldn't have taken the job if I didn't want to succeed. I'm very talented with marketing campaigns, as you know, and I hope you can use my talents elsewhere."

He raised his eyebrow and smiled.

I added, "For your business."

"Should we start over?"

"If you want to, but it really isn't necessary. I have a feeling you'll slip somewhere along the way and say something inappropriate or crass. Let's just move forward."

He gestured to the seat next to him and said kindly, "Sit."

I took that as his olive branch and calmly sat down next to him, waiting for his instruction.

When he was seated, he immediately launched into the schedule for the event. He slid a schedule over to me and asked, "Did you read over everything Sol sent you?"

"Yes, on the plane this morning."

"Good. You remember the headset Erin was wearing and what she was doing? Checking everyone in? Getting their starting positions?"

"Yes."

"Good. Everyone will switch roles every three to four hours. It's exhausting to have to stay in one place. You'll start at the check-in desk, give the competitors their welcome bags, and then hand them off to an escort."

"Why am I the only one here right now?"

"Because you are the only one who hasn't done this before."

I dumbly responded, "Oh."

He continued. "Then you'll escort, then you'll stage monitor. If you need a break, call on the headset, and we'll send a runner to relieve you. The runner will show up for your scheduled break so you can eat lunch."

My head was spinning. "Where's lunch?"

"Here, in this room."

"Where will you be?"

"Here, or in the sound booth, or with the judges. Wherever I'm needed."

My eyes were blurring a little as I read the schedule, and I suddenly felt like I hit a wall. "Paxton, I'm ready to work this weekend, I am. But I'll be honest, I've had a pretty hectic three days—six, really—and I could use a rest." I rushed on. "I don't mean to be high maintenance or anything, but do you think we could head back to the hotel and then maybe go over it again at dinner?"

"Are we going to dinner?"

I blushed again. "Aren't we? I just assumed."

He reached for my hand and held it gently, rubbing his thumb along the backs of my fingers. "I was just teasing, Charlotte. Yes, we can have dinner together."

We both looked at our hands. Heat rushed through my body. He slowly released my fingers and looked back down at his stack of papers.

Without looking at me, he started putting his files back into his bag. One of his files fell to the floor, and I bent to get it for him.

I tried not to look, but the papers were court summons for Paxton with a Mr. and Mrs. Something-or-Other as the plaintiffs, and it was hard to look away. I shuffled the pages back into the folder and handed them to him.

"Thanks."

He didn't make eye contact with me as he stuffed the file back in with the rest.

I waited expectantly for him to say something else. The only thing he said when he stood and put the bag over his shoulder was, "Ready?"

The mood between us had shifted. He had retreated back into his own private world. Ushering me out to the car, he actually held the passenger door for me and waited until I was situated before gently shutting it.

The ride to the hotel took less than three minutes. I was suitably impressed when he pulled into valet at the Brown Palace hotel. "Do you always stay in hotels that are this nice?"

"No, but we usually only need a place for one night. We'll be here until Sunday. I thought it would be a nice change."

A concierge came out to meet us. "Welcome back, Mr. Crown. Can I help the lady with her bags?"

"Yes, please," Paxton looked at the gentleman's name tag. "Mr. Ralston. Thank you. The lady's in room 417."

"I have a room already?"

He glanced at me briefly as he handed a twenty and the car's keys to the man. His hand at the small of my back, he ushered me into the lobby. "Are you hungry?"

I was caught off guard by the opulence and elegance of the hotel. The nine-story, open atrium lobby was reminiscent of an era when travelers would have afternoon tea.

Paxton took me to a set of settees and comfortable chairs. As soon as we were seated, a waitress came over with small menus.

"Good afternoon. We only have small plates on the menu until four o'clock. Can I get you something from the bar?"

She was clearly swooning over Paxton. So, because I was tired and feeling feisty, I put my left hand on his knee, making sure my engagement ring glittered up at her. "What do you think, darling, a Manhattan?"

He smiled broadly, keeping his eyes on me a moment longer than comfortable. Then he leaned forward, picked up my hand, and kissed my palm.

"Sounds delightful."

Then he looked back at the waitress, who looked properly chastised.

"Two Manhattans, please, and a soft pretzel."

When she walked away, Paxton laughed and drew an imaginary line all around him. "You just marked everything around me."

"That was petty, I know. She was just so blatantly fawning over you."

"And she's entitled to do so."

He was right, and I was obviously jealous. Sadly.

I was twirling my engagement ring around and around on my finger.

"When's the wedding?"

My twirling stopped, and I looked down at my hands.

"I, um, I called it off."

I was afraid to look at him. I expected to see a look of self-righteousness, maybe even a smug grin. Instead of laughter or passion, his eyes drooped in sadness. "I'm sorry to hear that."

My eyes stung. I blinked a few times to ward off the tears. "It was actually coming for a while. On my end, anyway. I think, in time, he'll see that too. We just want different things."

"What do you want, Charlotte?"

The waitress appeared with our drinks and the pretzel. "Mr. and Mrs. Crown, your drinks. I'll be back to check on you in a bit."

I stopped her. "Wait, we aren't married. We're just," I paused. "We're just friends. He's single if you're interested."

She shifted on her feet, her eyes darting between the two of us, and Paxton tried to contain his laughter. She said (in a voice she might have used to calm a crazy child), "Okay, thanks."

Paxton acknowledged her and thanked her for the drinks.

I reached for mine and took an unladylike gulp.

"You're goofy."

He shook his head as he sipped on his drink.

A comfortable silence sat between us as we sipped our drinks and pulled at the pretzel. In the corner, a pianist was playing lively afternoon music. The day finally caught up with me, and I relaxed back into the sofa.

Paxton interrupted my mindlessness, reminding me that I hadn't answered his last question. "Why are you still wearing the ring?"

"I don't have an honest answer for you. Forgot. Too busy. Denial. I don't know, Paxton, I guess I just am."

He nodded and didn't press for anything else.

My eyes started to close. The combination of the alcohol and the comfortable couch had relaxed me so much that I drifted off.

The couch depressed next to me, and I lifted my head, momentarily disoriented.

"Did I just fall asleep?"

"You did." He reached in his pocket and handed me a key. "I checked you in before I picked you up today. Meet me down here at seven for dinner?"

I nodded dumbly and stood from the couch, my brain foggy as I mumbled, "Seven. Down here for dinner?"

"Do I need to call and wake you up?" He was smiling at me.

I grabbed my bag and blinked him into focus. "That's probably a good idea."

"Have a nice nap, Charlotte."

Nodding once again, I headed toward the elevator and a nap.

CHAPTER 18

THE SHRILL RINGING of the phone woke me from my deep sleep. Rolling over, I reached for the hotel phone and held it to my ear. Without opening my eyes, I answered, "Hello?"

"It's time to wake up." His voice was husky. The low hum sent vibrations over my entire body. I imagined he was next to me, whispering in my ear. "Charlotte?"

"Mmm, yes?" I said and then smiled and stretched.

He chuckled. "It's time to wake up."

Coming out of my dream state, I sat straight up, taking the earpiece with me and pulling the phone to the floor with a disorienting clatter. "Oh, crap! Right. Time to wake up."

"I'll see you downstairs."

I started to ask if Solara had arrived, but all I heard was a dial tone.

Showering quickly, I wrapped myself in a towel and went back out to the bedroom to get my clothes. The valet had placed my luggage at the foot of the second queen-sized bed. I pulled one case up onto the mattress to find something to wear.

With the suitcase open, I froze. I had no idea what to wear.

This was dinner with my boss. In the past, I would have worn a nice cocktail dress or a pantsuit. But this was Paxton, and it was pole dancing.

I stared into my case filled with jeans, leggings, sundresses, shorts, and T-shirts. And then said, "Huh."

I dug around for the best sundress I had and decided it was better than jeans. And *certainly* better than leggings.

Gathering up my clutch, I stuck my room key in a side pocket along with my phone and a lip gloss. Before I could get out of the room, however, my cell phone started chirping from the bottom of my bag.

I frantically tried to get it before whoever was calling hung up. When I pulled it from the tiny clutch, my heart sank at the caller's name.

Mark.

Taking a deep breath, I picked up the call. "Hi, Mark."

"You didn't text me when you landed."

"We went straight to the job, and then I was really tired. I'm sorry."

He didn't respond.

"Mark?"

"Yeah, I'm here. I just wish you would let me know where you are."

"Mark, we broke up. I'm sorry if that doesn't fit with your plan, but..." I had to calm myself down. "Mark, I will be there for that gala. Please email me if you need anything."

"What about a job when you're finished playing stripper-girl?"

"Goodbye, Mark." I was half a second away from clicking the end call button.

"Charlie, wait."

I sighed heavily and waited.

"I'm glad you're safe."

"I'm fine, Mark."

"What do you want to do about the house?"

"Can we talk about that next week? I'll be back in Phoenix on Sunday. Maybe we can talk on Monday about what we should do."

"I'll call you Monday."

"Great. I'll talk to you then."

"I love you, Charlie."

Click.

I hung up on him.

I was shaking. Grabbing the pillow off the bed, I buried my face in it and screamed. Screamed until I was completely empty of air.

When I'd gotten it all out, I plopped down on the mattress and put the pillow down next to me. Now that I'd let that out, I wiggled the ring off my left finger and put it in my jewelry bag with my toiletries.

I heard Paxton's voice asking me why I was still wearing it, and I realized I was done. Over it. I would mail the ring back to Mark on Monday.

Shaking out my arms, I put a smile on my face, left my room, and headed down to the atrium to meet Paxton. When I stepped off the elevator and into the atrium area, I noticed it was now full with guests mingling and drinking.

I glanced around inquisitively, looking for Paxton, the thin watch on my wrist telling me it was a little past seven.

A voice called to me from the couch not fifteen feet in front of me. "Charlotte."

It took a second for my eyes to register that it was Paxton.

He stood. "Charlotte?"

My smile dropped, and I put my hand to my belly to calm the butterflies. Now I knew why he always used foul language. All I wanted to say was, *Oh, yes, please fuck me. I don't want dinner; I want you.*

He was dressed in slacks and a button-down dress shirt. His sleeves were rolled to the middle of his forearms, and his face was freshly shaved.

"Hey."

His eyebrows flicked up in amusement. "Is that your standard greeting with me?"

I blinked a couple of times. I might have shaken my head. "Sorry.

I wasn't expecting you to be so—I wasn't—I didn't think—" I stopped and focused. "You look very nice."

When he smiled, he looked boyishly charming. "Thank you. Are you hungry?"

Gah, what a silly question. "Starved."

"Do you want a drink first? Or, the hotel has a nice restaurant, and we can just eat here."

"Let's eat here."

He escorted me to the hotel dining room, and the hostess seated us in a half-moon booth near the back. The booth looked like it would seat six comfortably, and I felt awkward having to shout across the table at him on the other side.

Apparently, Paxton did too, because after the hostess left, he suddenly stepped out of his side of the booth and came over to mine. "Scoot."

"What?"

"Scoot over. I'm not going to shout at you all night. Scoot."

I moved closer to the middle until he stopped me by tugging on my hand.

"That's far enough."

My eyes grew wide when I realized he was still holding my hand.

"I want to be able to whisper."

I slowly pulled my hands from him. "You're giving me whiplash—*Boss*!"

He laughed robustly. "Fair, fair."

The waitress greeted us and handed Paxton the wine list.

She ran through the dinner specials. I had no idea what she was saying. I was so distracted by the man sitting next to me. I just nodded and smiled and said that sounded delicious.

Paxton indicated his bottle selection as he handed her the wine list, asking me, "Is that okay?"

I nodded.

"I'll give you two a few minutes to decide, and I'll be right back with your wine."

When she was out of earshot, Paxton commented on the fact that I wasn't wearing my ring.

"Were you looking for it?"

"No, I didn't feel it when I grabbed your hand. *Then* I looked for it."

I tucked my hand under my thigh, palm down on the seat. "Don't you want to start our conversation with something superficial and banal?"

"Do I strike you as the type who would squander time on trite conversation?" He reached for his water glass and took a small sip.

I teased him. "Oh, so you do know big words." In a deeper voice, I said, "Me, Paxton. You, fuck-buddy."

He almost spat out his water and then put his head back and laughed. "Is that how you see me?"

"You do have an overall pissed off, kind of caveman approach about you. At least, you did when we first met."

His eyes darkened, and his smile dropped a little. "You've uh… you've caught me at an off-time, Charlotte."

"Did you go to college?"

Cautiously, he responded, "Yes."

"Where?"

He guffawed and snorted at my attempt to lighten the mood again. Then he responded, "Arizona State."

I practically jumped out of my seat. "Me too."

"Yes, I know, but I was a few years ahead of you."

I deflated a bit. I certainly didn't want to play the 'Do you know so-and-so?' game with him.

"Right."

The waitress reappeared with our wine and expertly poured a small bit for Paxton to try. He nodded at her, and we waited until she finished pouring before ordering our dinner.

"What did you major in?"

He took his time responding—watching my face—a small smile forming on his face. "Economics."

"You did not." I thought he was teasing me.

His smile dropped a bit. "You've pre-judged me, Charlotte. You assume that your world is the only world, that we're all supposed to fit into boxes, and that your basic box is the important one we're all supposed to care about and adhere to."

He wasn't angry with me, but shame had me dropping my head. "I'm sorry. You're right, I did."

His hand reached out to capture my cheek, and he turned my head toward him. "Don't be ashamed. I've lived with those kinds of reactions my whole life. I usually don't care what people think."

I whispered, "Do you care now?"

His thumb was stroking my face.

"More than I want to.

I was drowning in him.

Slowly he pulled his hand away and scooted a few inches back. "So much for conventional conversation."

"Predictable."

He smiled at me, then said, "Unimaginative."

"Clichéd."

"Ordinary."

"Vapid."

He laughed heartily. "Vapid? I am *not* vapid."

Our waitress appeared with our dinner, and we both waited until she had left to continue talking.

"No, you are certainly not vapid."

We ate in companionable silence for a bit until I'd gathered up the courage to ask him who Charlie was.

"Tell me why you broke off your engagement, and I'll tell you who Charlie was."

Taking a small sip of my wine, I cleared my throat and smoothed the napkin on my lap.

"You were kind of right about my life. It has been stereotypically—basic. I'm an only child, and my parents are seemingly perfect.

Although, now that I'm older, I see their differences. But I also see how compatible they are in their values and love for each other."

"There was nothing dark or scarring about my years growing up. I followed the checklist: I went to college, I met Mark, I moved to Houston. That's that."

His eyes were kind when he said, "But that's not that."

"No."

Patiently he waited for me to continue.

"I never questioned what I was supposed to be doing. Then Mark suggested we buy a house and start thinking about getting married. There wasn't any reason I shouldn't say yes. It felt like what I was supposed to do next. Saying yes was easier than questioning why I would say no."

"That seems sad to me, Charlotte."

"To you, maybe, but to me, I didn't know any different. Then I got promoted at work, and suddenly I started feeling panicky. The world was moving forward with me, but not with my permission. I'd become a bystander caught up in other people's stories."

"You weren't making your own story."

"You must feel like that sometimes?"

He lowered his head and mumbled, "Lately, a lot."

I knew he would tell me soon, but I just needed to get my words out right now.

"I was working late one night and was getting really stressed out. Our discussions weren't going well, and I needed some air, so I volunteered to get everyone dinner."

My voice trailed off, and I started to relive the first time I'd stepped into the studio.

"The chandelier hanging from the ceiling caught my attention. I found myself looking through the window, captivated by the twinkling lights and sultry furnishings. It was beautiful frosting that needed to be touched, and I wanted to see what kind of cake was underneath."

"I went back the next day and met Erin. She showed me the studio, and something in me cracked. I felt like... I felt like I could breathe. I hadn't even realized how tightly I'd been holding on."

"And your fiancé?"

"Mark.

He raised his eyebrows as if to say, *You really want me to use his name?*

I chuckled under my breath. "I thought he would be excited about it. Supportive. Turned on. But he wasn't. He was demeaning and judgmental. His words were ugly, and his actions dismissive."

"Most people don't turn their whole world upside down for pole dancing."

"It was more than just dancing, though. I felt sisterly to Erin; I felt embraced by Solara. When I competed, as *cute* as it was"—I looked at him pointedly. — "as cute as it was, I felt a sisterhood. I felt accepted and encouraged to be..." I played with my napkin. "I felt sexy."

"You don't need to pole dance to feel sexy."

I blushed. "I know. But I did. And it was something Mark had never given me.

Paxton's eyes were boring into mine, and I rushed on. "When I spent last weekend with my parents and Solara talked to me about the job, I thought I could still manage both worlds. But when I was back in Houston, I knew I couldn't. It all just crumbled a few days ago. But I wouldn't change the outcome."

"You know the job is only for a few months, right?"

I sighed. "I know. And I don't know what's after that. But I know I'll be okay."

"You know, courage is way sexier than dancing."

I flirted with him. "Are you saying I'm courageous?"

"I'm saying you're sexy."

I inhaled sharply and couldn't take my eyes from his.

"Mark called me before I came downstairs for dinner."

"And?"

"It wasn't fair to continue wearing my ring."

"Fair to whom?"

I didn't answer. Instead, I took another sip of wine and said, "Your turn."

He groaned and looked at his watch. "Is it bedtime yet?"

I teased him. "No. You said you would tell me." Then, softly, I asked, "Who's Charlie? You always call me Charlotte when most people don't. I can't help but feel there's a reason."

"You have a beautiful name."

"That's not why."

Shifting awkwardly in his seat, he took a deep breath and then let it out slowly. His eyes glossed over a bit, and he looked away.

I reached out for his hand. "Paxton, I'm sorry, I didn't mean to pry. I mean, I did. But if it's something you really don't want to talk about, you don't need to tell me."

He picked up my hand, kissed my fingers.

"No, it's fine, I'll tell you. And yes, you did mean to pry."

My fingers tingled where his lips had touched them. When he released my hand, I pulled it back to my lap and rubbed it with my other hand.

"Only Solara and Max know. And Story. Well, my parents too, but for all other purposes, no one else at the studio."

My heart fluttered at his trust. I waited. When he spoke, I wasn't prepared for what he told me.

"Charlie's my son—

With a whisper, he added, "was my son."

"What?" My stomach clenched.

"My son," he repeated quietly.

"Paxton. I had no idea. I mean, I couldn't imagine that. What do you mean 'was'?"

"My wife—my ex-wife." He sighed heavily. "My soon-to-be-ex-wife didn't want children. She never wanted to get pregnant. By the time she realized she was, she was already almost eight weeks along."

"When was this?"

He looked upwards, calculating time in his head. "Almost two years ago."

"Did you want children?"

"I'd never given it much thought until it happened, and then I was thrilled."

I remembered that Erin had told me his wife had been in a motorcycle accident a few months ago. "What happened?"

"She started to withdraw. She didn't seem happy. She started to ignore me." He leaned forward, hands between his knees. "We went for an ultrasound and found out we were having a boy. I started calling him Charlie. I thought it was a cute name for a little boy."

He took a deep breath. "I started planning the room in the house. I found the little wooden train at a flea market."

Mention of his house momentarily tripped me up. Imagining him in a house, like a real person, made me more curious and intrigued by him.

"She came into my office one afternoon. I'd just returned from Los Angeles, and she was upset. Her words were fragmented, scattered, and coming out broken when she said she'd lost the baby."

He dropped his head. Tears welled in my eyes.

When he looked up from his lap, he smiled sadly and then said, "A few days later, a clinic called me, asking me how Myla was feeling. That was her name—is her name—Myla is her name."

He continued, "I was confused; I told them she was feeling fine. The nurse went on to say that abortions can take a while to recover from emotionally. She wanted to make sure Myla was seeing her therapist—and thought it would be good if the two of us went together."

My chest was shaking with uncontrolled tears for him. My heart was breaking.

He shrugged. "I couldn't believe what I was hearing."

He shook his head and laughed sardonically. "I put down the phone and went downstairs to the front desk. Myla was home that day. Story was working. I asked her if she knew, and she looked terri-fied. I screamed at her, asking again if she knew. She started to cry. I left and went home to talk to Myla."

"Myla met me at the door. Story had called her to tell her I was on my way. She was pleading with me to listen to her. She wasn't ready; she didn't want to ruin her figure—all kinds of nonsense. That day is kind of a blur now."

"I'm so sorry, Paxton."

"I kicked her out. We went back and forth for a few months, seeing a counselor—but it was dead. The relationship, my love for her, my son. Dead."

I wiped at the tears in my eyes and waited for him to continue.

"I filed for divorce a few months back, and here we are. That's that."

He had used my words, so I used his. "But that's not that, is it?"

His eyes were pensive and contemplative. He started to speak and then stopped, biting on the corner of his upper lip, and then exhaling. "No. But for another time. That's enough depression for one dinner date. And you did only ask me who Charlie was."

"And this wasn't a date."

"No. No, it wasn't, was it?"

I was struggling to keep my emotions under control. I couldn't believe what he had just told me. Never in a million years would I have imagined that he had suffered such great loss.

"I'm sorry about your son, Paxton. I'm sorry you had to go through that."

He nodded gravely.

"Why does Story still work for you?"

He rubbed his hands across his face. "Christ, you really intend to ring me out tonight, don't you?"

"Sorry."

"Myla and Story are sisters. They were both dancers. Myla *was* a stripper, and Story was a back-up dancer for bands and musicians.

Story wanted to get Myla away from the club life, so they both came to work for us. Story's smart, and she's really good at what she does."

"I thought, in Houston, that she had a thing for you."

He laughed out loud. "Story? Hardly. Story bats for the other team."

"What?"

He raised his eyebrows and shook his head a little, waiting for me to catch up. He saw the moment I figured it out and said, "A quick one, I see."

"Oh!"

"Yes, oh."

The waitress arrived to take our plates and left a dessert menu.

Wanting to bring us back to safer ground, I asked him what time we would leave in the morning.

"Well, if Solara would ever get here, we could talk about that."

"Is she coming tonight?"

"She texted me a short while ago. Said she was on her way."

Paxton reached his hand across the table, palm up. I reached for his hand, and he curled his fingers around mine.

"Thank you for listening." I said quietly.

"Thank *you* for listening." He responded in the same hushed voice.

The sing-song voice of one who could only be Solara sounded across the restaurant. "Paxton, Charlotte, I made it."

I pulled my hand from Paxton's and saw a brief glimpse of loss in his eyes.

Paxton addressed her as she approached the table. "Solara. Glad you made it."

She glanced quickly between the two of us. "Why the sad faces?"

"Charlotte is sad that I can't make love to her now that I'm her boss."

Solara squeezed in next to him, forcing Paxton closer to me. I scooted over a foot, making more room for both of them.

I was shocked. "Are you serious?"

"You asked me why not earlier. Did I misunderstand?" His eyes were teasing.

Solara spoke before I could respond. "Ignore him, Charlotte. I'm so happy you're here. And I'm so sorry I missed the flight this morning. Paxton had me running errands, and I just ran out of time."

I raised my eyebrows and looked at Paxton inquisitively. "Oh really, running errands? That's very interesting."

Paxton just shrugged, a little-boy-grin on his face.

CHAPTER 19

I'D JUST PULLED my hair up into a high ponytail when an incessant knocking pounded on my door.

Solara had pressed an eye up to the tiny hole in the door. I teasingly asked, "Who is it?"

In a too deep voice, she responded, "Room service."

She made me smile, and I swung the door open to her. "I'm almost ready."

"We have time. Paxton's on the phone screaming at the rigging crew. Did you eat breakfast yet?"

I'd gone back into the bathroom to finish getting ready and responded, "Just coffee."

She put a L.O.V.E bag on my bed and then made herself comfortable at the tiny table in the corner. "You aren't one of those 'I don't eat carbs' kind of girls, are you?"

"I'm not; I just haven't eaten yet."

After my response, I heard her on the hotel room phone ordering breakfast. She ordered two cinnamon raisin bagels, three sides of bacon, two Denver omelets with hash browns, coffee, and juice.

"I may not be a carb-free girl, but that's an awful lot of food."

"Trust me, you've never worked so hard in your life as you will today. You'll thank me later when it's six and you realize you haven't eaten all day."

I stepped out of the bathroom, mascara wand in hand, and said skeptically, "But Paxton said we would get breaks for lunch."

She looked at me with a dubious expression. "Paxton sits in the conference room or yells at the lighting crew. He doesn't have a clue what's going on with us."

Loudly, while I was finishing my makeup, I said into the mirror, "I'm excited for today, for this weekend. You aren't just going to turn me loose, are you?"

I heard her voice close by and turned to see her leaning up against the doorjamb. She was smiling at me, arms crossed.

"I won't let you flounder, I promise."

Letting out a sigh, I thanked her and finished with my makeup.

She kept watching me. "You and Paxton looked cozy last night."

I blushed. Not making eye contact with her, I said, "We had a nice dinner. He was…" I searched for the right word. "He was pleasant."

She laughed knowingly and turned back to the bed. "Come out here when you're finished. I have some things for you."

Turning off the light, I stepped out of the bathroom and joined her. "What's up?"

"This is for you." She handed me the L.O.V.E bag.

I took it from her and reached inside. It was a black, baby doll style, V-neck T-shirt with the L.O.V.E logo on the back and my name above the left breast. "Oh, I love it!"

Laughing, she said, "I'm so glad because there are three of them in there, and you need to wear one today."

"Oh, of course. I'll change right now."

"Wait, there are a few more things."

I reached in and pulled out a pair of black leggings. "For today?"

"Yes. I know you probably had jeans or yoga pants to wear, but these are so much more comfortable. And way cuter.

The leggings were ankle-length, but they had sheer black side panels that ran ankle to thigh. Sexy, yet not displaying too much.

I reached in a third time and pulled out a pair of red hot pants with the L.O.V.E logo on the butt.

When I raised my eyebrows at her, she shrugged. "For sleeping. I just thought you would like them."

Holding them lovingly to my chest, I told her, "I love them. They are the best gifts I've ever received." Then I sat on the bed and hugged her.

"You're teasing me."

"Kind of. But I do love them."

I stood and put them in the dresser drawer where I'd put most of my things last night. As tired as I'd been, I knew that if I didn't unpack after dinner, I'd be living out of a suitcase for the next three days.

Solara had made herself comfortable again at the table, waiting for breakfast to arrive, while I changed.

When I came out, room service was just being delivered. My stomach growled. Sitting down to join her at the table, I'd just taken a bite of bacon when there was another knock at the door.

I mumbled, "I'll get it, you eat."

I looked through the peephole and saw that it was Paxton. He was leaning on the doorframe and looking anxious. When I opened it, he looked down at my chest and then back at my face, grinning devilishly. "Good morning, Charlotte."

"Hey."

His eyebrows went up in surprise. Then he leaned in from the hallway, whispering in my ear, "One of these days, I'm going to get you to say, 'Good morning, Paxton.'"

The fresh scent of soap and laundry detergent was sharp, and I think I visibly trembled. "Do you want to come in?"

"Is my sister here?"

"Yes."

He teased. "Then no."

Solara shouted from inside the room. "Paxton, there's breakfast."

He responded, only loud enough for me to hear, "In that case, I never refuse the opportunity to eat." He leaned in, put his lips to my ear lobe, sucked on it gently before releasing it, and then ignored my squeal as he passed into the room.

Taking a few calming breaths, I slowly shut the door and then joined them at the table.

Solara pulled her feet up onto the chair and wrapped her arms around her knees. "Did Story make it?"

Making himself comfortable at the table, Paxton poured himself a cup of coffee and leaned back in the chair. "She's on her way. She got in late last night and went to her friend's house. She'll meet us at the venue."

I jumped into the conversation. "Where is Story? I thought she left earlier this week to come here."

Paxton looked down into his coffee, and Solara looked at me solemnly, then said, "She did, but she had to go back home for a family event."

I so desperately wanted to ask, but the look Paxton shot her kept me from speaking.

Solara looked back and forth between us and asked Paxton, "Did you tell her about Myla?"

"I told her she was Story's sister. And yes, I told her she was my ex-wife."

As only I imagined siblings could do, they were communicating without speaking the actual words. Was I missing something? I was about to ask when Paxton stood from the chair and slugged back the rest of his coffee.

"You two almost ready?" he asked as he headed to the door.

Solara forked a few more pieces of fruit into her mouth and mumbled, "I am."

I responded, "Yes, I just need to slip on my shoes and grab my bag."

The door locked behind me, and the three of us left together.

The SUV was parked out front of the hotel. Solara immediately jumped in the back seat. I gave her a little glare, and she simply smiled.

The drive to the venue was quick, and from the time I stepped out of the truck, it was a non-stop blur.

Paxton immediately disappeared backstage, and I went off with Solara.

I tried to remember everything Paxton had told me yesterday and listened intently to Solara as she showed me how to check everyone in.

"We have cool new headsets, so you don't need to wear that bulky pilot headset."

She clipped a transmitter to a belt that she wrapped around my waist. As she clipped, I held my arms up. "The downside to these sexy leggings? No place to put the transmitter."

When it was resting on my hip, I lowered my arms, and she handed me a headset with a small microphone. She talked while she slipped them over my ears, and adjusted the band where it rested at the back of my head. "You'll be on channel eight and talking primarily with the sound booth when stage monitoring. If Paxton or I need you, we'll just switch to your channel. *You* don't change your channel; we'll come to you. For now, we're all on channel two until the show starts."

My head was spinning, and my eyes were wide as she talked.

"Breathe, Charlotte. You'll be fine."

The vendors were starting to arrive, setting up booths of shoes and sexy outfits, costumes, stickers, poles for home use, makeup, and hair extensions.

Employees from the local and regional studios started to arrive, and I knew I wouldn't remember all their names. They were all so normal, and I nodded and smiled as I was introduced to them. I started to feel like a bobblehead.

Story arrived. Even though I didn't know her very well, and

thought briefly that she probably didn't like me, I almost hugged her when she handed me a venti coffee from Starbucks.

"You'll need it, doll." She winked at me. "Glad you're here."

"Thank you so much." I took a tentative sip of the hot liquid and saw Paxton come out from the hall that led up to the conference room.

Story handed him a coffee. "Everything okay this morning?"

"Yeah. The riggers lost the key to the spin pole, so I'm going to run to the studio and get another one."

"Want company?" Story was already handing Solara the coffee tray, and I felt a pang of jealousy.

"Sure. Let me grab my bag. Sol, you got this?"

He looked directly at Solara, and she nodded. Then he gave me a look that was tender and apologetic.

"You ready?" He asked me and sounded like he cared.

I nodded and took a deep breath, exhaling audibly. My chest rose, and I noticed he saw it too. With a quick glance and a sweet smile to me, he turned and addressed Story.

"Give me five minutes."

When he was gone, I avoided looking at Story and stepped behind the check-in desk. Solara started explaining how to use the computer system and that each girl would get a gift bag.

Paxton came jogging back out. He and Story left through the front door of the theatre.

Solara gently pulled on my elbow. "C'mon, I'll show you where the bags are, and we'll start bringing some of them out."

Solara and I spent most of the morning packing gift bags and getting the lobby ready. At noon, lunch was delivered, and we all went over the schedule for the day in the conference room.

There were about ten of us working, and I could feel the excitement building for the day. The girls that knew each other were friendly and happy. All of them were very respectful of Paxton and Solara.

Both of them intrigued me. They were so focused on their business and yet so patient and accepting of their employees.

Paxton never once indicated any overt flirtation, and I thought back to that day when I first met him. It seemed so long ago.

Tapping his knuckles on the table, he smiled at everyone. "Okay, let's have a great day. Let Solara or me know if you need any help."

We all stood, most of us cleaning up our lunch wrappers and walking back downstairs.

The girls checking in ranged from first-time competitors to professionals. Feeling bubbly and joyful, I couldn't stop grinning and welcoming them all to the event.

Some of them disregarded me. I wanted to tell them, "I'm a vice president," but I wasn't. Not anymore. I was staff, and that made me grin even more. Gaining more confidence in my abilities, I started to realize I didn't need the title.

When there was a break in the check ins, Solara turned and asked, "Why are you grinning so big?"

I shrugged. "I'm just happy."

Her grin grew, and she hugged me. "I'm glad."

When one of the local girls showed up to relieve me from the desk, I glanced at my watch, shocked to see that it was 6:00 p.m. Solara had been right: I was starving. "Solara, I'm going to run upstairs and get a bottle of water. I'm going backstage next, right?"

"Yes, and you'll do great!"

I nodded at her encouragement and ran quickly up the stairs to the conference room. Paxton was working on his laptop, and I tried to grab a power bar and a water without interrupting him.

Not looking up, he asked softly as he continued to type. "You doing okay?"

It was peaceful and quiet up here. I unscrewed the top to the water bottle and took a small sip. "I'm doing good. Thank you."

He lifted his head and smiled at me. "I'm glad."

We stared at each other goofily, my smile growing. "I have to, I have to go stage monitor now."

"Have fun."

Butterflies danced in my belly, and I practically bounced down the stairs. Almost skipping down the dark hall, I entered a dark backstage area filled with the next group of dancers. I was momentarily taken aback at not only how many girls were there but the adornments on their outfits.

The stage monitor I was relieving waved me over. "Charlotte, right?"

"Hi. Yes."

She handed me a clipboard. "The next six groups are all the exotic dancers. Each group is a different level and has three to four girls in each one. The last group should be finished by eight o'clock. Make sure you get their starting position and make some notes here on the side, so you don't forget." She pointed to the earlier schedule. "See how I just made some comments in the margins?"

I nodded at her and tried not to get distracted by the dancers. The crystals and sequins kept pulling at my attention.

"The girls know to check in with you, but if you get to the next group and you don't have any dancers, send one of the pole cleaners to the dressing room to find them. Have them enter from the back of the stage unless they tell you differently. Then when they are in their starting position, cue up your mic and say 'Texas, Texas, Texas.'"

I was confused by the use of the word. "Is that for me?"

"No, it's for the music guys to cue up the dancer's program."

"But why Texas?"

She looked at me. "Try saying Colorado three times fast."

I said it in my head and then said, "Yeah, that doesn't work."

She laughed. "We use Texas regardless of city or state. It's easy."

She left me to manage the stage, and I was caught up in a whirlwind of dancers and glitter.

The music selections ranged from techno to sultry, and I was entranced. The girls were confident and happy. Some of them were so ethereal, I found myself completely distracted by their bodies, their fluidity, and their every move's perfection.

At one point, I found myself moving rhythmically along with one of them until I was interrupted by a young girl trying to check herself in.

"Excuse me, I was told I needed to check in with you."

She was timid and shy. I spoke kindly to her, "Hi, yes, what's your name?"

"Ember Lynn. I'm Exotic Level 1." Moving beside me, she looked at the clipboard and pointed to her name.

"Is this your first competition?"

"Yes, and I'm really nervous."

"You'll be fine. You look beautiful. Just take a deep breath. I've been there before, and I know how you feel."

She nodded and shook out her hands at her sides. I asked, "Okay, Ember, what's your starting position?"

She told me, and I made notes in the margin of the paper. When her group was called, I walked with her to the back of the stage and waited until the pole cleaners finished wiping down the poles.

The announcer called her name, and I smiled gently at her, telling her she would do great. She teetered out onto the stage and stood in her standing position. Clicking on the microphone, I said, "Texas, Texas, Texas," and her music started.

Once again, I was captivated by the dance. This was not the nervous, shy girl I'd just talked to; this dancer was gorgeous and seductive. My mind shifted, and I thought, *I can do this. I'm going to do this.*

A feeling of calm settled over me. I finished the shift exhausted and yet oddly invigorated.

Ending the day was a flurry of boxing things up and locking them in the conference room until tomorrow. Paxton had ordered catering for dinner. By the time I reached the upstairs conference room, all the girls were stuffing their faces with breadsticks, salad, pasta, and grilled shrimp.

I filled a plate, took a seat at the end of the table next to Paxton, and inhaled my food. He was twirling side to side in his chair, talking with the studio manager from Denver. He gave me a brief, sexy smile before turning back to his conversation.

Now that I'd stopped moving, a deep tiredness snuck in. My eyes started to close, heavy from the long day.

"Wake up!" Solara said exuberantly as she plopped down in the chair on the other side of me.

"I. Am. So. Tired."

"You'll get used to it. And you'll learn to eat breakfast. You almost ready to go?"

I looked at my watch and saw it was past nine. "Wow, this day flew by!"

"And we have two more, so we need to get back and get to sleep." She put her palms together against her cheek, closed her eyes, and started to snore.

I chortled and sat back in my seat.

Out of the corner of my eye, I saw the manager get up to leave. Paxton rolled his chair closer to Solara and me. Leaning over, elbows on his knees, hands clasped in front of him, he asked, "You two ready to go?"

My belly tightened. I wanted to reach out and ruffle his hair. Instead, I simply nodded.

Solara stood, grabbed her bag, and swiped two more cookies off the catering tray. "Ready."

The three of us were the last to leave. The theatre was eerily quiet, except for the cleaning crew. Once again, Solara rode in the back, and we were quiet on the ride to the hotel.

After Paxton gave the valet the keys, he told us both to be downstairs tomorrow at 9:00 a.m. "First event is at noon. We need to be ready."

Solara looped her arm through mine and then saluted him. "We'll be here."

He gave us one last glance, holding my eyes as he spoke. "You did good today, Charlotte. I'll see you in the morning."

I tried to speak, and my words got stuck. I cleared my throat and tried again. "Thank you. See you in the morning."

Solara pulled me toward the elevators. "I'll ride up with you."

I was physically exhausted. I wanted a bath and bed.

"You really did do a good job today, Charlotte. You just fit right in."

She hugged me at my door. I felt safe and... oddly, loved.

"Thank you. I had a good time."

She squeezed me again and turned toward her room.

I stopped her. "Solara?"

"Yes?"

"I was thinking—" I stopped, and she raised her eyebrows. "I was thinking I might do an exotic. For Irvine? If you think I could." I stuttered a bit. "I mean, I would still work the show, but maybe I could practice when I'm not working. "

Her grin grew wide. "I think that's a great idea. You should talk to Story; she can choreograph an amazing routine for you."

"Okay." I nodded assuredly. "Okay, I will."

"Good night, Charlotte."

"Good night."

I let myself into my room and fist-bumped the air.

CHAPTER 20

AFTER MY BATH, I dressed for bed in the red hot pants and tiny tank top Solara had given me, pulled a wine out of the minibar, and poured it into one of the water glasses.

I opened the blinds and sat down at the window to watch the twinkling city lights. My body relaxed as I sipped the wine. For the first time in what felt like forever, I felt centered.

A light knock was at the door, and I dropped my feet from the windowsill, startled.

Slowly placing my wine on the desk, I padded to the door and looked through the peephole.

Paxton.

My heart raced, and I jumped back as if he had singed me through the door. I looked around my room frantically, as if I could hide.

I couldn't let him in—or could I? I was hoping he couldn't tell through the peephole that the table lamp was still on.

I calmed my racing thoughts and sat down on the edge of the bed, bringing myself back to the moment. We'd had a nice day today. He had been... He'd been normal.

"Charlotte?" he called softly through the door.

I stood and paced, wringing my fingers together. Was I ready for this? Was I overreacting?

My phone buzzed on the nightstand. When I picked it up, it was a text from Paxton: *Charlotte?*

Hi, I texted back.

Are you out?

No, I'm sleeping. That should work.

In your room?

I paused before responding. *Yes.*

I grimaced and closed my eyes.

My phone was silent. I sat back down on the edge of the bed and waited.

When nothing came through, I went to the door and looked out again. He was still there, but farther away, closer to the railing. He was looking at his phone, then out toward the open atrium, then back at his phone.

He started to text again.

My phone pinged with an incoming text, and I ran back to the bed to read it. *You left your headset in the truck.*

Oh, my God. This sexy, hard-ass, beautiful man was nervous. I giggled and touched my fingers to my mouth.

I ran to the door and then stopped a few feet from it, taking a deep breath. Slowing my pace, I took the last few steps to the door, took another deep breath, and then hesitantly opened it.

He turned when he heard the click. Slowly, he walked toward the door, giving me time to admire his, well, everything. When he reached me, I noticed (for the first time) that he really did have my headset in his hand.

My smile dropped, and I said flatly, "My headset."

He held it out toward me, a wickedly humorous smile on his face. "You shouldn't leave it behind."

"Right."

I took it from him and watched as his gaze slowly ran the length of my body. I flushed and felt my breasts perk.

Taking a chance, I waited until his eyes came back to mine.

"You could have given it to me in the morning."

Our eyes were locked. Stepping back a few inches, I opened the door a bit further.

He stayed in the doorway. "I could have."

His pupils were dilated. Sexual energy radiated between us as he put his arm up on the doorframe and rested his forehead on his arm.

I knew he was torn, but I wasn't going to beg.

He stood up straight and stared down at the headset, then back into my eyes. He took a step forward, and I had to back up to make room for him.

When he had cleared the doorway, I let go of the handle. The door swung shut. He caught it just before it banged closed, gently letting it lock.

I stood against the wall. He reached out to lightly run the back of his fingers on the skin of my belly, below my tank top.

I inhaled and sucked in my stomach, my breaths now coming in short pants.

My arm fell to the side, the headset dangling to the floor, and I dropped my head. I stared at his fingers, spellbound, as they ran back and forth across my skin. When they went under the waistband of the short-shorts, I sucked in my breath and lifted my head, whispering, "Paxton."

"Charlotte, I'm going to kiss you."

"Are you asking permission?" I flirted, heat radiating between my thighs.

He lowered his head, his breath hot as his lips moved closer to mine. "No, I'm just letting you know."

Breathily, I said, "Okay."

His mouth descended to mine. Full, soft lips met mine, and I put out my tongue to taste him. He moaned and deepened the kiss, wrapping his arms around me and pulling me close. His hands spanned across my back, holding me tight.

He walked us backward into the room. My calves hit the bed.

Gently, he lifted me up and lay me on the bed. Hands around his neck, I held on until he had me lying flat.

I scooted back and smiled at him as he reached for the hem of his shirt and pulled it up over his head.

"Holy Mary. You've been hiding this?" I sat up and ran my fingers down his chest to his belt buckle. He had an eight pack and hints of a "V" low on his belly.

His grin was devilish. "If you knew, would I have had you that first day?"

I put my finger to my lips and looked heavenward, pondering the question.

He pushed me back farther on the bed, crawled over me, and then said on a laugh, "I think not."

Kissing up my belly, he pushed my tank top up and over my head.

I closed my eyes and let him kiss me all over. One hand gently teased my breast; his tongue circled around the other. When he took it in his mouth, I closed my eyes and arched, moaning out loud.

His mouth left me, and then he blew softly on my wet skin. My nipples tightened, and I thought I would die if he didn't kiss me again.

Settling his body between my thighs, he looked down at me and whispered, "Gorgeous."

I reached for his face and pulled him down to kiss me.

He paused before kissing me again, searching my eyes.

"Paxton, please kiss me."

That was all the permission he needed before pressing his mouth to mine and giving me everything. He was an expert at this—maneuvering gently and then adding pressure. His tongue dancing with mine and reaching every depth of my mouth. He bit my bottom lip, then gently sucked on it before kissing me deeply once again. The weight of him was delicious torture. My hands ran across the strong muscles of his back, holding him close to me.

His mouth left mine and traveled down my body. Kissing. Blowing. Nipping. Licking. He licked his way down between my legs.

He knelt down at the foot of the bed, taking my panties with him as he went.

I raised up on my elbows. "Paxton?"

"Please let me give you pleasure."

I couldn't breathe. This man. Who was this man? I nodded and lay back.

Pushing my knees apart, he pressed his palms to my inner thighs, and caressed me with his tongue. I sighed as his tongue slid up into me. Then, he took me in his mouth, sucking and licking until I was squirming underneath him. Strong hands gripped my bottom pressing me up to his mouth as he loved me greedily.

I reached for his head, held him in place as I shook, my toes curling, and then shattered, calling out his name.

Like a wet noodle, I went limp on the bed, panting with my release. I had to blink a couple of times, and then he was all I could see above me.

I smiled up at him. "Thank you."

He swooped down to kiss me again. "You're welcome."

Reluctantly, he pushed himself up off me to stand, walking to the head of the bed to pull back the covers.

Pulling myself to a sitting position, I asked. "Are you going to stay?" I was a little confused.

"No, you need to sleep."

He picked me up, carried me to where he had prepared the bed, gently placed me on the mattress, and then covered me with the blankets.

"Don't you want to... you know?" I looked at the bulge in his jeans. I wanted to run my hands over his broad shoulders, kiss every golden freckle I could see.

He leaned down to kiss me chastely on the cheek. "Yes, I do want to... you know—but we have time."

"Are we...?"

He smoothed back the hair from my face and buried his head

in the crook of my neck. He inhaled and gripped my hip under the blanket. "You smell so fucking good."

Laughing, I said, "Oh good, I'm glad we fit that word in here somewhere tonight."

He was nuzzling my neck; it tickled. Whispering in between kisses, he said, "I don't know what we are, Charlotte, but I have been enchanted by you since I stepped into that limo and saw you looking at me from the window. Let's just breathe for now, okay?"

I teased him. "Well, I need to rest, and you're bothering me. You should leave, or I'm going to be super tired tomorrow. I don't want to get in trouble with the boss. Now go."

He reached under the blanket and caressed my bottom again. He whispered back, "I'll see you in the morning."

When he stood, I propped myself up on my elbow and watched him put his shirt back on. "I'll see you in the morning."

He leaned down to kiss me again.

When I heard the click of the door shut behind him, I rolled over to sleep, smiling like a teenager.

The next morning, I ordered breakfast from room service and ate as Solara had instructed. When I met the two of them downstairs, my eyes went to Paxton as soon as I stepped off the elevator. He was sitting on the couch watching for me, and his smile grew as I approached them.

The smile softened his face, and it was hard for me to imagine he had been such an asshat to me.

He stood as I got closer. "Good morning, Charlotte."

"Good morning, Paxton." My grin was so big I thought my face would crack.

From the couch, I heard, "Really?"

Solara had been working on her laptop. I looked down to see her smiling up at us, eyebrows raised.

I included her in my greeting. "Good morning, Solara."

"Apparently."

Paxton grabbed his bag from beside the chair and put it over his shoulder. "You two ready to go? We have a long day."

Solara packed up her things, and we all headed out together to the venue.

The day was long and exhausting, but it didn't seem so stressful since I now knew what I was doing. All the Denver girls had started including me in their conversations, and I felt like I was really part of the team.

My thoughts frequently turned to Paxton, and I had to shove them back down so I didn't humiliate myself. All I wanted to do now was touch him and kiss him. But this was work, and I had to be a professional.

I did my best to avoid him during the day, which was easy since he never came backstage.

When we returned to the hotel that night, both Paxton and I held back in the lobby, waiting for Solara to head to her room.

Solara asked us if we wanted to get a glass of wine.

"No," we responded at the same time.

Solara glanced back and forth between the two of us—and started laughing. "C'mon, Charlotte, I'll walk with you to your room."

It was all I could do not to say no. Instead, I said good night to Paxton and went with Solara up the elevator. We said a quick good night, and I let myself into my room.

As soon as the door was shut, I pulled out my phone. Grinning to myself, I texted Paxton: *I forgot my headset.*

Five minutes later, there was a knock at my door.

This time I didn't hesitate; I flung it open to let him in.

He rushed through the door, scooping me up in his arms and burying his head in my neck. Frantically kicking off his boots, he said, "She totally cock-blocked me."

I laughed as he threw me to the bed and climbed over me, kissing my face and neck, everywhere he could get to. "No, she was protecting me."

Slowing his kisses, he took my face in his big hands and looked me directly in the eye. Softly, he said, "She might be right to do so."

I shook my head gently from side to side and whispered, "No."

His lips lowered slowly to mine, pressing gently as we melted into each other. We kissed and kissed and kissed for what felt like forever.

With finesse, he took my T-shirt and leggings off, planting kisses on every inch of skin he could reach.

When he rolled me over on top of him, I reached behind me and took my bra off.

He pulled me to him for a kiss while plunging his hand into my silk panties and slowly, gently slid his fingers inside me. I moaned into his mouth as he stroked me, loved me, and pressed the heel of his hand up against my sex until I arched my back and came, calling out his name and collapsing on top of him.

His hand gently rubbed up and down my back. His chest rumbled with subtle laughter.

He flipped me over, so he was hovering above me, and I looked at him with sleepy eyes.

With amusement, he asked, "You okay?"

I reached up and touched his cheek, marveling at him. "Mm-hmm. Stay with me tonight."

He planted a quick kiss on my forehead. "I can't."

"Why?"

"Because. You. Tempt. Me," he said, between kisses to my face.

"Isn't that what I'm supposed to do?" I pulled back and stared at him, batting my eyes.

He was sitting on the edge of the bed, putting his boots back on. He stood and tucked his shirt back into his jeans.

"Charlotte." His tone was laced with something I couldn't pin down. Frustration? Warning?

I sat up and pulled the sheet over me, feeling exposed. "What's the matter?"

He put his hands on his hips and looked up to the ceiling, letting out a breath.

I pressed. "Is it your wife? Are you staying married? Is this just a game to you?"

He rushed to the side of the bed and sat down, pulling me to him.

"No," he said, and then more emphatically, "No!"

"Then what? What is this?"

He dropped his forehead to mine. "I'm not staying married. But it's complicated, and I don't want to burden you with it right now. Just please be patient with me."

I took his face in my hands and pressed my lips to his, breathing life into him. I said against his lips, "Okay."

When he pulled away, a cold draft ran over my shoulders.

"And now, you really need to let me go, or I will fuck you six ways from Sunday, and neither one of us will get through the day tomorrow."

I stepped out of bed. Wrapping myself in the sheet, I walked him to the door.

He kissed me again, and I whispered, "I can't wait to get to Sunday."

CHAPTER 21

MONDAY MORNING, I sat at my dad's desk in his home office, rubbing my thumb back and forth across the screen of my phone, reminiscing about the weekend.

I needed to call Mark; I needed to tell him that I wanted him to buy me out of the house. But I was daydreaming about Paxton.

The rest of the weekend in Denver had been exhausting.

Paxton and Solara had treated all of the Denver crew to dinner Saturday night. I'd listened attentively to all of their unique stories, enthralled by their colorful past—sometimes crass, sometimes endearing, but completely authentic.

I'd tried so hard not to stare at Paxton, but it was difficult not to. He'd been so much more relaxed. I loved the way his eyes crinkled when he laughed, and his face softened.

Story had sat next to me at dinner, and I'd asked her if she would help me with an exotic routine.

"Are you kidding me? Heck yes! I would love that."

Her response had surprised me. I hadn't expected her to be so enthusiastic, and I told her so.

"Why would you think that?"

I'd fiddled with the napkin on my lap. "You didn't seem too keen about me in Houston."

She'd stared at me blankly and jerked her head forward. Then she shook it and blinked rapidly. "What? I'm so sorry. I don't even really remember Houston; it's kind of a blur to me. My family is going through a difficult time. If I gave you the impression that I didn't like you or disregarded you, I am so sorry."

My phone had pinged in my pocket. I pulled it out and looked down to see it was Paxton. A grin had spread across my face. I'd looked up to see him completely engaged in a conversation.

Story was briefly pulled into another conversation so I texted him back. I waited to see if he would look at his phone.

I didn't wait long. He glanced at it, smiled briefly, and went back to his conversation.

We went back and forth a few times, flirting and lamenting about how we wanted to be anywhere but at dinner.

In the truck, on the way back to the hotel, I'd texted him from the front passenger seat: *I'm going to do an exotic in Irvine*

Solara had sat in the backseat, talking about the show in Phoenix next weekend. I'd heard her say things like "one day," "small," and "easy." But I'd been more distracted by the dark look that had come over Paxton's face at my last text.

When we stopped at a light, he texted: *Why?*

Solara abruptly interrupted my thoughts. "You two know you aren't being subtle, right?"

I dropped my head and grinned.

He reached across the center console and grabbed my hand.

Instead of going to my room that night, we'd sat in the atrium and talked. Solara had hugged us both, said good night, and gone up to her room alone.

I'd sat on the couch, legs pulled up under me, facing him.

After the cocktail waitress had delivered our wine, I asked him why he was so upset by my comment.

His head was resting on the back of the couch, and he was holding my hand in his lap. He rolled his head over to look at me.

"You know you don't have to dance."

His comment hurt me. I didn't need anyone else in my life disapproving of me.

"I know I don't have to, but I want to."

He reached his hand up and held my cheek in his palm. His thumb caressed my cheekbone, and I reached up to keep his hand in place.

Scooting closer to me, he said, "I'm just saying, you don't need to prove anything to anyone. You are exquisite just as you are."

I swallowed the lump in my throat. I was falling for him. I was falling hard.

"I need it for me, Paxton." I leaned down to kiss him and whispered against his lips. "I need it for me."

When he was silent, I continued. "Are you worried about me being like Myla?"

The sad look he gave me told me I was close to right.

I squeezed his hand tightly and said, "I can't pretend to know what motivated her, but I'm not doing this for attention. I really am doing it just for me."

He whispered back, "I'm not comparing you."

I looked at him with an amused expression, and he laughed.

"I'm not."

He kissed my fingers and added, "If you want to do an exotic, then you should do it."

He pulled me under his arm, snuggled me up alongside him on the couch, and kissed the top of my head.

We each went to our own rooms that night, lingering only a little longer before saying good night. The next morning, he was all business again.

He had helped us with our luggage, checked us in at the airport, and driven me home after we landed back in Phoenix. He was the perfect gentleman—until he wasn't. And that was fine with me.

A tiny woodpecker landed on the windowsill, pecking its beak against the window frame and jarring me out of my daydreaming.

Sitting up straight in my dad's chair, I turned on my phone and called Mark.

He answered right away, and I asked him if this was a good time to talk.

"Yeah, yeah, just let me close my office door."

I waited a second for him to get settled, and he asked me how I was doing.

"I'm good. It's nice to be home." He sighed heavily, and I rushed on. "I'd like for you to buy me out of the house, Mark. I can get Suzanne to pull everything together for us. You can keep all the furniture. I'll send movers for the rest of my things in a few weeks."

"Do you have a place to stay yet?"

"No, I was in Denver for the whole weekend, so I didn't give it much thought. I'll stay with my parents for a bit and start looking in a week or two."

Our conversation was so dry, so unemotional. Like we'd been business partners instead of lovers. Thinking of being lovers brought Paxton to mind, and I relaxed.

"Charlie, I'm going to be honest here, I don't really understand what happened. One minute we were fine, and the next, you're gone."

"I can't explain it, Mark. I don't know what else to say. Honestly, I just… broke." I flailed my hand in the air in frustration. "But I can't go back." I rushed on. "I don't want to go back."

There was silence on the other line.

"Charlie, do you love me?"

My stomach clenched. Hot tears pricked my eyes. "No." A thick tear fell. "I'm so sorry."

"Did you ever?"

"Mark, please. It doesn't matter now."

His voice was soft. "It matters to me."

Could I lie? Did I even know? I think I did. I couldn't hurt him anymore. "I did, Mark. I did love you." I remembered good times that we'd had together and knew it wasn't fair for me not to explain.

"I felt like you didn't really see me anymore though. When I started taking classes and hiding it from you, I think I knew you would never approve. After dinner the night I met you after a class, when you told me I couldn't do the competition, I felt trashy. Not because of the competition, but because of your words. Your words and your tone made me feel bad about the dancing. Not the dancing itself."

He was silent on his end, and I continued. "I can't go on with you, Mark. I can't be with you knowing you are silently judging me."

Neither one of us spoke for a moment.

Mark cleared his throat. "Don't worry about the house. I'll get with Suzanne and take care of everything for you."

"Thank you, Mark."

"Will you be at the gala in a few weeks?"

"Yes, I'll be there."

"We don't need to make any formal announcement. I'll let you tell whoever you want."

I nodded—not trusting my voice—and then I realized he couldn't see me. "Okay."

"Okay."

This was awkward now. "Well, I'll see you in a few weeks."

"Take care, Charlie." And he hung up.

Absentmindedly, I sat staring out the window, sitting completely in the moment. Despite the call with Mark, peace settled in my heart. All of the desert flowers in my parents' backyard appeared more colorful, the cacti greener, and I started to laugh. And laugh. And laugh.

There was a knock on the doorframe of the office, and I turned to see my mom. "Charlotte, are you okay?"

I caught my breath and controlled the laughter. "I'm great!"

"Are you sure? You seem a little hyper." She approached me tentatively, holding out a mug of coffee.

"I'm so good, Mom. I am *so good!*" I looked heavenward.

"Was that Mark on the phone?"

"Yes, and I think we're going to be okay,"

"Are you getting back together?" Her voice was high, shocked.

I spoke quickly. "No, no! I just meant... I think we'll be able to move on amicably. He sounded sad, but he also sounded resigned. And I've known him long enough to know when he's done with something."

She curled up in the corner of the leather sleeper sofa. In a conspiratorial tone, she said, "And what about the man who dropped you off last night?"

My cheeks grew warm and I shrugged. "That was Paxton. He owns the studio. He's my boss."

"Uh-huh. I don't recall you ever kissing any of your other bosses."

"I thought you were asleep." I twirled back and forth in the chair, grinning at her. "And how do you know he kissed me?"

She started to laugh. "You just told me."

I picked up my dad's stress ball and threw it at her. "I don't know why I still fall for that."

"You look shiny this morning."

She wasn't wrong; I felt shiny this morning.

Last night when I arrived home, all the lights had been turned off. I'd thought my parents were sleeping. Apparently not.

Solara and Paxton had both had their vehicles at the airport. Solara lived in a loft downtown, so Paxton had offered to drive me home.

As we'd gathered our bags from baggage claim, Solara had asked me, "Charlotte, will I see you tomor—"

"I told her to come in on Tuesday. She needs some time to get settled." Paxton said.

Solara wasn't fazed at all by his declaration. She'd hugged me, given me a kiss on the cheek, and told me she would see me then.

After pulling into my parents' driveway, Paxton had shut off the engine, and we'd sat quietly in the car talking about the week.

"Take your time, Charlotte. Come in on Tuesday when you're ready."

"There's a show this weekend, right?"

"Yes, and you'll do great." He had turned in his seat and was leaning up against the door, watching me.

"What?"

"I just can't believe you're sitting here."

"Are you... happy about that?"

His eyes crinkled at the corners. "A little."

My heart raced, and I'd wanted to crawl over the center console into his lap. However, he'd turned and opened his door, jumping out and getting my bags out of the back.

Sighing at having to leave our intimate cocoon, I'd directed him to the front door.

We'd entered quietly, and he'd put all my suitcases in the front entry. He'd whispered, "This is a nice house."

I'd whispered back, "Thank you."

"Where's your room?"

He'd wrapped his arms around me and started nibbling on my neck.

In a hushed tone, I said, "I'm not showing you."

"Where are we gonna make out?"

"In the living room, where all good daughters make out with their boyfriends."

Laughing, he'd lifted me up against him and walked me backward into the living room. When he pulled me down next to him on the couch, he'd said, "This is fun. It's like high school."

He slid his hands under my shirt, and I got goosebumps from his feather-light touch.

"We could go to your house," I purred as his thumb brushed over my nipple and it perked to attention.

He'd hesitated a moment before simply responding, "We could."

We'd made out on the couch until I'd found myself yawning.

Kissing my belly, he'd said, "We should do something a little more rigorous next time so you don't fall asleep on me."

"I'm so sorry. I just got so sleepy."

"I know you're tired. "

As he planted gentle kisses all over my face, I'd felt myself just melt into the couch.

"I'll let you rest."

I'd felt a draft between us and realized he was standing to leave.

"I'll walk you out."

He held his hand out to me, and we walked to the front door together, holding hands.

Taking me into his arms, he grabbed my face and kissed me deeply, consuming me, claiming me. I held on to his belt buckle, pulling him into me.

Slowly, he'd pulled back and whispered, "I'll see you Tuesday."

I'd slept so well after that. Now I was being interrogated by my mom, who'd tricked me into spilling my guts.

"I am shiny today, aren't I?" I grinned a cheesy grin.

She stood from the sofa, saying that she was going to a yoga class and my dad had a business dinner that night, so I was on my own.

I spent the rest of the day unpacking my things and looking for a townhome or rental. Eventually, I would need to think about a real job again.

Tuesday morning, I arrived at the studio and was greeted by both Solara and Story. They both shouted, "Welcome to your first day! Yay!" Then they handed me a tall coffee.

I felt ridiculous *and* welcomed. "Thank you. Where do I put my things?"

Solara stepped out from behind the desk. "Come with me, I'll show you."

I followed her up the stairs to a small kitchen and break room. It was painted a comfortable blue-gray, and a couch sat against the sidewall, facing a mounted TV. Against the back wall were lockers for my things. A cherrywood table (with four cream-colored leather chairs surrounding it) sat in the middle of the room.

"There are some girls that work in the evenings, and I wouldn't want your stuff to disappear." Solara rushed on, rambling.

"Not that I don't trust them, but... well, you just never know."

Carefully placing my bag in one of the lockers, she waited until I was ready and then showed me where to find coffee and snacks.

"Let's go back downstairs. Story will walk you through the classes, the reservation system, and show you everything that needs to be done to get ready for the event this weekend."

I followed her back down the stairs and saw that Paxton had arrived. He was leaning casually against the front desk, speaking softly with Story. Now that I knew their history, it didn't bother me so much, but I did feel a little jealous at their apparent comfort with each other.

When he looked up and saw us, his face softened, and a small smile formed on his lips. Standing up straight, he asked if I'd gotten settled all right.

I tried not to fidget.

"I did. I'll stay at my parents' for a bit and then start looking for a place—once I figure out what I'm going to do. Long term, that is. I mean, I know this job is only for a couple of months, so I do have to figure out what to do after."

The three of them were all staring at me. Paxton's smile grew bigger, and Story looked at me like I'd grown a third eye. I took a deep breath and spoke, "I got settled just fine. Thank you."

Solara started to laugh. "Paxton, don't you have boss stuff to do?"

"Why, yes, Solara. I do." He turned to Story. "Do you want to take care of that other thing tomorrow afternoon?"

She nodded solemnly. I lowered my head, not wanting to intrude on the rest of their private conversation.

He rapped his knuckles on the counter, hitched his bag up higher on his shoulder, and headed toward the stairs. It was all I could do not to follow him with my eyes. Instead, I stepped behind the counter, smiled at Story, and told her I was ready to learn.

It was her turn to laugh at me. "Enthusiastic, I see."

"I want to get to the part where we can choreograph my dance." I beamed at her.

Solara turned to follow Paxton up the stairs, and Story started my training by showing me the computer system.

The day passed by quickly. Story showed me how to work the computer systems, schedule classes, bill people, and check them in. I met almost a hundred people in just one day: a whirlwind of long hair, short shorts, leggings, smiles, and surgically enhanced breasts. The ballerinas came in to use the gym; the hip-hop dancers came after work. By the time the evening girl came in to work the front desk, I was so tired I thought I was going to fall off the high stool behind the desk.

There was another college-aged girl who came in to clean the studios and the locker rooms. She was quick and efficient; I didn't even recognize that it was her when she asked me to check her in for the five o'clock floor class.

"Charlotte. It's me, Vivian." She was looking pointedly at me.

"Oh, my goodness. I didn't recognize you with your hair down."

"That's okay. I know you're new." She smiled kindly at me. "You'll get it."

Audibly sighing, I thanked her. "There were so many people that came through here today. I had no idea. Is it always this busy?"

"Worse on Saturdays. But yes, this studio is really popular."

"I see that."

"You're from the Houston studio, right?"

"Yes. Kind of. I took classes there, but I'm originally from Scottsdale."

She smiled again. A soft, accepting smile. "Well, welcome home."

The impact of her soft, kind words smacked into me. The simple 'welcome home' told me I was right where I needed to be.

I tilted my head. "Thank you."

She left me to work and walked up the stairs to the second pole dancing room.

After everyone was checked in for the five p.m. classes, I went back upstairs to get my things and leave for the night.

I'd seen Solara and Paxton briefly in the conference room, but other than that, they'd been noticeably absent. I'd missed seeing them. After spending so much time with them this weekend, I now felt abandoned.

When I reached my car, I turned the air conditioning on full blast. The hot Arizona sun had turned my car into an oven, and I waited until it had cooled down before removing the sunshade from the front window.

As I tried to fold the screen back into its tiny, round bag, I saw Paxton leaving the building. His head was down, and he was looking at his phone as he crossed the parking lot.

He didn't see me until he was seated in the front seat of his SUV, and then his eyes found mine.

My heart was racing. I wasn't even sure what we were, and I felt a little silly for sitting in my car in the parking lot.

He was the first to look away.

A few seconds later, my phone pinged. It startled me, and I looked down to see a text from Paxton: *Do you want to have dinner with me?*

I started to respond with something snarky but then realized I wanted this to be real. I wanted this to be something. I looked up and saw him watching me. Waiting.

I simply responded: *Yes*

Through the windshield, he smiled. Then his response came through.

Follow me.

CHAPTER 22

HIS HOME WAS set up in the hills above Phoenix—in a remote area of one-acre lots. The long driveway was edged with a two-foot rock wall and desert shrubs.

Surrounding the house were Arizona ash and desert willow trees; they provided shade to the front walk and around the back.

The garage door rose as Paxton approached. I stayed behind in the driveway, admiring the one-story house with the white-painted stucco and burnt sienna-colored clay tile roof.

I could see dark wood, double front doors at the end of a tiled front patio, and a fleur-de-lis water feature off to the side.

Stepping slowly out of my car, Paxton was waiting for me in the garage. "You can come in this way if you like."

"I'm impressed with your house."

His grin grew, and he tilted his head toward the garage door into the house. I followed behind him as the garage doors shut behind me.

We went through a laundry room and into an open floor plan with windows that looked out toward the McDowell mountains. He slipped his shoes off at the door. I followed his lead, kicking mine off and tucking them next to his.

The kitchen had beautiful white oak cabinets and stainless-steel appliances. It was spotless; only a coffee cup and a spoon sat on the counter next to the sink.

Paxton put his bag down on a chair at the kitchen table and told me to make myself at home. "I'm going to change, and I'll be right back."

I'd wandered into the living area. "Uh-huh." My back was to him. I turned so he could see me. "Fine. Okay. I'll be here."

A look of amusement crossed his face as he stood staring fondly at me. "Do you like waffles?"

"You're feeding me waffles for dinner?" I crossed my arms and smiled back at him.

"Not just any waffles—chicken and waffles."

"Isn't that a Southern thing?"

He walked off down the hall and said over his shoulder, "Then you should enjoy it.

I took my time admiring his house. The Spanish-style terracotta flooring was a beautiful contrast to the white walls and exposed wood beam ceilings.

The living room furnishings were large and comfortable. Cushions were propped up at the end of the couch, making it appear as if he had been reclining and watching the large screen TV that hung above the fireplace. Imagining him alone, relaxed in his home, made me flush.

Against the wall, next to the fireplace, was a driftwood-style bookcase. I gently touched the pictures lining one shelf.

A family picture was set center stage, and I lifted it from its place of prominence. They were in Sedona with ATVs lined up behind them. The backdrop was the beautiful fiery red rock formations of the Colorado Plateau.

Solara was a chubby young girl, and Paxton and Max looked like teenagers.

Max was the image of his dad: tall, lean, and blond. A proverbial golden boy. Paxton was tall and broad. His curly black hair was mussed and long, brushing the top of his shirt. While I would have expected him to look angry, his smile was carefree and happy. Max had his arm around his shoulder, and Solara was sitting on an ATV in front of them. A wide, cheesy grin spread across her face. Her eyes were squinted closed, and her face was raised to the sun.

His mom somehow looked elegant, even though they were all dressed for the outdoors. Standing directly next to Paxton, his step-dad looked protective and sturdy. His air of ownership extended to all three of the kids. My heart squeezed. He had the coloring of Max, but the hold around Paxton's shoulders—and the sparkle in his eyes—told me everything I needed to know. Paxton's step-dad loved him.

"What do you think?"

Still holding the picture, I turned and inhaled sharply when I saw him. He was dressed in joggers and a short-sleeved, gray T-shirt.

He wasn't looking at me. Instead, he had continued on into the kitchen and was pulling out the items to make fried chicken and waffles.

"I think... I think you have a lovely family." I put the picture back on the shelf and took a seat on the kitchen counter's barstool.

"They're all right." He took a pitcher of iced tea from the refrigerator. "Tea?"

"Please."

He poured me a glass and set it on the counter in front of me.

I took a small sip. "Thank you."

He nodded and settled into cooking. Making small talk, he asked me how my day was. "It was good. Busy. I didn't realize how much business went through there until today. I enjoyed it."

"We're trying to build another full-sized studio in California, so that could grow the business even more."

"Is that what Max is working on?"

I took a small sip of my tea and watched as he slowly walked around the side of the counter.

Turning me in my chair, he leaned down to kiss the side of my neck. He stepped in close to me and pushed my legs apart. "Let me be really clear about something. You might not be ready for us, and I might not be ready for you, but you will never belong to my brother."

Leaning back, I looked into his dark, heated eyes and saw possession and desire. All I could do was nod as he leaned down to kiss me.

He put his hands on the back of my pants and gently squeezed my bottom. When he pulled back from me, I had to shake my head to clear the lust-induced fog.

I whispered, "I was just making small talk."

He kissed my nose. "And I just wanted to be clear."

He went back around the counter to finish cooking, moving effortlessly as he pulled out plates and silverware.

I waited until the energy crackling between us settled down, and then I asked, "What do you mean when you say 'I'm not ready for us.'?"

He pulled the waffle from the iron and split it in half, placing two pieces of fried chicken on each plate and carrying them to the table. "C'mon. Grab the syrup, if you would, please."

Taking the syrup to the table with me, I sat next to him and waited for him to answer me.

He noticed I wasn't eating and put his fork down on the side of his plate. He reached for my hand and kissed the tips of my fingers. "You are everything good for me. Everything I could lose myself in. I see you, and I see love and flowers and light. I can't risk losing you before I even have you. You just came out of something pretty significant—a lot of things significant—and I need you to be grounded when I'm ready for you."

Emotion bubbled up inside me, and I burst into tears. I wrapped an arm around my middle and buried my face in my other hand.

"Charlotte. Oh, my God, don't cry. Why are you crying?"

He slid the legs of the chair back, and then he was lifting me in his arms, carrying me to the couch. He cradled me across his lap, my head buried under his chin.

I could hear his heartbeat as my tears slowed, and he mumbled good-naturedly, "I guess we won't be eating chicken and waffles."

"I don't know what happened. I'm so sorry."

"You don't need to apologize." He lifted my chin with his finger. "Charlotte, we are going to be lovers. We just need time."

My head was resting against his arm. He wiped the tears from my eyes with his thumb.

Tentatively, I asked, "What did you mean when you said 'When you're ready for me.'?"

Groaning, he leaned his head on the back of the couch and smiled at me. "I never should have invited you to dinner."

"You don't have to tell me if you don't want to."

With a heavy sigh, he said, "My divorce from Myla isn't final. You know I filed. We'd been separated for much longer. I guess I was just lazy. She'd already moved in with her boyfriend, and she didn't want anything from me, so it was pretty straightforward." He shifted a little bit so he could get his arms around me. "Myla was in a motorcycle accident a few months back or so." He looked pensive and shook his head. "Honestly, I can't even remember the date."

I wanted to tell him I knew, but I didn't want to get Erin in trouble for gossiping.

He stared blankly across the room and continued. "She's on life support, and because I'm still her husband, I have to sign the papers to suspend artificial heart and lung function."

My face froze in a mask of shock and empathy. "Paxton, this is awful. I'm so sorry."

His eyes focused on me. "Hardly first date conversation." He added teasingly, "Or is this second date?"

I ignored the rhetorical question. "What are you going to do?"

"I couldn't *do* anything. Her parents sued me to prevent me from signing the forms."

"Can they do that?"

"They can—but they won't win. Story's on my side, and Myla wouldn't want to live like this. For all intents and purposes, she's gone. She's brain dead. She won't recover."

"Her poor parents. They must be heartbroken."

"I'm sure they are. They won't talk to me. We talk through our lawyers."

The papers that had fallen out of his briefcase in Denver made sense now. So did the love from his mom, the meeting with Solara on the steps, and all of the support and love for Paxton.

My eyes teared up again. "How is Story doing?"

"She's sad. Angry. She's been sleeping around a lot." He laughed.

"And you?" I prepared myself for his answer.

A moment passed before he responded. His eyes met mine, and I couldn't look away. "I haven't been with anyone since I met a brown-haired, provocative, doe-eyed, sensual woman in a hallway at one of my studios. She has the sexiest bit of ass that peeks out from her dance shorts, and I haven't been able to think of much else since I touched her. She gasped when I held her, and I can't wait for the day when I hear that sound again."

"Paxton."

He looked to my mouth. "And now you know why I'm such a mess."

We were both breathing heavily; his words had turned me on. "Would you really have... Would you have, you know, at the studio?"

"Would I have fucked you? Yes." He tightened his hold on me. "I'm not proud of that, Charlotte. I'm not. But I was in a weird place." He put his forehead to mine. "I'm still in a weird place, but I don't want to let you go."

I reached up to pull him down to me, and he adjusted himself so he was lying on top of me.

"Do you find it odd that your mom was my ballet instructor?"

"No." He was kissing my neck and working his way down my shirt-front. "You have too many clothes on."

"I thought we were waiting."

"Your skin is so soft."

He was totally distracted, and I giggled when he nipped at my belly. "I think I want my waffle now."

"You can have them for breakfast." And then he kissed me.

I didn't sleep at Paxton's house that night. We made out on the couch for a while, and then I left, promising to text him when I got home. He promised to make me breakfast soon.

On Thursday, Story and I discussed training for the Irvine show and decided to start the following week.

We were sitting at the front counter in between classes, and she told me to start listening to music. "Pick something dark and sexy. Something that you feel in your soul. I want you to be so into it that you don't even know you're on stage. You should feel like the music is taking every last drop of your sexuality with it—and that you just had the best sex of your life when the song ends."

"Am I blushing?"

She winked at me. "You will be." She pulled out her iPhone and started playing some recommendations for me. "Seriously, Charlotte, you totally have this. I promise I will make a routine for you that is so sensual, and tasteful, you won't feel ashamed at all. I promise."

The rest of the week flew by after that.

Max came to town on Friday, and I had a chance to talk with him a little more. He was friendly, but I could also tell he was here for business, not to get to know me.

By the time Saturday arrived, I felt like I'd worked for the studio forever. Girls were greeting me by name, joking with me, and getting to know me.

I spent a lot of time talking with Vivian, and I learned she was a marketing major. I told her I was in sales and marketing as well, and that I would be happy to mentor her.

She had looked confused when I told her, so I had to explain that it was in a previous life. After that, I tried to keep it to myself. I didn't want anyone feeling weird around me.

I came to realize that Paxton and Solara always took the event crew out to dinner after an event. The Phoenix show was no exception.

After the show, the girls all changed into swanky cocktail dresses, and we all met at The Beverly. Vivian joined Story, Solara, and me, and I was happy to add her to the list of my new friends.

The bar was sleek and elegant with prohibition-era décor. Black leather, half-moon couches with deep button rivets lined one wall. I was suddenly craving a Manhattan.

Max and Paxton got us all a booth, and I slid in next to him. Story sat next to Max, and Solara and Vivian spent most of their time at the bar.

After a waitress delivered our drinks and Paxton ordered some appetizers, Max asked me about my previous work.

"You worked in finance, right?"

"A financial planning services company. I was in sales and marketing. Not quite the math whiz, but good with people."

"Did Paxton tell you we were expanding to California?"

I glanced to Paxton, trying to gauge how much I was allowed to tell them. He was relaxed and smiling, so I figured it was okay. "He did. That sounds exciting for you guys."

"If you don't have anything lined up after competition season, we could use your help. Paxton told me you set up some pretty good marketing campaigns before the Houston show."

"Actually, Erin set them up. But yes, we brainstormed together."

Paxton took a sip of his drink and smiled at me. "Charlotte was Erin's 'thought partner.'"

Story asked, "What's a thought partner?"

Paxton and I both laughed, and I explained what it was.

Glancing around the bar, I thought to myself that I finally felt... happy.

Max and Paxton had started in on the new business plan, and I excused myself to use the ladies' room.

Two girls were already in there applying lipstick; I stepped around them to wash my hands.

The one closest to me was blabbering on about two girls at the bar. "Did you see how desperate they looked? They kept looking at the two hot guys in the booth."

My back was to them in the vanity mirror, so they couldn't see me. Slowing my hand washing, I listened to the rest of their conversation.

"Seriously, they look like prostitutes." She smacked her lips in the mirror. "The skinny one looks like a stripper. Those guys would never go for that."

My face flushed. I was so angry I almost pulled on the back of her head.

They left the bathroom. The bleach-blonde one muttered, "See if you can distract the blond one from the girl with the shorter hair. He's totally my type."

Their profiles were visible as the door swung shut behind them. I took a couple of deep, calming breaths.

Following them back to the bar, I braced myself up against the counter to the left of the one with the fake eyelashes and bleach-blonde hair. Solara and Vivian were on my other side.

From afar, she'd looked pretty. Up close, she just looked mean.

As sweet as sugar, I said, "Hello. How are you guys tonight? I'm Charlotte."

They were pleasant but wary. The blonde one told me her name was Susan. In my head, I rolled my eyes. *Great, now I will never forget her.*

"Nice to meet you, Susan. I just saw you in the bathroom. That's a lovely lip color. What's it called—'I'm a bitch.'?"

She looked confused for a second and then challenging. "Lovely dress. Goodwill?"

"Oh, I'm so sorry, I didn't introduce you to my friends." I stepped back so she could see Solara. "Solara, this is Susan. Susan, this is Solara, Chief financial officer for L.O.V.E Enterprises: a National fitness equipment supply company."

I glanced back at Paxton, and he tilted his head in a bemused way.

Next thing I knew, he was standing between Susan and me. "Everything okay?"

Susan turned to look at him, puffing out her inflatable chest. "Actually, no. This woman here insulted me, and I don't even know who she is. Maybe you could get the manager to ask her to leave."

I was infuriated. I pointed my finger at her, raising my voice. "You insulted my friend in the bathroom. You don't know anything about this woman, judging her because she doesn't look like you. She is incredibly smart, and kind, and talented, and she can do things on a pole you only wish you could do if you were strong enough to heave your skinny ass up on one."

Solara had stepped up beside me and was pulling on my arm. "Charlotte, it's okay. C'mon, it's okay."

I was shaking.

Smoothly, Paxton leaned into Susan. Silkily, he said, "What do you think I should do about her?"

"I think we should have the manager ask her to leave. She was rude and offensive. And then, maybe you and I could get a drink." She purred the last words. Bile rose in my throat as adrenaline rushed through me.

He glanced at me over his shoulder and grinned wickedly before turning back to Susan. He moved his head closer to her. "Well, the woman you insulted is my sister, and you probably owe her an apology. And the feisty one? That's my girlfriend. I think I might go fuck her. She just became so painfully beautiful to me for defending her friend and my family. You should consider that. And no, I won't be having a drink with you."

Her mouth dropped open as Paxton stood and addressed us. "You guys ready to leave?"

I grabbed my purse from the booth and stormed out the front door—with Solara and Vivian right behind me. A laughing Max and a stunned Story followed.

I turned in a circle when I stepped out onto the sidewalk.

Pleading with Solara to forgive me, I started to cry.

She laughed her bold laugh and hugged me. "Charlotte, you don't need to apologize to me. You were my champion tonight. How can I not love you for that?"

"It was so unprofessional and rude. I should have just ignored her. I acted like a child."

Story had her arms crossed but was smiling. "Apparently, you got a boyfriend out of it."

I looked at her apologetically, sighed, and then said, "Story—"

"Don't worry about it. I'm not blind. He had to move on sometime from my sister."

Paxton came boldly out the front door. "I paid everyone's bill. Thank you very much."

We all stood staring at him, waiting for him to say something else about the incident.

Putting out his arms, palms up, he said, "What?"

Solara and Vivian both hugged me, and we burst out laughing.

Max just shook his head. "This is what I'm missing?"

I went to Paxton, trying to control my laughter. "I am so sorry."

His response was a deep kiss, consuming me and letting everyone know he was serious about me. He held my cheeks in his large palms. "Nothing to forgive."

Solara interrupted us. "Charlotte, I can honestly say that was the most entertaining after-party ever."

Paxton tucked me in close and whispered, "C'mon, I'll take you home, Rowdy."

CHAPTER 23

THE GARAGE DOORS had not even fully shut before Paxton and I were tearing each other's clothes off.

His mouth was on mine as he held me with one arm and opened the door to the kitchen with the other. Against my lips, he muttered, "I can't wait, Charlotte. I need you. Please say yes."

Between kisses, I responded, "Yes, yes, yes."

We fumbled in the kitchen, trying to get our shoes off, and then came back together to kiss some more. Paxton walked me backward down the hall.

I tried to get his buckle off, but he pushed my hands aside and pulled my dress up and over my head.

He groaned and stopped for a moment in the hallway. Pushing me up against the wall, he lowered his head to kiss the tops of my breasts. His hands reached behind me and gently lowered my panties so I could step out of them.

He kissed my belly on his way back up, and then he lifted me up so I could wrap my legs around his waist. His mouth was all over my chest and neck as he walked us further down the hall into his bedroom.

He was leaving a trail of my clothes behind. I whispered, "My panties."

"We'll get them later."

It was pitch black in the room, and he stumbled into the door, lowering my feet to the ground. I stood in darkness.

"Stay right there."

I heard him shuffling through the bedroom. Then a click as he turned on the lamp on the nightstand.

Prowling back toward me, he left me no time to look around. His mouth came crashing down to mine, his tongue skillfully dancing with mine. I remembered the feel of his tongue on my sex and moaned as he reached around me and unhooked my bra.

My breasts fell free, and he lowered his head to give each of them a lick, moaning in delight. He growled my name, "Charlotte."

Closing my eyes, I leaned my head back and just let him love me. One of his hands roamed down my body, and then he gently slid a finger inside me. Then two. I gasped, my knees buckling.

"Oh, you're so fucking wet!"

I couldn't hold myself up any longer. "Paxton."

"Right here, baby. Right here."

He carried me to the bed and gently placed me on the end. Dropping to his knees, he put his mouth to me. I was so turned on, I came instantly, holding his head in place and calling out his name.

My feet dropped to the floor, and he whispered huskily to me to scoot back. He removed the rest of his clothes in a flurry and then climbed over me, so he was resting between my legs.

Bracing himself above me, he reached over me to get a condom out of his nightstand. I lifted my head to kiss his chest, gently touching his sides with my fingers, while he was busy ripping the wrapper open.

He paused briefly—his tip at my entrance—and I squirmed beneath him, granting him permission. Dark eyes bored into mine. I parted my lips on an inhale as he slowly penetrated me, filling me, burying himself in me.

"Keep your eyes open." Slowly pulling out, he waited. Then, he pushed back in until he was pressed up against me with great control, rolling his hips and applying perfect pressure.

I couldn't look away, but I also could barely keep my eyes open during this sweet torture.

Again. And again. He pushed into me, then out—taunting me, teasing me until my toes curled and that familiar tingle intensified. He thrust faster and then reached between us, rubbing his thumb over my clit. I came so hard my back arched, and I bucked beneath him, screaming, "Oh, fuuuucckkkk."

Then I collapsed as he hammered against me. He tensed, lowered his head, and buried it in my neck, groaning my name.

Slowly, he climbed off me and went to the restroom. When he returned, he flipped me over and ran his hands all over my back. He rested them at my bottom—squeezing and massaging. He slapped me gently, then ran his hands softly over me, soothing. Finally, he slid his hands between my legs and pushed his fingers in me again. I was turning to putty, my mind in a foggy bliss. It only got foggier when he whispered,

"So sweet."

He left me for a second. With my face pressed into the mattress— and my body buzzing from my recent orgasms—I couldn't be bothered to even turn my head to see where he had gone. When he returned, I heard the foil of another condom being opened, and then he knelt between my legs, gripped my hips, and pulled me up onto his lap. My back was flush against his chest as he pushed into me again. I dropped my head back onto his shoulder.

His arms circled me. I was floating in a euphoric state. Enraptured by him, filled with him, I pushed myself down, taking him deeper.

His deep voice whispered in my ear, "Touch yourself. I want to watch you come."

I reached between my legs and rubbed the spot that would spiral me out of control. Harder and faster, I panted and then crashed. I barely had time to relax before he was pushing me over and slamming into me from behind like a piston.

I'd never been fucked like this before. Now I knew why I'd felt branded that day at the studio when he'd looked at me—I'd known he would.

He came again, gripping my hips. Kissing my back, he whispered over and over again, "Beautiful. So beautiful."

Gently, as if he was handling a fragile doll, he turned me over and kissed me on the mouth. Sweetly and lovingly.

"Don't go anywhere. I'll be right back."

He kissed my nose. I watched as he went into the bathroom and came out a minute later, dressed in drawstring pajama bottoms. He was holding a T-shirt and a wet towel.

Sitting down next to me on the bed, he caressed me with the warm towel. He wiped the sweat from my chest and shoulders, trailed down my hips and legs, and then rested between my thighs to both clean and comfort. I gazed at him as he lovingly looked at every inch he covered.

When his eyes returned to mine, I smiled tentatively.

"You're beautiful, Charlotte."

I tried to say thank you, but the words got stuck in my throat. I mouthed them.

He threw the towel on the ground next to the bed and quietly told me to sit up. Slowly, he put one of his T-shirts on over my head; I lifted my arms to help him.

His palm stroked my head, smoothing back my hair, pulling it free from the neck of the shirt. I watched him, transfixed, as his eyes skimmed my face. The soft material smelled like fabric softener, and it caressed my skin.

With mock seriousness, he said, "You're going to need to stay the night."

I giggled and said, "Now that I have been thoroughly debauched?"

"Not thoroughly—but we can fix that later. Scoot over. You wore me out."

I slid over on the mattress. He crawled in behind me, snuggling up and wrapping me in his arms.

In the middle of the night, his hands caressed me. His fingers gently separated my folds and caused me to wake; I squirmed against him in my half-awake state.

The T-shirt was pushed up against my waist, and his hardness pressed up against me. I raised my leg just a bit and pushed back, inviting him in.

When he slid into me, I closed my eyes and let him take me. In my dreamy state, I felt him everywhere. In. Out. And again, until my orgasm roared, and I drifted back off to sleep, wrapped up in him like a cocoon.

I was momentarily disoriented when I woke up in the unfamiliar room, in the unfamiliar bed—alone.

The exposed wood-beam ceiling was visible above me. Lying on my back, I stared up at the ceiling fan and smoothed the covers over me, resting my hands on my stomach. The dark walnut headboard matched the executive-style desk placed in front of a large picture window looking out to the desert. An antique rose-patterned chair sat at the desk.

Gold lamp shades covered the bronze lamps, and gold-colored, Victorian-style curtains covered the windows. They should have looked feminine. Instead, they gave the room a cozy, romantic contrast to the bed and desk's manliness. Multi-colored, Native American area rugs covered most of the tile flooring. This room was eclectic and yet perfect.

The house was silent. I rolled over to Paxton's side of the bed, burying my head in his pillow and inhaling. Just his smell turned me on. I sighed and tucked the pillow into me.

"Hey, sleepyhead."

I lifted my head and saw him in the doorway, shirtless and sweaty. "Hey."

He came to me and sat down on the edge of the bed. "I thought we'd moved on to 'Good morning, Paxton.'"

I lay back, stretched, and smiled. "Good morning, Paxton."

He leaned down to kiss me. "Good morning, Charlotte."

"You stink."

"I went for a run." He left the bed and headed for the shower. "Give me five minutes, and I'll make us breakfast. Coffee's on if you want some."

The shower spray turned on, and I heard the familiar click of the door opening and shutting.

Pulling his T-shirt off, I threw it on the bed and followed him into the bathroom.

The laminated glass fogged from the steam. He was humming, and I smiled as I opened the door and stepped in behind him.

His face was to the spray. He rubbed his hands over his face and turned to look at me. "This is a nice surprise."

My hands rested on his chest, massaging him. Then I trailed one hand down to cup and stroke him. He grew in my hand, and I smiled knowingly up at him.

Looking at him coquettishly, I said, "It's Sunday."

"Waffles?"

"You said, and I quote, 'I will fuck you six ways from Sunday.'"

He reached around me, pulled me close, and then lowered his mouth to bite on my earlobe. "I did say that, didn't I?"

"Mm-hmm. And by my calculation, you owe me two."

He reached behind him, turned off the water, and lowered himself down to his knees. Pushing my legs apart, he ran his tongue up inside me. Then, pulling back for just a moment, he looked up at me wantonly and said, "Then I should get started."

And he did.

Later that week, I found myself alone at the studio.

Not completely alone. Vivian was there, and a few dancers were in and out practicing routines. But Solara, Max, and Paxton had left the office together Tuesday afternoon, and they hadn't returned on Wednesday.

Tuesday night, Story gave me instructions on closing the store and told me she would call the next morning to check on me.

"Are you sure you want me closing the studio?"

Story looked at me like she didn't have any patience left. "You're completely competent, Charlotte. I think you can handle it."

I was taken aback by her abrupt tone. "Story, did I do something to offend you?"

She rubbed her temples. "No. Just family issues I'm trying to work through."

I wanted her to confide in me, so I took a chance and said, "If you need someone to talk to, I…" I jumped right in, "I'm a good listener."

Looking at me like I was an alien, she grabbed her bag and headed toward the front door. "I'll call you later."

I was left staring after her, not really sure what had just happened.

On Thursday, none of them had returned. We had a competition in Las Vegas that weekend, and we were supposed to leave Friday morning.

I texted Solara at noon: *Coming in today?*

They'd all deserted me.

Next, I texted Paxton: *Hey.*

That should get his attention.

Sitting at the front desk, I was reviewing the event agenda for the weekend when Vivian came running down the stairs screaming. "Charlotte, come quick, come upstairs."

I jumped off the stool and met her at the foot of the stairs. "What's the matter?"

"The girl… That girl that was practicing… I don't know her name. She fell. She fell."

Her words were broken, and I told her to calm down. "Take a breath. Tell me what happened."

She talked as she led me back upstairs to the larger of the two-pole studios. "She was practicing a split hip hold. You know what that is, right?"

We continued to the top of the steps. I nodded and rolled my arm in a "keep going" gesture.

"Right. Well, she was practicing the hold, and somehow, in transition, she slipped and fell from the top. She definitely broke her arm, but she might have also cracked her collarbone."

I entered the dance room, and the girl was on her back crying. I knelt down beside her. "Hey. Hey, you okay?"

Tear-filled eyes met mine. "I think I broke my arm. And my hip hurts too."

Oh, goodness. I looked around for Vivian. "Vivian, will you run back downstairs and get my phone?"

She bolted from the door, and I looked back at the girl on the floor. "I'll get you taken care of. Get you to the hospital."

When Vivian returned with my phone, I immediately called Paxton. No answer.

"Ugh! Where are you guys?" I said to myself.

I tried Solara. No answer.

I tapped my phone in my palm, looking at the girl but not really seeing her, trying to figure out what to do.

"Do you have someone you can call…?"

I looked at the girl with raised eyebrows, and she responded, "Hope."

"Do you have someone you can call, Hope?"

Her eyes teared up. "No."

"I need to call 911."

"No, please don't."

There was fear in her eyes. And then I realized. She was a stripper. She didn't have anyone, and she probably didn't have any way to pay for an expensive ambulance ride. My heart hurt.

With as much consolation as I could muster, I told her we needed to get her to the hospital.

Tears welled in her eyes. "I know. Okay."

I turned to Vivian. "Vivian, can you please drive Hope to the hospital?"

She whispered, thinking Hope couldn't hear her. "I can't, Charlotte. I have class this afternoon at three."

Unbelievable. "Okay." I turned to Hope. "I guess it's you and me."

Vivian asked, "Why don't we just call 911?"

I stood from my kneeling position. "Ambulances are too expensive, and I can't let her go to the hospital alone."

"I can stay until I need to leave for class, and then I can close up for you."

"Yes, please. And can you call anyone registered for the evening classes and cancel them? I don't know where everyone is—and emergency room visits always take hours."

"I can do that."

I turned back to Hope. "Can you stand, Hope?"

She tried to get up and winced in pain. Vivian ran to my side, and we both gently lifted her from the floor.

Vivian got Hope's bag from the locker room, grabbed my purse and keys, and met us at the front door.

I texted her my cell number. "Call me if you have trouble locking up. If anyone complains about the cancellations, tell them we will give them a free private lesson with Story."

Her eyes bugged out. "Are you sure?"

I laughed sardonically, "Oh, yeah, I'm sure."

On the drive to the hospital, Hope told me she didn't have insurance.

"That's okay. They have welfare programs for these types of things. Don't worry about it. Just..." What on Earth was I thinking? "Let's just get you taken care of, okay?"

I parked in the emergency room parking lot and helped Hope inside.

It was, thankfully, not that busy. The administrator behind the desk checked us in and gave me a bunch of paperwork to fill out.

I sat next to Hope in the blue, wood-framed waiting room chairs and started asking her all the questions on the forms. "What's your date of birth, Hope?"

She told me, and I put down the pen.

"You aren't even eighteen." My voice was laced with frustration.

Not getting a response from her, I sighed and continued with the paperwork.

When it came to the parent/guardian signature, I groaned and put my name. My life was getting messier and messier.

I returned the packet to the lady behind the desk and sat back down to wait with Hope.

"Charlotte, my arm hurts."

"I know it does. They'll get to you in just a few minutes."

Or hours, I thought.

She leaned her head on my shoulder, and I stared blankly at the TV mounted on the wall. One of those real-life court drama shows was playing, and I was momentarily grateful I had a day job. Then again, I didn't. Not really. My life had been so much neater before.

Without disturbing Hope, I pulled my cell phone out of my pocket and tried to send another text to Paxton and Solara. The signal just kept spinning.

"Hope? Sit up, sweetie. I need to get some coffee."

"Should I wait for you if they call me?"

"No, go ahead and go in. I'll be right back. I'll find you."

I left her sitting by herself and meandered down the hospital hallways, trying to find the cafeteria or a Starbucks.

Following the signs that pointed toward the cafeteria, I came around a corner and saw Paxton staring into a vending machine.

He wasn't moving. Just looking blankly at the selections. His hair was mussed, and it looked like he hadn't shaved since last weekend.

I walked toward him.

"Paxton?" He wasn't even registering that I was calling his name. I said, a little more emphatically, "Paxton!"

When he lifted his eyes to me, I jerked back in surprise. His eyes were haunted. Pained. Despondent.

I ran to his side and held on to his arms. "Paxton, what happened? What's the matter?"

His eyes were glassy. He swallowed a few times before speaking. "It's... She's..."

CHAPTER 24

I TUGGED ON his arm and pulled him alongside me, searching for an empty room.

Down a hall from the vending machine wall was a locked door. I pushed the access button, heard a loud buzzer, and the double doors electronically swung open.

I had no idea where we were, but at least someone had let us in.

He followed dutifully alongside me as I peeked surreptitiously into room after room until I found an empty one.

I pushed him in before me and then shut the door. The lights were off, and the room had a gray hue to it. Half-opened aluminum blinds let in the only light from outside.

He took a seat on the single bed, buried his face in his hands, and started to cry.

I had no idea what to do, so I simply sat next to him and rubbed his back.

After a brief moment, his tears stopped abruptly, and he sat up straight and braced his hands on his knees. Staring up at the ceiling, he blinked a couple of times and swore. Then he stood and went into the bathroom, grabbed a hand towel, and wiped his eyes. "Ah, fuck! This sucks."

When he stepped out, he put his hands on his hips, puffed out his cheeks, and then exhaled. "Hi."

I frowned at him. "Hi?"

"What are you doing here? Did Sol call you?" He appeared dazed.

"No, Paxton. No one called me. No one's called me since Tuesday. Story left the studio Tuesday night, and this is the first I've seen of any of you."

"How did you know to come to the hospital?"

"I came because one of the girls that practices solo fell from the pole, and I needed to have her arm looked at. I think she broke it."

"Did you get her to fill out a statement?"

"Paxton! What is going on? Why are you here? Is it Myla?"

At the mention of her name, tears pooled in his eyes. I waited while he made himself comfortable on the hospital bed. He pulled his feet up onto the mattress, bent his legs, and then rested his wrists on his knees.

I pulled one knee up and sat on the end of the bed. Waiting.

"She..." He cleared his throat. "Monday morning my lawyers called. They said her parents had dropped the suit. Story had been begging them to let her go—to let them, let me, let her go."

His chest was shaking as he worked to control his tears. Resting his head back on the inclined mattress, he stared off at the wall. "On Tuesday, we signed the papers to unplug everything. Story was supposed to let you know."

His eyes met mine; they were filled with sadness.

Quietly, I said, "She didn't. She ran out Tuesday afternoon. I thought someone would be back yesterday, and then when I couldn't get a hold of anyone... well, I was getting a little pissed off. Why didn't you let me know?"

He reached out his hand, and I scooted forward. He pulled me between his legs, held my head to his chest, kissed it, and then stroked my hair.

"I'm sorry. The days have blended together this week. Everything moved so fast, and I didn't want to burden you. I wasn't thinking clearly. Forgive me?"

"Is she…Is she gone?"

He laughed derisively. "I have no idea."

I sat up and looked at him. "What do you mean you have no idea?"

"I have no idea." He laughed again. "The doctors keep saying, 'It's almost time, it's almost time.' My parents have been here all day; Solara and Story have been here all day. And she just keeps breathing. It's like she's intentionally torturing me."

"Paxton, that's an awful thought."

His tone turned somber. "I know. I'm just so tired."

I tried to make him feel better. "I've heard it could take hours or days. I've heard. I don't really know."

"Hmm. I guess."

He put his head back again. "I'm glad you're here."

I stood from the bed. "Actually, I should get back. They might have taken her back already, and she needs me."

"Who is it?"

"Hope."

He shook his head. "I don't know who that is."

I stood from the bed. "She's a young girl. She doesn't have anyone."

He had zoned out again.

I reminded him about the Vegas show.

He stood and came to hug me. Burying his head in my neck, he said with grief, "Solara will go with you. Story and I need to stay behind."

"Paxton." I didn't really know what to say.

"I know. I'll call you later. I promise." He took my face in his hands and placed a gentle kiss on my lips. "I'll walk out with you."

He held my hand, and we stepped out of the room.

The nurses at the station saw us and addressed Paxton. "Mr. Crown, your family is looking for you."

I whipped my head up to look at Paxton. "She's here? In this ward?"

He nodded wordlessly.

Solara came around the corner. "Paxton! Where have you been? You've been gone for almost an hour." It took her half a second to realize I was standing right next to him. "Charlotte? What are you doing here? Did Paxton call you?"

Paxton spoke for me. "No one called her. She's been running the studio for two days without any of us."

She looked at me in surprise. "I thought Story told you."

I shook my head. "No."

"Oh, Charlotte, I'm so sorry." She enveloped me in a hug. "We're having a bit of a family crisis. Are you—"

"She's here with one of the solo members. She fell and broke her arm." Paxton said.

"Really?"

I looked at her, perplexed, and nodded my head. "Yes, Solara, really."

Solara rubbed her temples. "I'm sorry. This has just been a really rough week."

"I know. I'm sorry too."

She looked back at Paxton, with sadness and compassion. "It's time, Paxton. Really. It's time. Her parents are asking that we're all there with her."

A deep sorrow settled in my heart.

He turned back to me, stroking my cheek. "I have to go."

I nodded, and he leaned in to kiss me chastely. My chest tightened as I held in my tears.

Solara took his hand, and the two of them walked off. Paxton's back was straight, and his head was head up, steeling himself for what was to come.

Shaking off the solemnity, I remembered I needed to get back to Hope.

I made my way back to the emergency room and learned Hope had been taken back to X-ray. The nurse led me to the room they had reserved for her. I waited on the reclining chair they had in the corner for visitors.

She was wheeled back in half an hour later, her arm wrapped in a neon orange cast.

The grandfatherly doctor smiled at me as he entered. "You must be Charlotte?"

I stood, wiped my hands on my pants, and shook his hand. "Yes, sir. How's our girl?"

He smiled at Hope. "She's going to be fine. Broken arm and a bunch of bruises, but otherwise intact."

"She said her clavicle hurt. It's not broken?"

"Not broken. But no more dancing for a bit. She needs to heal. And I want to see her back in four weeks."

He turned his attention back to Hope. "You'll be back dancing in no time. But try and stay away from the top of the pole, if you can. It's a long way down."

I was so impressed with his non-judgmental demeanor. It was refreshing to hear, and I was so grateful for his acceptance of her.

She smiled tentatively at him, and I said, "Thank you, Doctor."

"My pleasure. The nurse will be in shortly with her prescription and discharge papers."

After the doctor left, Hope started to cry.

I rushed to her side. "Why are you crying?"

She hiccupped. "I don't have another job, Charlotte. If I can't dance, I can't pay my bills, my rent, or my groceries."

Inwardly, I seethed. This girl was a minor, and someone had allowed her to live like this. "We'll figure it out, okay? Maybe you can help out at the studio? I'll talk to Paxton and Solara. Don't worry. You just focus on healing."

By the time we returned back to the studio, and Hope's car, it was dark. The studio's only visible lights were the flooring lights that went up the stairs from the lobby to the top's open area.

Hope had fallen asleep, her prescription pain meds shoved in the top of her bag.

I gently nudged her. "Hope. Hope, wake up."

She woke, wiping drool from her cheek. "Where are we?"

"Back at your car. I don't think you should drive, though. What's your address? I'm going to drive you home."

"No. I'm fine."

"No, you're not. What's your address?" She mumbled it, and I put the car back in drive.

The neighborhood was not the most desirable, and the apartment complex looked shabby even in the dark. I could only imagine its deplorable state during the day. A group of teens was smoking in the parking lot. Hope's head hung in shame as I circled through the parking lot.

She pointed toward the last building. "It's the second one on the left, up ahead."

I drove right past the building, left the complex, and turned on the main road that lead to my parents' house.

"What are you doing?"

"You're coming home with me. You need someone to take care of you, and I'm going to be out of town this weekend. I'm taking you to my parents."

"You live with your parents?"

Her tone was laced with disdain, and hearing it from her point of view, it did seem a little embarrassing. I should accelerate my own apartment hunting. If she only knew what I used to have.

Interesting how easy a teen could shame me. "I just moved back a few weeks ago and haven't had time to find a place of my own."

She stared out the car window and mumbled, "Fine." A sullen expression flashed on her face, but her body visibly relaxed.

I was doing the right thing.

When we reached my parents' house, I gave her a brief tour that ended in the kitchen. I told her it was okay to help herself to whatever she wanted. My mom had heard us rustling around in the kitchen and came in to greet us.

"Hi, Mom. This is Hope. She's going to be staying here for a week or so."

"Hi, Hope."

"Hi, Mrs. Chase. Thank you for letting me stay."

I shook my head at my mom from behind Hope's back, hoping she wouldn't ask me anything just yet.

My mom was gracious and asked if we were hungry.

Hope responded that she just wanted to go to bed.

"Okay, dear. I'll see you in the morning."

Hope said good night. I showed her to the guest room, got her settled, and gave her something of mine to sleep in.

When I returned to the kitchen, my mom had made me a cup of tea and a half sandwich.

She waited until I'd taken a few bites and washed them down. "Oh, my God! This is either *so good* or I am just *so hungry*."

Resting against the sink, she said, "Are you going to tell me what's going on?"

I relayed the events of the day. By the time I reached the end of the story, my mom had made her way to the stool beside me and was holding my hand. "Oh sweetheart, how terrible for them. I am so sorry. You had a rough day, didn't you?"

"Not as rough as Paxton and Solara, but yeah, this is one for the books, for sure."

"What are you going to do about the girl?"

"I have no idea. I wasn't really thinking clearly, but as soon as we drove by her apartment, I knew I couldn't leave her there."

She laughed. "Aren't you leaving for Vegas tomorrow?"

I looked at her sheepishly. "Can you take care of her until I get back on Sunday? I promise I'll figure something out while I'm gone."

She patted my hand and said, "Sure. I can do that. But she's not a lost dog; you can't keep her."

"I know, Mom, I know." I stared at my plate. "Life was certainly more peaceful in Houston."

She patted my hand again and then left me for bed.

By the time I changed into my pajamas, brushed my teeth, and crawled into bed. I felt like I was a hundred years old. How had life turned so fast?

Solara was late for the plane. She was the last to board, and she looked horrible: tired and wrung out.

I waited until she was settled in the seat next to me before asking how she was doing.

"I'm okay. I stayed with Story last night. She's not doing well."

"And Paxton?"

I was hurt that he hadn't called me.

Solara looked at me with sad eyes. "He's okay, Charlotte. Just give him a little time. I know he cares about you. I can see it. I can feel it. But he just, from his point of view, killed his wife. Ex-wife, kind of, but that's a burden no one wants."

She took my hands in hers and turned sideways in the seat. "I knew you were someone special as soon as he came home from Houston. He complained about you when he told me you would be calling, but he was standing up straighter, and his eyes weren't flat anymore. There was something there, even though he was fighting it. Don't give up on him. Let him get through this."

I put my head back on the seat, squeezing my eyes shut so I wouldn't cry.

"And now, we need to tough through this weekend. It's just me and you and the Vegas crew, so it will be crazy busy. But we can do it. We're strong." Solara said.

"Fake it until we make it?"

"Fake it 'til we make it."

The flight to Vegas was uneventful. As soon as we landed, Solara shifted into professional mode. She was much better at it than I could have been, and I simply followed her lead.

I knew what to do now, so I wasn't a burden to her, but it was certainly taxing on just the two of us.

By the time the event was over Saturday night, we both looked like we hadn't slept in a week, and neither one of us wanted company. But Solara was determined that we would press on. We would take the crew to dinner with smiles on our faces—and no complaining. This was their event, and we were going to celebrate them.

When the evening ended, and Solara and I were comfortably settled in an Uber back to our hotel, the smiles dropped. We both audibly sighed.

"You did good this weekend, Charlotte. Thank you for being here." Her eyes were closed.

I whispered, "You're welcome."

We both went to our own rooms at the hotel, and we agreed to meet in the lobby the next morning for breakfast before the flight back to Phoenix.

Flinging myself face first on the bed, I was out.

Shortly after midnight, my cell phone buzzed in my hand: Paxton.

I answered. "Hello?"

"Sleeping?" His voice was slurred.

"No."

With a masculine laugh, he asked, "How was the show?"

"Uneventful."

We were both silent.

"How are you, Paxton?"

He groaned. I imagined he was sitting in his bed, leaning back against the headboard.

"I'm okay. I wish you were here."

I closed my eyes and whispered, "Me too."

Another moment passed, each of us listening to the other breathe.

"I'll call Solara in the morning, but I wanted you to know that the funeral is on Monday. I'm closing the studio on Monday and Tuesday. We don't have anyone to work with, and I know you and Sol will need to recover from the weekend. I asked Story to send an email to our clients."

This wasn't the time to tell him I had someone in mind to help out at the studio. Instead, I simply responded, "I understand."

"Do you want to get dinner this week?"

My heart broke for him. He was trying to be normal.

"I'd like that."

"I'll call you in a few days."

"Good night, Paxton."

"Charlotte…" I waited. "Good night."

CHAPTER 25

WHEN I CAME to work on Wednesday, I breathed a sigh of relief that Hope's car hadn't been towed. By the looks of it, I couldn't imagine anyone would want it anyway.

When I'd come to work that day, I'd brought Hope with me. The morning I'd left for Las Vegas, I explained to my dad what I'd been doing, the help Hope would need, and a plan for getting her into a safe environment.

"I can't bring her back to that apartment, and I know she can't stay here forever. But since I'm traveling, I don't have time to help her just yet."

Both my parents had been supportive: they took her in and were willing to act as caregivers. My dad had given me a big hug. He passed no judgment and told me, "As long as you're happy."

Hope had had plenty of rest over the last few days with my parents, and her fresh face now showed her younger age. She was excited about helping out at the studio, talking incessantly on the ride in about how she really liked most of the girls that worked there.

I'd talked with Solara on the plane ride back from Vegas, and she was more than happy to have the extra help.

She'd pointed her finger at me. "But she better not screw us over and show up late."

"I'll stress that point."

"Vivian has been with us for almost a year now. I'll start moving her to the front desk, and Hope can start off cleaning." She was musing to herself.

"You do know she has a cast on, right?"

"Can she Swiffer?"

"I guess so."

"Then she and Vivian can work it out."

And that had been the end of the conversation.

Getting back into the routine of work was easy. My former life only slightly crept in around the edges—when I bothered to think about it at all.

After lunch, Story asked me if I wanted to start choreographing my program.

She was sitting next to me at the front desk, and a pad of paper sat on the counter in front of her. She idly twirled a pen between her fingers and swung her crossed leg back and forth.

"Are you sure?" I said, trying to be respectful of her grieving. "We can wait if you need more time with your family. Or, whatever."

In a rare moment of vulnerability, she said softly, "I'm fine, Charlotte. It will help me keep my mind off things."

"I'm really sorry."

Her eyes glazed over. "Thank you."

"And if you want to take a break, or need a day, just let me know. I can work extra days or shifts. I've never lost someone close to me, so I can't imagine what you're feeling. But I'm here for you if you need me."

A tear fell, and she brushed at it with her finger. "You're just going to make us all fall in love with you, aren't you?"

Adrenaline shot through me. I didn't want to dwell on what she'd just said, nor did I question it. Happiness filled me that I might just fit in here. Instead, I turned on my phone and pulled up YouTube. "I think I found a song. Do you want to hear it?"

She nodded.

I found the tune, pressed play, and Story closed her eyes, moving her hands and shoulders to the rhythm. The breathy, reverberating words hit me in the pit of my stomach. This was my song.

Story's eyes opened when the song had ended. "Perfect."

A slow grin grew on my face, turning into a full-blown smile. "Perfect."

She jumped off the stool, grabbed her pen and paper, and walked toward the dance studio. "Let me draw something out, and we can start tomorrow."

My smile dropped. "Wait, what? What do you mean 'draw something out'?"

"I need to make a mind map. Get all the moves written down that will flow with the music."

My enthusiasm for this project escalated. "A mind map? I love mind maps. I use them all the time in advertising. Can I help?"

She laughed. "You don't even know what the moves are called."

"Please, Story, let me do it with you. Please?"

"Okay, okay. You can help."

She sat back down with me at the front desk. We stayed there all afternoon, listening to the song and talking about the moves. Some of them I could do. Others, she would need to teach me, and I would need to practice. I could sit on the pole and spin, but the upside-down moves made me nervous, especially since Hope had just broken her arm.

"Bring dance clothes tomorrow. We'll practice in the morning before the noon classes."

Both Story and Solara were back at work, so I sat at the front desk alone. I was energized to start working on my choreography, but at the moment, I had nothing to occupy my mind. I became obsessed with checking my phone, waiting on a text or a call from Paxton. Nothing.

I knew I should give him time, but his silence was making me crazy.

Doodling on the pad of paper Story had left behind, I found

myself mapping out a strategy for marketing. I laughed at myself at how easily I could shift back into business mode.

As I conjured plans out of the air, my phone rang. Richard's name was on the screen. I couldn't begin to imagine what he wanted, and I certainly wasn't going to take the call while I was working.

Letting it go to voicemail, I kept writing my proposal for a new marketing campaign for L.O.V.E.: one that would bring in moms, professionals, and people who had preconceived ideas about pole dancing—but wanted to try it regardless. My mind was working at a feverish pace. By the time I looked up from my frenetic writing, it was almost five o'clock, and students were starting to arrive for evening classes.

I checked them in with learned efficiency, greeted almost all of them by name, and smiled broadly at them. A couple of them whispered over the desk, asking me how Paxton and Story were doing.

I nodded. "They're doing fine." I kept it at that not wanting to gossip about the family.

When the last of the classes had been checked in, I left for the night, checking my voicemail before driving home.

Richard wanted to talk to me about my job; he asked me to call him. I was a little confused. What job did he want to talk about?

As soon as I turned on the car, the phone connected automatically, and I returned his call.

He answered right away, his boisterous voice booming through the car speaker. "Charlotte! Thank you for calling me back."

"Hi, Richard. How are you?"

"Good, good." He shifted from joviality to his business tone. "I don't like how we left things the last time we met. To be frank, I was surprised you ended things so abruptly."

I was stopped at a red light, staring at nothing. This was a conversation I didn't want to have. I imagined clicking the end button and just continuing my drive home. How rewarding would that be—to just hang up on him?

"Charlotte, did you hear me?"

I shook my head. What had he asked me?

"Sorry, Richard. My phone was on mute." *Think, Charlotte, think.* "I'm doing well, Richard."

"I'm sure you are, but we'd like to talk about bringing you back. You were an invaluable member of the team. We'd like to have you back."

I was speechless.

Exasperation laced his tone. "Charlotte?"

"That is…" I paused. "That is intriguing, Richard. I'm flattered."

"Should I send you the contract?"

"I'd like some time to think, Richard. Can you give me a couple of weeks?"

"Take the time you need. Let me know at the gala."

I pinched the bridge of my nose; I was getting a migraine.

"Thank you, Richard. I'll give it very thoughtful consideration." I agreed I would have an answer by the gala, and we hung up.

The call reminded me that I hadn't talked to Suzanne in weeks. She would be knee-deep in planning the gala, but I still owed her a call.

Her elegant voice came over the speaker in the car. "Hello, stranger."

I chuckled. "Hello, friend."

"I thought you'd disappeared forever. Mark and I placed bets on whether or not you would actually be coming to the gala. Please tell me I'm going to win."

"I'm still coming."

"Damn!" I heard her snap her fingers.

"What do you mean? You actually thought I wouldn't come?" I was kind of hurt.

She sighed. "Charlie, you left your job, your fiancé, this beautiful house, and I haven't heard from you in weeks. Can you honestly tell me you're coming back?"

So many thoughts fired through my brain all at once. The one that pushed to the front, though, was that she had called me Charlie. My entire identity had been wrapped up in that name. No one called me that here. Not even my mother. But I was still Charlie—just a different version of her. Secondly, maybe she was right. Maybe I didn't really want to come back at all.

"Well, I was planning on it." My tone was petulant, and I resented her a bit for thinking bad things about me.

"I won't turn the win over to Mark just yet," she said jokingly.

An image of her standing in my kitchen—Mark's kitchen—came to mind. "How is Mark?"

"He's good. I have some paperwork to send you about the house. I need a few more days, and then I'll FedEx it to you."

I'd meant about our breakup, so I found it odd that she shifted so quickly to the house. A tingling at the back of my neck forced me to imagine something I never had before. Or, if I had imagined it, I'd chosen to ignore it.

I must have taken too long to respond. "Charlie, are you still there?"

"I'm here." I wish I could've seen her face when I asked quietly (and with some reservation), "Suzanne, are you sleeping with Mark?"

She didn't respond, and I inhaled sharply. She hadn't immediately denied it.

In almost a whisper, I asked, "Are you?"

"Charlie, this isn't a phone conversation." Her voice was shaking.

"How long?"

"Charlie." She was almost pleading.

I screamed, "How long?"

I pulled over to the side of the road and stared at the speaker. "How long, Suzanne?"

Her voice was soft when she said, "A few months. A year or so, maybe. It just happened."

My eyes welled up with tears, and I choked on a cry. "Oh, my God!" I put my fist to my chest.

"Charlie, we didn't mean for it to happen. We—"

"Stop. Just stop. I don't want to hear a reason. You're my best friend. *Were* my best friend." I shook my head and stared out the window. "I gotta go."

"Charlie…"

"You can claim the win. I'm not coming to the gala."

I hit the end call button and sat on the side of the road for a moment longer, processing what had just happened.

This was unbelievable. How had I not seen this? All those times I'd confided in her.

I dropped my head on the steering wheel and started to cry. I cried over the loss of a best friend. I cried over the loss of my relationship. I didn't want any of it back, but it still hurt.

My phone pinged, and I looked at the screen on the console. It was a text from Paxton: *Dinner tonight?*

Oh, goodness. I can't handle all this.

I texted back: *I can't tonight*

The phone rang, and I hit the answer button on the screen. "Hi."

"You okay? I thought we were going to get dinner this week?"

My words got stuck around the lump in my throat, and I had to swallow hard not to break down and cry. "You know, Paxton, maybe you were right. Maybe I'm not ready for us."

I was met with silence, so I continued. "I mean, I just got out of something. You just got out of something. Maybe this isn't the best thing right now."

Gruffly, he asked, "Where are you?"

"What?"

"Where are you?"

"Um, I'm sitting on the side of the road in my mom's car. I'm on my way home."

"I'll see you in ten minutes."

And he hung up.

I stared at the phone as if he was going to pop out of it. This was certainly a busy drive home.

He pulled his SUV in right behind me as soon as I turned into my parent's driveway.

I locked the door with the key fob and walked to his driver's side door.

Lowering his window, he said, "You've been crying."

"It's not important."

"Come with me."

"Let me give my mom her keys so she doesn't think I've been kidnapped."

He waited until I returned, and then he drove higher up into the hills, winding through the neighborhood and out toward the desert.

"Where are we going?"

He rested his forearm on the steering wheel and glanced quickly at me sideways, grinning mischievously. "I thought we would stick with the whole high school vibe you have going on at your parents' house—and we would go park."

He waggled his eyebrows, and I laughed.

When he finally pulled over, he rolled down the windows and turned off the car. The sun was setting, and it would be dark soon. When the sun set in the desert, it got dark fast.

A light breeze blew through the cab. I unbuckled my seatbelt, pulled my foot up on the seat, and turned to face him, my back against the door.

As he was unbuckling his seatbelt, he asked, "What happened today, Charlotte?"

"First of all, how are *you*? Are you okay?"

He relaxed his legs, scooted over in the seat, and placed his back against the door, so we were facing each other. "I'm okay. The ceremony was quiet and small. A few of her old friends came. Friends I'm happy to be rid of." He turned to look out the front windshield, reflecting, and then turned back to me. "Why did you want to cancel dinner?"

I didn't tell him about Richard since I didn't even know what my response would be. But I told him about my call with Suzanne, and I shared all the clues I should have seen along the way.

He just listened. At one point, he reached out to take my hand, intertwining our fingers across the center console. He played with them. Over and over, he rolled my fingers between his, creating a calming rhythm.

A tear dropped. "I just can't imagine why, after all this time. She was so supportive of me. And Mark, oh my goodness! He was so awful to me; he constantly shamed me. Why didn't they just come out and tell me? Why did he have to make me feel so bad about myself?"

"He doesn't deserve you, Charlotte."

"I know. And I don't regret calling things off. *Obviously.*" He smiled at me, and I continued. "But I feel so stupid. And embarrassed."

When I was done talking, he stopped his twirling and held my fingers tight. "Charlotte, I think you already know how I feel about you."

My heart hurt. "Paxton, please don't say it. I'm not ready to hear it."

"I know you're not." He chuckled in amusement. "And maybe you're right. Maybe we aren't ready for each other, but it doesn't change how I feel. I'm sorry your friend did that to you."

I thanked him. "Me too."

Letting out a heavy sigh, he said, "This is probably the worst possible time to tell you this, but…" He tightened his hold on my fingers. "I need to go to California for a few weeks. Max needs my help with negotiations on the new studio. I need to go."

Pulling my lips in between my teeth, I simply nodded. But I could feel my chest tighten, and I had to hold my breath so I wouldn't break down again.

He pulled me over the center console and into his lap, whispering my name lovingly, "Charlotte."

I burst into tears.

He rubbed the back of my head and held me close, soothing me. "Shh. We'll be okay. You'll be okay."

I lifted my head, and he held my face with both his hands. Wiping the tears from my eyes, he leaned in to kiss me. Our lips pressed together, and I could taste the salt from my tears. We simply breathed.

The softness of his full lips against mine was so erotic—not moving, just feeling—until he parted his lips slightly and pulled my bottom lip between his.

I sighed and shifted, our bodies clumsily trying to get closer to each other. Slanting his mouth against mine, he deepened the kiss, and I melted into him.

His deep laugh vibrated against my lips. He started to smile.

"What? Why are you laughing?"

"Because I really do feel like I'm in high school. We're too old for this. Come home with me."

I nodded silently.

Awkwardly, I managed to get myself back to the other side of the truck. I adjusted my leggings, which had shifted across my waist.

He was grinning at me.

Sullenly, but teasingly, I said, "I'm hungry. Are you going to feed me?"

Wickedly, he grinned at me. "Oh yeah, I'm gonna feed you." He started the truck and put it in drive, turning it back down the hill. "All night long."

CHAPTER 26

"CHARLOTTE! LEAN AWAY from the pole. You keep leaning into it. You look like a monkey."

Story had been trying to get me to keep my body away from the pole, and swing around with my feet apart, all morning. I was so tired I could barely even hang on.

"Lean out!" She shouted at me. Then she mumbled to herself, "We need to work on your core."

Resting my hands on my knees, I bent over to catch my breath. Paxton and I had stayed up until late in the evening, talking. Eventually, we'd gone to bed. He had made love to me with adoration and care. Instead of being rough and consuming, his touch was emotional and healing.

"I'm sorry, Story. I'm just so tired."

"Fine. Let's try a cross knee release. We need to get you high on the pole, so you can do the layout and hanging spins toward the end of the song. Climb up, and then hook your knee tight before you lie back."

I followed her lead and found myself hanging upside down on the pole. Stuck. "Story, I can't get back up."

The door to the studio opened. All I could see from my upside-down position were male dress shoes and the bottom leg of trousers. "Hey, Story, I was looking for Charlotte. Can I have her for a minute?"

Frustrated, she responded, "Sure. Maybe you can help her down."

"Hi, Paxton." I tried not to move too much from my upside-down position, fearful of falling.

I heard him chuckle, and then he squatted down and tilted his head to see me better. "Hey, darlin'. What are you doing?"

"I'm practicing."

"Do you need some help getting down?" His words were laced with laughter.

"That would be *great*."

He stood, put one arm behind my shoulders and the other under my bottom. "Let go."

I wrapped my arms around his neck and then relaxed my legs, so they came off the pole.

He held me close, and I buried my head in his neck, inhaling his masculine scent. I whispered, "You smell good."

His chest rumbled in laughter. He set me down gently, kissing the top of my head. "You do too."

I stepped back a step so I could look at him. "You look nice."

He didn't acknowledge my compliment. He looked sad. "My plane leaves in a few hours. Max and I have an investor dinner tonight as soon as I get off the plane."

Scanning him from head to toe, I teased, "You look very professional."

Tucking my hair behind my ear, he gripped me by the back of the neck and pulled me close. My hands rested on his chest.

"Charlotte, I know this is a difficult time for you." He paused, and I wondered where he was going with this. He looked uncomfortable. "I don't want to be the reason you don't go back to the life you're meant to have."

"But you're not."

He released me and stepped back a bit. "You think that now. I'm going to take some space while I'm gone. I think me leaving is for the best."

"The best for what?" I crossed my arms.

His eyes never wavered from mine. "I don't think we should continue… right now. What you said last night about us both getting out of something? You may have been right."

I shook my head. "So, you're just leaving? And I won't even get to talk to you? Thanks for the sex; gotta go?"

"Max and I are going to be very busy."

I slapped him.

He turned his head and put his palm to his cheek. He didn't even look angry. He just took it, accepting my anger. Somehow, that hurt even more.

I was livid. "And yes, this time I meant it.

He didn't respond. Didn't even fight me.

Looking around, I noticed Story had left us alone. I grabbed my water bottle and towel and left the room. "Good bye, Paxton."

I went straight to the locker room and cried quietly in a changing room.

This was bullshit! He wanted to leave? Fine. But I had started something, and I was going to finish it. I didn't know if I was going back to my job, but I knew that I wanted to compete—and that I loved being here.

I dried my eyes and then placed a cool towel on them to lessen the stinging.

When I left the locker room, Paxton had gone. Story was waiting for me at the front desk.

She looked at me questioningly, her eyes wary. "Wh—"

"I don't know." I cut her off.

She looked at me as if I was a fragile doll. I didn't want her pity, and I said a little too tersely, "I don't know, but we have a dance to finish."

Her chest started to shake. She giggled.

I barked at her to keep myself from breaking down. "Well, don't just sit there."

Pulling her lips between her teeth to curb her laughter, her eyes lit up with admiration. "Yes, ma'am."

The next few weeks were a blur of travel, practice, work, repeat. I trained Vivian so she could work the studio while Story, Solara, and I managed the remaining three competitions before the final show in California.

Story, Solara, and I became a tight-knit force. We were seamless in our management of the shows. I started to realize what real friendship looked like—and what it felt like—respectful boundaries and trust.

After the final event in Chicago, I told them about the offer to return to my former position. After the celebratory dinner, the three of us went to the outdoor pool at the hotel, paper cups and a bottle of wine in hand.

The moon was shining bright, giving just enough illumination to the unlit outdoor area. I reached for the handle to the gate, but it was locked. "Do you guys want to just head back to my room?"

Story looked to our left and stepped up on the flower pot. "Nope." She effortlessly leaped over the gate and unlocked it from the inside.

I jokingly asked, "Were you a delinquent?"

Grinning mischievously, she said, "There were some times."

The three of us settled in the lounge chairs, and I poured us each a glass of wine. "I can't believe how fast the time has gone. Irvine is in two weeks already."

Solara had closed her eyes.

She took a deep breath. "I hope you're planning on staying. We like you. I'd love to have you do more marketing."

This was my opportunity to come clean. "I haven't really decided what I'm doing next." I swung my legs over and sat up on the chair. "My former boss called. He offered me my job back."

Story stilled, and Solara opened her eyes, rolling her head over to look at me. "What did you tell him?"

"I told him I would have an answer by the gala, but then that went to shit. I guess I just need to call him soon."

"What do you mean 'that went to shit?'" Story asked me.

I hadn't told them about my conversation with Suzanne, so I elaborated. Then Solara laughed. And laughed. And laughed.

"It's not that funny, Sol."

"It's kind of cliché, really."

I lowered my head and said morosely, "Yeah, I know."

Then, slowly, I started to laugh too. And soon, the three of us were laughing so hard I couldn't breathe.

When our laughter subsided, I poured the rest of the bottle into our cups and gave a toast. "To new friends. May they never sleep with your boyfriend."

Story raised her glass. "No worries here, chica."

Solara raised hers as well. "Me neither."

And then we laughed all over again.

We eventually stumbled back to our rooms, and Solara stopped with me at my door.

Kindly, she said, "Paxton will be at the show in California."

"That's nice. It'll be good to see him."

She looked at me knowingly. "Have you heard from him?"

"No."

"Maybe you should text him. Just say hello."

I smiled sadly. "I think it's best if I don't. I'm not sure what I'm doing next, and the whole thing with Myla... I don't know. It's just..."

She took my hands in hers. "It's just life. Things happen, Charlotte. We can't plan to fall in love."

"I don't know, Sol. He was pretty clear that it was for the best."

"I think he thought it was the best for you, and you misunderstood. He didn't want to burden you with his mess, even though he needs you." She added, "Desperately."

"He was so sure of his decision." Tears welled in my eyes.

"Have you considered that... maybe he knew you needed time to figure out what you were doing? So that when you were ready, you would fight for the two of you?"

The tears fell.

"He's been alone for a long time." She rolled her eyes, realizing what she meant to say. "Well, you know, not *alone* alone, but without someone who really cared about him. Even when he was married to Myla she used him."

My heart was hurting so much, nausea churned in my stomach.

She continued. "But you... you challenged him. You fought back when he was, quite honestly, a total asshole. Your heart, Charlotte. Your heart. When it came to Erin, Hope, and me? And even Story. You showed him how good you are. But you still don't know who you are, and he can't go through that again. He wasn't leaving you because he doesn't love you. He left because he does."

All I could do was nod.

"Just send him a text. Something."

She enveloped me in a hug.

"I'll see you in the morning." As she walked off, I heard her say, "I can't wait to sleep in my own bed."

Before I fell asleep that night, I lay on my side and buried under the covers, staring at the blue screen of my phone.

What would I say to him—I miss you?, I love you?

As much as I wanted to, I couldn't.

Maybe Paxton had been right in leaving. If he'd stayed, I might have gotten lost in him. I might not have been able to make the right decisions for me. Being with him was fun, exciting, challenging, and intense. I needed to make sure I was ready before talking with him.

I turned off the phone. Rolling over, I placed it on the nightstand, plugged it into the charger, and closed my eyes to sleep.

The next day, after our flight landed back in Phoenix, Story had me back in the studio to practice. I swear she was trying to kill me. She never stopped shouting.

"Charlotte, you are so good technically, but you have *got* to work on your transitions. They are key to the sensuality of the program. Stay fluid and elegant."

She stood up from the bench she was sitting on and demonstrated what she was talking about. "Transfix your audience. Pull their eyes along your body. They didn't come to watch a soccer player; they came to be seduced, entranced, and transported into a fantasy. Lure them in from one move to the next."

Walking around the pole a couple of times, she did some leg circles and then a sunwheel. "Don't just fling your leg up. Get enough momentum that you can smoothly lower yourself to the ground. Make sure you drop your hips back when you spin; otherwise, you will just drop to the ground like a weight."

She stepped back. "Now you try."

The music played, and I did as she said, getting my back leg high enough that I spun to the ground in a stag position.

She shouted again. "Tighten your butt, Charlotte. Pull your abs up!"

I did as she said, and I instantly felt my form improve.

"Again!"

I was exhausted and covered in bruises. But I did it again.

She started clapping. "Good! Good! Now gently lower yourself to the ground, and we'll start the floor work."

For the next hour, we worked on the moves from one pole to the next, with the plan to start on the static pole and finish on the spinning pole.

"It will make for a more dramatic finish." Story said.

Afterward, we sat on the studio floor and talked through the sketches she had laid out on the floor.

"This is really challenging. Do you think we can get it all finished in two weeks?"

"We need to work every day. You're kind of soft."

Looking down at my stomach, I pinched the tiny roll that was under my belly button. "I'm not going to lose this overnight, Story."

"I'm just teasing you, Charlotte. But we do need to work every day. This is going to be fabulous."

I nodded at her. "Got it."

She reached out and squeezed my hand. When I looked up at her, admiration and respect were shining in her eyes. "You'll be ready, Charlotte. You'll be ready."

CHAPTER 27

STORY, SOLARA, AND I arrived in sunny Orange County the day before the show and headed directly to the venue from the airport.

I'd never been to California, and I was struck by the perfectly sunny weather. Not humid like Houston and not scorching-hot like Phoenix. The air smelled like fresh-cut grass and oranges.

When we stepped outside, I lifted my face to the vibrant sun and inhaled deeply, letting the aroma seep into my lungs. I was feeling jittery and anxious about seeing Paxton, and the warm rays of the sun helped to relax me.

The theater was a short twenty-minute drive from the airport. Solara was on the phone as she stepped into the front seat of a black SUV limousine. Story and I rode in the back, and I noticed she wasn't saying anything. At all. She was staring out at the palm trees passing us by, far away with her thoughts.

"You okay, Story?"

She turned her head to look at me. "Hmm?"

"Are you okay? You seem distant."

"This was Myla's last show—last year. It's bittersweet being here. I don't really like California."

She turned back toward the window. I reached out to hold her hand, and she took it, continuing to look at the city.

When we reached the theater, I followed Solara to the large

conference room where we were all meeting. My eyes widened at the number of men and women sitting around an oval-shaped table. And in chairs against the walls.

Paxton was standing at the head of the table in his usual competition wear: a black T-shirt, black jeans, and black boots.

My stomach clenched from nerves. I felt like I'd been punched in the gut, and my heart squeezed from adrenaline. I wanted to run to him and tell him he made a mistake—and that I loved him—but now was not the time.

He caught my eye, and I smiled tentatively. He jerked his head briefly in a greeting and fumbled around with some papers in front of him. He appeared nervous. For some reason, that made me grin.

From behind, someone's shoulder bumped me in a friendly gesture. "Hey, Charlotte, good to see you again." Max pushed me a little forward, trying to get by me.

"Oh, hey, Max. You too."

Paxton called for everyone's attention and proceeded to pass around the schedule. "This is our last big event for the season. I know you've all worked hard during your individual shows, and we're grateful to you for volunteering your time to work this final event. Solara and Story have done their best to accommodate those of you that are competing. If we missed someone, please let us know, and we'll find someone to work your slot."

I quickly looked for my name and noticed that I was left off the work schedule during my event. My role was primarily working the check-in desk, and I was fine with that. The stage monitor position kind of stressed me out.

Paxton continued talking, and I watched everyone in the room as he spoke. They were listening intently; they respected him. No one cracked jokes or made googly eyes at him. Like I'm sure I had.

Paxton, Max, and Solara were esteemed. It was obvious they were running this business—and running it well. Goosebumps broke out on my arms.

"We've made arrangements for a party Saturday night at The Deck on Laguna Beach. It's right in front of the Pacific Edge Hotel, for those of you that are staying there. Max, Solara, and I hope you'll all join us to celebrate the end of the competition season."

He ended by answering some questions and then disappeared out the side door. Solara came to me. She said the driver would take Story and me to the hotel to check in. Max, Paxton, and her had some work to do. She gave me instructions for the morning, and then she told me that Story had the company card to check in to the hotel.

"Are we on our own for dinner tonight?" I asked her.

"Probably. We'll be late."

"Okay. Have you seen Story?"

"I haven't. Check the dressing rooms. She might be helping some of the girls get ready for the morning."

I nodded at her, and then I headed down the hall to the back stairs that led to the stage and the dressing area.

When I hit the last step, I stood in the shadows of the backstage area and saw Paxton assessing the poles and the rigging. He was double-checking the work to make sure no one would get hurt.

He stood and walked in my direction, not yet seeing me.

I stepped from the shadows. "Paxton."

Stopping short, he took all of me in at once, and I almost melted. "Hi, Charlotte."

"I was looking for Story. She was going to ride with me to the hotel."

He looked over his shoulder to the stage and then back at me. "I haven't seen her."

This was a bit awkward. "Well, it was good to see you. And, I guess I'll see you tomorrow." I turned to leave through the exit doors, stuttering a good-bye.

"Charlotte, wait."

Quickly walking toward me, he shoved his hands in his back pockets when he stopped abruptly in front of me.

My palms were sweaty, and I wrung them in front of me.

Standing still in front of him, I waited patiently for him to speak.

"I..." he paused. Then he leaned closer and whispered, almost in a growl, "Charlotte, I've missed you."

I reached out tentatively, putting my palm to his chest. I whispered back, "I've missed you too."

That one touch was all he needed to reach out and pull me close. He buried his head in the crook of my neck, and then he placed one palm on the side of my face. He wrapped the other one around me—and then kissed the side of my neck and my cheek.

He whispered, "We need to talk."

I breathed him in. This felt like heaven. After nodding, I pressed my body against his.

He groaned. "This is such a bad weekend. We're so busy. Saturday okay?"

"Saturday." I agreed, and we stood holding each other, cheeks pressed together tightly.

A cheerful voice came from behind us, and we broke apart. "There you are, you little tart. C'mon, I want to get checked in, and we need to go over your routine." As an afterthought, she added, "Hey, Paxton."

"Hey, Story." He put his hands in his front pockets, but he was grinning.

I floated off like a butterfly, grinning back at him as Story dragged me out the front door.

Story and I checked in, and she showed up at my door a few minutes later. "We are going to be so busy the next two days. I don't know when we'll have time to practice your routine. Run it through tonight in your mind. When you have a few minutes every now and then, try and find one of the practice poles to do a few segments."

Sitting at the tiny table on the balcony, she pulled up the music. I stood in the middle of the room, ready to run it through in my head.

"Ready?"

I closed my eyes and nodded. She started the music and called out the steps.

"Do your leg circles. Now sunwheel. Change pole sides, and do the side roll. Do the leg hook to a sit and then layout. Lower to the ground…" Her voice droned on, and I moved in a circle, imagining the movement from the static pole to the spinning pole. When we came to the end of the song, I opened my eyes and saw her smiling at me. "Just make sure you are tight on that last layout spin. It's fast, and the pole will be moving. You don't want to fall."

"Great! Thanks for that."

She stood, looking uncomfortable, and I was embarrassed by my sarcastic response.

She paced in front of me.

I went to her with concern. "Are you okay?"

"Actually, um…" She cleared her throat, struggling to control tears. "I wanted to thank you. You have been kind and supportive during your time with us. About my sister. You don't know us very well, but I can see how much you care about Paxton and Solara. And Paxton and Solara care about you. I wanted you to know that I do too. You can count on me as a friend."

"Oh, Story. Thank you." I put my hand to my chest. "That means a lot."

"Well…" She composed herself. "Get a good night's sleep. The next two days might find you cursing all of us."

She let herself out. I went through my regular nighttime routine: laying out my clothes and making sure my competition outfit was ready. I wanted this new life more than anything. And I wanted this dance to be damn near perfect.

Exhaustion was looming. If there was one thing I knew for certain, it was that, come Sunday, I was going to want to sleep for 24 hours.

The last three days had been a blur. I'd had no idea people were so invested in this sport. I ran errands. I got coffee. I checked women, men, and others in. Not once did I ever see Paxton, Solara, or Max waver from the business of keeping things moving.

When it was time for me to start getting ready, Solara showed up with my replacement. She took me to another dressing room on the other side of the theater.

"Where are we going?"

"Shh. I'm not supposed to give privileges. But I know how important this is for you, so I finagled a private dressing room from the theater." She was dragging me down a hallway, and we stopped at a door that had a star on it.

I pointed to it. "Did you do that?"

She giggled. "You deserve it."

"Thank you."

She opened the door, and we went inside. "I brought all your things from the other room." She showed me where my outfit was hanging on the back of the door. "It's not much, but it's private, and you can do some visualization. I'll come get you when it's time."

"Thank you, Solara. Thank you." I hugged her tightly.

"See you in a bit."

The room was quiet, serene, and small. It was furnished with a small loveseat and a dressing table with a tri-fold mirror. I undressed from my work clothes, and then I put on an oversized button-up flannel that would be easy to remove when I was ready for my outfit.

I started with my hair. Using a flat iron, I made it as long and sleek as I could. Parting it down the middle, I brushed it back into a low ponytail at the nape of my neck. Story suggested that I pull my hair free during my last segment; this ponytail would make it easy to do.

With expert care, I applied the stage makeup, contouring my facial features and highlighting where needed. My eyes were my best feature. I had thick, black lashes (that I accented with liquid liner) and fake lashes that made my eyes pop. I shaped my eyebrows with pencil and applied a shimmering pink eyeshadow to my brow ridge. Cherry red lipstick completed the look.

When I was satisfied that my face was complete, I took off the flannel and put on a nude bra. Silver and black sequins covered just the right places, giving the illusion that I had nothing on. The thong bikini was next, decorated in the same fashion, but with darker straps that could be seen from the front and back. A black and silver garter belt went around my waist, and I left the straps to hang down the top part of my thighs.

The most beautiful piece of my outfit was a black corset, covered in Swarovski crystals so that it would shine and sparkle in the stage lights. It was sexy and seductive, and I put it on with care so I wouldn't lose the crystals. Instead of hooks, it had Velcro in the front, so I could easily remove it.

Throughout this process, my breathing was calm and intentional. I kept myself in the moment and savored every fluid move, every touch of the fabric on my skin, every rasp of Velcro, and every snap of the bra. I sat back down on the dressing room chair and carefully pulled on the black mid-thigh stockings, rolling them delicately over my feet and gently up my leg. I left the garter belt unattached since I would be removing it later in the program.

When the stockings' elastic band was secure around my thigh, I put on the black, faux-leather ankle boots. They were open at the toe and laced up the back. The six-inch platform heels were embellished with silver rhinestones.

When the second boot was on, I stood and stared at the girl—the woman—staring back at me in the full-length mirror that hung on the back of the door.

I felt strong and powerful. Sexual and dominant. I felt like I finally owned my life.

My black satin gloves were on the dressing table. I pulled them on, delicately rolling them up my arm and completing the look.

A knock at the door pulled me from my musings, and I told whoever it was to come in. The door cracked open.

A cheerful Solara asked, "Are you decent?"

"I am."

Story and Solara both peeked around the door, stepping inside and shutting it behind them. When I came into their line of sight, they both gasped, and Story covered her mouth in surprise.

Solara couldn't move. "I... Oh, my gosh, Charlotte! You are..." She shook her head. "You are exquisite."

"Thank you." I could feel myself blushing.

Story lowered her hand; she was smiling. "You ready to go?"

I simply nodded.

They walked in front of me. A measured pace, so I could keep up in my heels. I felt like a rock star. We went down the hall, behind the stage, and around to the practice area. My guardians, my protectors, my tutelaries.

Story had me do a few stretches, which were difficult in the corset, but I tried.

I peeked out from the side and saw Paxton pacing in the back of the theater. It made me smile. I was so ready to do this.

"Cute, my ass!" I muttered to myself.

Solara, Story, and I stepped back into the shadows and waited. The two of them held my hands, and we breathed silently, waiting for my name to be called. The lights on the stage dimmed to the purple and red I had requested, and my name was announced.

I opened my eyes, and Story and Solara squeezed my hands.

"You got this!" they both said.

I stepped out of the shadows onto the stage. With my back to the audience—I raised one gloved arm high above my head—and held onto the pole. I grabbed my elbow with the other hand, cocked my hip, and waited for the music to start.

CHAPTER 28

THE SULTRY, MELODIC lyrics of Billie Eilish's "You Should See Me in a Crown" enraptured me. I swayed my hips, walked seductively around the pole, and used every movement to pull the audience in. Just like Story had said.

Story's voice was in my head as I came around the front of the pole. Slowly, deliberately, I removed my gloves—one finger at a time—and then flung them to the side on a beat.

With my back against the pole, I did a few sultry, slow squats to the floor, gyrating my hips. Low to the floor, I put my chin to my shoulder with a flirty smile and enticed the audience into the erotic moves.

Soon, I no longer heard Story's voice telling me what to do. I was so entranced by the music, I found myself spellbound by my own alluring dance. My body moved on its own, remembering the routine.

With my back to the audience, I swung my hips around, pushed my bottom out behind me, and removed the corset.

I grabbed the pole with both hands, swung my legs up, and hooked myself to the pole, ankles crossed. Turning my legs, I pulled myself into an upright position and seductively climbed the pole.

The techno indie song drew me along, and I erotically maneuvered myself back to the ground—crossing and uncrossing my legs as I spun my way back down. The moves and spins were strategically choreographed to hit each of the seductive beats of the music.

When I reached the stage floor, I flipped my legs up and around so I could inch my way across the stage to the other pole. With my arms braced behind me, I scooted myself along by doing leg twists, and my stockings sparkled provocatively in the lights.

Reaching the spin pole, I pulled myself up, turned once again to the audience, and removed the garter belt. I stuck my finger in my mouth in a shameless come-hither way.

The music picked up in tempo, and I prepared myself to finish the routine.

I flipped up and climbed the pole, alternating my legs, hooking and swinging. I did the splits; the only contact with the pole was my inner thigh. Then I lifted one leg up and connected to the pole with my ankle.

When I could, I let go of the pole with one hand, grabbed my ankle, and pulled it down. I put myself into the layback and forced the spin faster.

The layback was the move I loved the most now. I soared; energy pulsing through me.

I was spinning and spinning, losing myself to the suggestive routine and the thumping bass of the song, and then everything in me broke. I felt the energy running from my fingertips to my toes as I spun around and around. Finally, my chains of confinement and expectations broke free and liberated my soul. They flew off of me; broken by my own sacrifice.

As the music slowed, I reached out to grab the pole, hooked my knee around the inside of my elbow, and gradually circled back down to the ground. Slowing my movements, I was spent and replete.

I was immune to the crowd, only feeling the music and my own heartbeat.

Settling myself down to the ground, the music ended. Everything was quiet, including the audience. Not sure if I was finished. Not wanting it to be over. With childlike sleepiness, I put my forehead to the floor and let everything go. All of my emotions drained out of me, and I stayed like that, feeling the weight of all the decisions I'd made these last few months disappear. They radiated out of me, onto the floor and away—never to be captured again.

For a moment, I almost forgot where I was. At that moment, I knew I was irrevocably changed.

The audience erupted. Clapping and cheers reverberated throughout the theater, but it all sounded far away. The lights were shining down on me when I lifted my head, and I was almost brought to tears. Instead, I laughed. Standing as elegantly as I could from my floor position, I slowly bowed, reveling in my newfound strength and sexuality. And then I left the stage, gathering my corset and garter as I went.

Solara and Story were jumping up and down, clapping and grinning from ear to ear.

"You did it! Oh, my goodness, you did it!" Solara squeezed me tight.

Story wrapped her arms around the both of us. "And you didn't fall."

When I stepped back, I was still grinning. "And I didn't fall." I fisted my hands, closed my eyes, raised my face to the ceiling—and exhaled. "I did it!"

They both laughed and hugged me again.

"I need to go change. I'll see you back at the hotel?"

"You did great, girl." Story said to me as I went back to the dressing room.

When I got to the private room, I took off my shoes and wrapped myself in the bathrobe I'd brought with me.

I curled up on the couch and took my phone from my purse. I had a phone call to make.

After a few rings, his gruff voice answered. I greeted him as professionally as I could, without sounding too ecstatic. "Richard, how are you?"

"Good, Charlotte, good. What can I do for you?"

"Well, sir, I'm not going to be coming back to Houston for the gala, so I thought I should call you personally with my decision."

His booming voice said, "Tell me the good news."

"Unfortunately, sir, I can't do that. I won't be coming back. I truly appreciate the offer. I know it was extended with sincerity. But I have found a new job that I love, that fits me, and that makes me incredibly happy."

As I said the words, I knew them to be true. A sense of peace and finality that had been lacking the last time we talked settled within me. That job was in my past.

"I am sorry to hear that, Charlotte." I heard acceptance, resignation, and a little bit of pride. "You will always have a friend—and a reference if needed—in me.

"Thank you, Richard. I appreciate that."

We hung up, and I sat in the quiet of the dressing room, reflecting on the call. I did feel at peace. Grinning broadly, I jumped up off the couch to go find Paxton.

Stealthily, I crept around the back of the stage, keeping my bathrobe tied tight.

Climbing the back stairs to the conference room, I stepped inside and saw Paxton sitting at the head of the table, leaning back, expecting me.

I locked the door behind me and sauntered over to him.

With a wolfish smile, he asked, "Did you come to gloat?"

Feigning ignorance, I flirted and asked, "Whatever could you mean?"

He pushed back from the table, legs spread, and I stepped between them, leaning against the table. I put my hand to my heart, surreptitiously untying my belt on the way up. "Oh, you mean that *cute* dance?"

His eyes glittered, and he stood, stalking his prey, lifting me up and setting me on the table. Stepping between my legs, he pushed the sides of the bathrobe away from me.

I rested my hands behind me, leaned back, and smiled up at him, waiting for approval.

His eyes raked over me, and he brushed the backs of his fingers along the soft skin of my inner thigh. When one of his fingers slipped underneath the sequined underwear—and he pushed it inside me—I gasped, and my smile dropped.

He whispered huskily, "It didn't look cute." Oh, how I had missed him. He paused as he bent down and kissed the side of my neck, teasing me with his fingers. "It looked, Charlotte, like you wanted something."

I was too turned on to speak, so I just nodded.

Slowly, he pulled his fingers from me, and I almost wept from the loss. To prevent him from stepping away, I hooked my legs behind him and pulled him toward me. I reached for his arms and placed them around me in a hug, and I hugged him back.

He kissed the top of my head. "You beautiful, gorgeous woman, go change. I'll see you back at the hotel."

Smiling, I gently pushed him back from me and slid off the table. Before I left, I said, "Did I communicate my message effectively?"

He laughed, "Loud and... sparkly."

I practically skipped to the door.

After I changed back into my work clothes and packed up my outfit, I met Solara at the check-in desk. The competition was almost over, and she told me to have the driver take me back to the hotel.

"Are you sure? I can wait for you."

"You go ahead. We need to make sure everything is packed up before we get to the party. We'll be right behind you. We won't take long."

Back at the hotel, I showered and took my time getting ready.

When I was dressed in jeans and a T-shirt, I sat outside on the balcony, which looked out over the Pacific Ocean. My room was on the hotel's top floor, and I could see down toward the outdoor restaurant where the after-party was being hosted.

The patio had several tables, an L-shaped bar, and a standing area with cocktail tables. Solar lights crisscrossed over the deck; they would illuminate the patio in a romantic glow when the sun went down later.

Solara, Story, and many scantily clad local girls started to arrive: They were all broad smiles, wagging hips, completely oblivious to the attention they were getting and, most likely, not caring. I waited for Paxton and Max to descend down the stairs to the deck before heading over.

As I descended the stairs, I caught Paxton's eye. He was standing at the bar, and he raised his glass to me in a toast, smirking naughtily.

Just as I hit the bottom step, I was engulfed in hugs and coaxed along to a large table situated by the balcony. Food had been ordered, and I noticed that many of the girls were already heartily eating from tiny appetizer plates overflowing with nachos and grilled shrimp.

Solara poured me a glass of wine while she continued to talk about the new studio with the current manager here in California.

Laughter and chatter surrounded me, and I'd never felt more at home.

The warm ocean breeze fluttered my hair.

I took a small sip, thanked her, and she smiled at me. Everyone was smiling and celebrating, and I realized I was happy. For the first time in a *very* long time, I was truly happy. Everyone was bathed in light from the setting sun; its warm glow wrapped us in a bubble of happiness.

I looked up to Paxton, knowing he was part of it, but also knowing it was all the girls surrounding me as well. Their friendship, their acceptance, and their genuine personalities.

As the sun dipped down over the horizon, the solar lights illuminated the area. They cast a warm glow over everyone and highlighted the party atmosphere.

Excusing myself, I stood, left my glass of wine on the table, and made my way to Paxton.

With one foot on a stool rung, the other stretched out in front of him, he rested his elbow on the bar and watched me cross the patio to him.

I scooted close to him, belly to the bar, and waved at the bartender.

The young surfer-type came over, wiping his hands on the towel at his waist. "Hey, beautiful, what can I get y—"

"She'll have a Manhattan." Paxton said, brusquely.

At Paxton's territorial tone, the bartender visibly shrank back from overt flirtation. I smiled at Paxton, trying to tone down the moment.

I turned back to the barman. "I'll have a Manhattan, please." When he had turned to make my drink, I turned a chastising look back on Paxton. "That was kind of cocky of you."

He pulled me toward him, and I stepped between his legs, completely uncaring that everyone could see us. He responded, ignoring my statement, "You were so beautiful today."

My hands around his neck, I tilted my head inquisitively, "Did you watch the whole thing?"

He leaned forward and kissed me sweetly. "I did."

When he pulled back, we simply gazed at each other.

His tone turned serious. "Charlotte, I'm sorry about how I left Phoenix."

I put my finger over his lips. "Shh. Not tonight. Tonight, I want to celebrate and be with my friends. Be with you."

He let go of my hands and pulled something out of his back pocket. Under the bar, he reached for my hand.

I quickly glanced down and saw he was giving me a room key. "It's your choice. I want you. I want you more than anything I could've ever imagined. I want to make love with you. I'm yours, Charlotte." I took the key from him. He spread his hands out to his sides and said quietly, "Yours."

I couldn't speak. I swallowed around the lump in my throat and nodded.

Max came up behind me, picked me up, and twirled me around,

jarring me out of our intense moment. "There she is! You were fantastic today."

When he set me down, I laughed, and he stumbled a bit. "Thanks, Max."

"Hey, Max, you hungry? You want me to walk you to your room? You might have had a bit too much to drink already." Paxton was laughing at him.

Max slurred his words in response. "Yeah, I guess so." He pouted like a little boy.

"Okay, man, let's get you something to eat, and then I'll take you back to your room."

I looked at Paxton over Max's head. As Max sat down at the bar and asked the bartender for a menu, I looked at Paxton and mouthed, "Is he okay?"

He mouthed back. "Girls."

I covered my mouth to keep from laughing, nodded, and then whispered, "I'm going back with the *girls*." He rolled his eyes.

The music had been turned up on the patio speakers, and some of the girls had stood up to dance—silly, girly, fun dancing. I kept an eye on Paxton, noticing when he headed our way to tell Solara he was taking Max back to his room.

She high-fived him and slurred, "Great job this weekend, Paxton! Great job!"

"Yeah, yeah. Not too much more, okay, Sol?"

She grabbed his cheeks. "I love you so much!" Then she kissed him soundly on the cheek.

"I love you too, Sol."

I watched him leave and fingered the key in my pocket. Did he really think I wouldn't come? I heard Solara's voice in my head: *He didn't leave because he doesn't love you. He left because he does.*

I stared at him as he ascended the stairs, guiding Max. I loved Paxton. Deeply. The forever kind. I knew with certainty I was supposed to be with him. He was giving me a chance to choose him.

Startling me from my daydream, Story sat down next to me. "Hey, girlie, I have a gift for you."

I scooted my butt back in the chair and sat up straight, surprised. "A gift?"

"Yes. You were amazing today, and I'm so proud of you."

I blushed at her praise. "Thank you."

"And you do know that you need a name, right?"

"A name?"

"Yeah, a dancer name. Like Story. But you can't have that one because it's mine."

"Story isn't your name?"

"Does that sound like a name a parent would give a child?"

I thought about it. "Actually... yes."

"Well, it's not, and now you need one."

"What is your name? Your real name?"

She harrumphed. "I'm not telling you. Now here, open your gift. You can think of a name later."

"Is it Margaret? Or Agnes?" I couldn't stop teasing her.

"Just open your gift."

With great care, I unwrapped the beautifully packaged present and carefully pulled out a crystal butterfly. Shards of light reflected back at me as I held it in the palm of my hand, admiring its beauty.

Story shifted uncomfortably, and I realized I hadn't said anything. "It's beautiful. Thank you!"

"I saw it and thought of you—that you were becoming a butterfly."

I stared at it in wonder and whispered, "Chrysalis."

"What?"

Lifting my eyes to her, I said, "My name. Chrysalis."

"What's a chrysalis?"

I looked back at the crystal butterfly in awe. "It's the hard shell around the butterfly that protects it while it's transforming." I lifted my head slowly to her, smiling. "Chrysalis."

Knowing exactly where I wanted to be at that moment, I stood abruptly from my chair, leaned back down, and kissed her on the cheek.

"I love it! It's perfect. I have to go. I'll see you in the morning."

She looked at me with confusion. "Uh, okay. See you in the morning."

Leaving the party, I stopped briefly in my room to drop off the butterfly and comb my hair.

Paxton's suite was on the bottom floor, and it had a deck that looked out toward the ocean. Under the outside entry's glowing lamp, I stood at the door and tentatively put the key on the lock.

Opening the door, I saw him reclined in one of the chairs, hands folded in front of him, arms resting on the side of the chair.

He was looking directly at me, waiting.

"Hello, Charlotte."

"Paxton."

He stood and walked toward me. "What took you so long?"

Not giving me time to answer, he grabbed my face and kissed me.

CHAPTER 29

THE NEXT MORNING, I woke before he did and stretched quietly so I wouldn't disturb him.

He was sleeping peacefully on his back, one arm thrown over his head. Small puffs of air escaped from his parted lips.

His dark beard had grown in over the past few days. I smiled to myself, remembering how the coarse hairs had felt last night, tickling the soft skin of my inner thighs.

He'd let me take over, allowing me to remove his jeans and push him gently back on the bed.

Patiently, he lay back, grinning mischievously at me as I removed my jeans and T-shirt. Glancing down at my nakedness, his eyes darkened, and his smile dropped. He reached for me, and I stepped out of reach, teasing him.

"No. Let me."

He relaxed—with intense effort—and I crawled onto the bed. I took him in my mouth, humming with the pleasure of loving him. His eyes were hooded as he watched me, his low groan blending with mine.

With his palm on my head, he gently followed my motion, muttering words of love and praise. Slowly, he pulled me off of him.

He whispered, "Slow down, baby."

I crawled up him and straddled his lap. I placed my knees at his sides, leaned down and kissed his chest, planting soft, hot kisses all the way to his beautiful mouth.

Teasing him, I ground my hips against him and whispered, "How do you want it? Is this what you want?"

He grabbed the back of my head and pulled me down to him. "I want you any way I can have you. Slow and easy, fast and crazy. I'll love you anyway I can." He slammed his mouth to mine, took over, and whipped me into a sexual fever.

Our kisses turned frenzied. Our tongues danced. I couldn't get close enough to him.

I pulled back briefly—so I could sit up and put him inside me. Gradually, he filled me, and I threw back my head and moaned. His pleasured groan followed mine. I placed my hands on his chest and closed my eyes, frantically grinding against him.

His hands had gripped my hips, and he slammed up into me, gripping my flesh hard. "That's it, baby, so good."

I moved faster on him, bracing myself with one hand and rubbing myself with the other. Sensations swept through me, building and tightening, bringing me higher and higher to the exquisite release. Everything in me tensed and tightened. I hovered at the place of sweet torture, shaking, holding on as long as could.

I pushed down hard one last time. His hardness filled me, and I threw back my head and screamed, "Paxton!"

"Yes, baby, come. That's it."

I collapsed on top of him, and then he flipped me over onto my back, hitching my knee over his elbow. "Enough of that."

He pushed into me again—over and over—until he tensed and growled my name. He buried his head in the crook of my neck, shook with his release, and then finally collapsed on top of me.

And then we laughed. And laughed. Our chests rumbling against each other.

When our laughs subsided, he rolled over onto his back and tucked me up against him. I turned so I could lean on his chest. He was running his fingers up and down my back, drawing circles, mellowed in the moment. His tone was laced with humor when he said, "You're so naughty."

I propped my chin up on his chest and smiled up at him.

He reached out to hold my hair, forcing my head up as he held it in place. Looking at me with adoration, he said, "You have no idea what you are getting into. You're driving me crazy in the best way."

Scooting up closer to his face, I said, "If you keep looking at me that way, I can't be responsible for what happens next."

"Challenge accepted."

He flipped me to my back and settled his face between my legs.

The memory of that brought attention to all of my sore muscles. I casually stepped out of bed, stretched again, and dressed for a walk.

It was still early. The sun was not yet up, and the morning sky was still a dark blue-gray, transitioning to the day's upcoming brightness.

Dressing and slipping my feet into my sandals, I grabbed his black hoodie and put it on. It fell to mid-thigh, and I took a deep inhale of the fabric. It smelled like him.

I put the room key back in my pocket and quietly let myself out, careful not to wake him with the clicking of the door.

The deck steps led directly down to the beach, and I left my sandals on the last step.

I could feel the dew of the early morning on my face, and the sand was cold between my toes as I trekked down toward the waterline.

The fog was still heavy over the water, and the smell of salt was bold in the air. A few dogs rushed past me, their owners a few paces behind them for early morning jogs, but other than that, the beach was relatively deserted.

At the end of the beach was a coffee shack I'd discovered a few days ago, and I walked toward it for my morning coffee. The young worker looked like he hadn't yet been to sleep.

I almost said, 'I understand, dude,' but instead, I just smiled and thanked him.

Casually making my way back to the hotel, I saw Paxton walking toward me on the beach, hands in his pockets. His jeans were rolled up at the cuff and a blanket looped through his arm at the elbow. His hair was a mess, looking inadequately finger combed, and my heart expanded with pure joy.

My smile grew as he approached me.

He stopped when he reached me. "Hey."

My eyebrows raised, and I chuckled. "Good morning, Paxton."

"You left me." He pouted, wrapped the blanket around my shoulders, and pulled me close, rubbing my back. "It's freezing out here."

"Such a baby."

We turned and started walking back to the hotel. I held my coffee in one hand and kept the blanket knotted around me with the other; he rested his arm around my shoulders.

We walked in silence a bit before he stopped and turned to me. Looking nervous, he pushed his hands back into his front pockets. After he hitched up his shoulders, his black down jacket bunched around his neck.

"Charlotte, before we go any further, I need to apologize to you. I left Phoenix in a really shitty way. I can only say that I've been kind of a mess—well, you know that." He shrugged and continued. "I wanted you to have room to breathe. I didn't want you to choose me because you had nothing left."

I tilted my head a little. "That's not putting a lot of confidence in my ability to know how I feel."

"I know, and I'm sorry. But here's the thing—I love you, Charlotte. I love you." He dropped his shoulders and stepped closer to me, making sure he had my attention. "We may not always be in the same place, and this business is going to get even crazier with the new store, but I want to be with you. I know you were offered your old job back. If you want to take it, that's fine. I'll move to Houston. I want to be wherever you are."

He paused, looking uncomfortable again. Then, pulled his hands out of his pockets and splayed them out in front of me. "Whatever that looks like."

"How do you know I was offered my job back?"

"Story told me." He looked sheepish.

He didn't know I'd refused it.

I stepped a little closer to him, shrinking the gap, smiling up at him. "So, let me make sure I heard you correctly. You love me—and you will move wherever I go?"

"Yes?" He looked like I was getting ready to trap him, and I laughed.

"It's not a quiz. I'm confirming."

"Yes."

Looking around at the houses lining the beach, I said, "We *should* move here. It's really beautiful."

"Did you hear what I just said? You can take your job back if you want. I'll go to Houston with you."

"Yes, I heard you. And I think I'd like to live here."

"In Laguna Beach?"

"Why not?"

"But what about your job?"

The sun was starting to rise, the fog was lifting, and the sky was turning a blue-violet.

"As of twelve hours ago, I don't have one. I'm unemployed and homeless."

He looked confused. "You didn't take your job back?"

I wrapped my arms around him, blanket and all. "Paxton, I love you. With everything I am. You are everything I didn't know I needed, and I can't imagine taking another breath without you in my life. I love you."

He picked me up and twirled me around, kissing my neck and laughing.

I laughed and held the coffee away from him, so it didn't spill down his back.

He tucked me in beside him when he put me down, and we continued walking back to the hotel. He started rambling about what we should do next. "Maybe we should move here. It will make it easy to get to the new studio. You can do our marketing and plan the launch party."

I stopped, halting him. "You want me to work for you?"

He turned back and said to me lovingly, "Work for me, work with me, boss me around." He paused. "Marry me."

My heart stopped. "Marry you?"

"Charlotte, I know you just came out of an engagement, but I think you didn't marry him because you weren't who you were supposed to be. I'm who you're supposed to be with. Marry me."

"That is a very confident statement."

"You love me."

"I do."

"See, you already have it down." He smiled at me. "Share my life with me." He smiled again. "Practice making babies with me."

I paused, watching him intently. He was serious, and I realized I would marry him today if that was what he wanted. "Yes."

"Yes?"

I laughed and started walking again. "I didn't stutter." He jogged to catch up with me, and I said, "Maybe I could teach."

He took my coffee from me and reached down to hold my hand. "You want to teach?"

"Sure. Maybe I could just do beginner pole for now."

"That would be fun. You're *much* better than when we met."

"Thank you very much," I responded sarcastically.

"You can do whatever you want."

I laughed out loud. "Story said I need a name."

"That's for strippers."

I let go of his hand and punched him teasingly in the arm. "I don't know about that. Story isn't a stripper. It might be fun, like a…" I rolled my eyes. "Okay, maybe like a stripper name."

"Do you have one in mind?" He reached for my hand, not wanting to be disconnected from me for very long.

We were both looking straight ahead as we walked, hands intertwined.

I couldn't imagine being anywhere else but with him. He *had* become everything to me. This *world* had become everything to me. I knew I was right where I needed to be—and in the life I was supposed to be leading. I had transformed, but I was still the same person, and so I looked up at him, smiling, and simply said, "Chrysalis."

ABOUT THE AUTHOR

Rie Anders grew up in the Pacific Northwest and has led a very colorful life. After successful careers in the country's aerospace program and corporate America, she picked up a pen and left the nine-to-five life. She wove her knowledge of aviation, Pacific Northwest culture, commercial fishing in Alaska, and the West's rugged landscapes, into beautifully crafted, happy ever after, contemporary romantic fiction novels.

Rie lives in Texas with her husband and competitive figure skating daughter. She is sure there is a story there as well. On the daily drives to and from the ice rink, Rie enlists her daughter's input on many things: character development, possible actors to play her feisty heroines on the big screen, and new songs to inspire perfect scenes are just a few.

If you want to know more about Rie, when she will release her next book, and where you can find her, please visit her website at
www.rieanders.com
and follow her at
https://www.bookbub.com/profile/rie-anders
https://twitter.com/RieAnders.

WHERE TO CONNECT WITH RIE

Bookbub
Goodreads
Facebook
Twitter
Instagram
Amazon Author Page

And don't forget to join her Romance Newsletter
on the homepage at www.RieAnders.com!

***

CPSIA information can be obtained
at www.ICGtesting.com
Printed in the USA
BVHW080931130421
604813BV00004B/280